Even though he'd spent his life pretending nothing bothered him, many things did. It bothered him that because of how he talked people thought he was special needs. It bothered him when people snickered at his clumsy size or whispered and pointed at the discs magnetically attached to his head. It bothered him that he had no friends, and it bothered him that there'd been no group outside of his family where he'd ever fit in.

That could all change now. In his mind he was dressed in shoulder pads and a helmet, and he was marching out onto the field with his teammates, a band of brothers.

That's all he wanted: to be, at long last, one of the many.

LEFT OUT

TIM GREEN

HARPER

An Imprint of HarperCollinsPublishers

Library of Congress Control Number: 2016936327
ISBN 978-0-06-229383-1

Typography by Andrea Vandergrift
17 18 19 20 21   OPM   10 9 8 7 6 5 4 3 2 1
❖
First paperback edition, 2017

For my beautiful and amazing wife, Illyssa,
the kindest person I've ever known

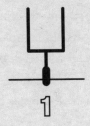

1

The moving van pulled away from the curb, puking a char-coal cloud that spilled down onto the street. The only thing darker than the diesel exhaust was the sky, boiling now with purple clouds and the distant rumble of thunder. Amid shouts of "good-bye" from neighbors and friends, a breeze kicked up, scattering leaves and the exhaust into the yard next door.

Moving was a good thing. Landon's mom had gotten an even bigger job in an even nicer place. At least, that's how she and their dad had tried to sell yet another move to Landon and Genevieve.

Landon glanced over at his little sister, who leaned out the car window taking pictures of her teary-eyed friends on the front lawn. Good at everything, she was like Landon's oppo-site. Genevieve had so much power over her friends that as they waved they were careful to shout not only, "Good-bye,

Genevieve, we'll miss you!" but also, "Good-bye, Landon! Good-bye!"

Landon could only guess what Genevieve had done to get those good-byes for him. He could easily imagine her threatening that if they didn't think cheering up her brother was important, obviously they wouldn't mind if Genevieve removed them from her list of friends. Landon wouldn't allow himself to enjoy the attention. He saw the show, felt a pang of jealousy, and turned his attention to the book he was reading on his iPad.

Genevieve nudged him. With tears in her eyes, she pointed out the window. "Look, Landon. They're saying good-bye to you, too."

Landon shrugged and went back to his book, feeling a bit guilty, but knowing that if he acknowledged *her* friends it would be too painfully obvious he had none of his own. Kip Meyers, standing there with his mom, didn't count. Landon knew Mrs. Meyers had insisted that Kip make a show of saying good-bye. Her son stood slouched, his hand held up half-heartedly, his beady eyes hidden under long, shaggy hair blown by the wind. Although he had hoodwinked his own mom and Landon's parents into thinking he was nice, Kip was among the worst of Landon's tormentors at school.

"Creep!" "Doofus!" Those were the best of the taunts Landon endured. And he had to admit that with the big earpieces he had to wear along with the thick magnetic discs stuck to the sides of his skull so he could hear some sounds, he often felt alien himself. Like the Wookiee from *Star Wars* or some other weird monster.

Whenever he could, he tried to hide the cochlear implants that were attached to his head by wearing his Cleveland Browns cap. But hats weren't allowed in school, and his mom insisted they not ask for the rules to be bent.

"Rules are made to be followed, Landon." His mother would pucker her lips in a prissy manner. "We don't want anyone to think you need to be treated differently than anyone else. Asking for exceptions suggests 'special needs,' and you're *not* that."

The phrase "special needs" was a red flag in Landon's home, mostly because of his mother's guilt. Because she had refused to have Landon tested for any problem when he was a baby, at age four he was diagnosed as a special needs child. People said he would not do well in school. But Landon's mom insisted he was smart and that the doctors needed to figure out what was really wrong. They finally did, and discovered that Landon couldn't hear—he was deaf in both ears. After months, he was fitted with cochlear implants, devices that helped him to hear. But the training involved in using them forced him to begin school a year late. That's why he and his little sister were in the same class. Even though he got good grades, most people still mistook his trouble with hearing and his slightly garbled speech as a sign of mental slowness that meant he had special needs, so whenever those words came up his mother denied them with great gusts of anger.

The downside to his parents' insistence that he not be different was that Landon couldn't wear his cap in school to cover his implants, but the upside was that he could play off his mom's guilt just like other kids. That age-old strategy of parental manipulation had created a wonderful opportunity when his mother announced that she'd gotten a great new job at SmartChips, which wasn't a high-tech company but one that made organic snacks.

When she told him and Genevieve about their next move, from Cleveland to New York, over a dinner of spaghetti and meatballs, Landon faked distress and sadness, but in that instant he'd decided to make a big change. His mother didn't know that, though.

Over the next few days, he played the role of a victim with heavy sighs and frowns—all with one big goal in mind. And then he made his move, asking for his mom's commitment that when they arrived in Bronxville—where she could take the train in and out of the city to work each day—he would be allowed . . . to play football.

Landon loved football. It was a visual symphony sprinkled with violence that looked like it didn't really hurt because of all that padding. Landon watched religiously: Sunday, Monday, and Thursday nights. His team was the Browns, but he'd watch anyone and visualize himself in the midst of the fray. Being big was one of the most important things about football, and Landon knew he was big—really big. But what attracted him most about football was that its players were heroes, universally beloved by the cities in which they played and sometimes nationwide. Landon craved that same universal acceptance and felt sure his goal of being liked would be achieved by becoming part of his own football team.

As she had every time he'd brought up the idea of playing football in the past, his mom argued again about the dangers of the sport. But Landon insisted that he'd do what she wanted and stop sulking about the move, *if* she would let him do what he wanted when they got to their new home. He tried to reassure her by saying, "Mom, look at me, I'm huge. I'll be great on the line."

"Well," she finally said, "you and your father have tired me out. I don't know if it's even possible with your implants, but if a doctor says it *is*, then I don't see why not."

His mother now sat ramrod straight in the driver's seat, ready for action and adventure. Laura, Genevieve's best friend, kept waving good-bye to Genevieve, and her mother, Mrs. Meyers, leaned in through the window with one arm on the roof of the car. As if on cue, a crack of lightning split the sky and the girls shrieked and headed for the garage overhang. The wind whipped even harder.

"Well, Gina." Mrs. Meyers leaned in for a good-bye hug and then glanced up at the sky. "You and Forrest timed it perfectly, getting out of here in front of this storm."

Landon's mom angled her head to assess the weather up through the windshield.

"Actually," she said, "it looks like we're heading straight into it."

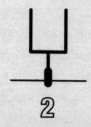

2

As they left the Cleveland suburb with its wide old streets, thick trees, and bright green lawns amid the crack and rumble of thunder, Landon leaned his head against the window and thought about what was to come. He smiled to himself and kept thinking back to his mother's expression when he made his big move to talk about football.

"Football?" Her face had gone from shock to amusement and she'd nodded her head like a bobble-head doll before giving him a knowing look. "Your father never played football, you know?"

Landon had nodded. He knew all about his father, a great big bear of a man who was nearly finished with his third unpublished novel. At six foot ten, Landon's father was a gentle giant, with fists the size of holiday hams, a peaceable man without a

6

violent bone in his body. Landon's mother never tired of comparing him to his father.

"He's so . . . so . . . calm. That's Landon. Calm as a summer day!" his mother would say, beaming at him and then back at whoever she was speaking to.

But Landon knew better. Although he'd never thrown a punch in his life, he fantasized often about getting revenge on his school tormentors on a football field. And what was so pleasant about a summer day? Swimming was the only plus he could see. Give him a pool and a diving board and he became an impressive human cannonball. But because of the extra weight he carried around and the fact that summer heat made his implants more noticeably uncomfortable, he liked fall better. The air was cool and crisp and the surge of football gushed from the TV. Now at his new school, he'd be like one of the NFL stars he'd watched but could never think of being.

He stared at his mother's dark curly hair as she guided their Prius carefully out of town with two hands firmly on the wheel, eyes glued to the road, lips tight. In the passenger seat, his father sat hunched over and squished by the confines of the little car, the back of his head snug against the roof and hands folded in his lap. His father would sit that way for hours on end without a peep of discontent. In fact, he'd be wearing a simple smile as he soaked in the nearness of his family and agreed with Landon's mom on a barrage of ideas.

Landon leaned toward his sister, who was still looking back, saddened by the loss of so many friends.

"It will be okay, Genevieve. You'll make new friends. I know you will." He gave her arm a squeeze. "It will be good. You'll make friends and I'll play football. Yes!" he said with a grin. "That's what I really want to do."

In the mirror he saw his mom's face tense up, and she shot a glance at Landon's father as if the whole thing was his fault. "Are you happy now, Forrest? Landon's looking forward to football. *Foot*ball."

"Right," his dad said. "He's a big boy; he'll be fine, Gina. Watch, it will be good for him."

"I told him *you* never played."

His father laughed. "I told him they couldn't find a helmet big enough for me, and I wasn't all that keen on it anyway, so I played the tuba in the marching band. Talk about good times. . . ."

"A marching band . . ." Landon's mom drifted into a blissful state as she obviously imagined the delights of the marching band.

"Well, I can't play music," Landon reminded them. "But I bet I can block and tackle."

Before his mother could reply, the dark sky opened up with a torrent of raindrops that hit the car like bullets. She redoubled her grip on the wheel and set her body against the storm, leaning into it like a hunter. They were on the highway in the passing lane, and a tractor-trailer raced up behind them blaring its horn.

Landon's mom made it into the right lane, and the ghostly shape of the truck cruised past like a sea monster, its taillights barely visible through the backsplash.

As they crawled along in silence, hazard lights blinking on

and off, Landon grinned to himself about his victory in being able to play football. The idea of beginning practice in just two short weeks gave him goosebumps.

Over an hour later, they finally got clear of the storm and his mother was able to increase their speed. Then she picked up right where they'd left off.

"What do you know about blocking and tackling, Landon?" she asked.

Landon took a breath and surprised everyone. "Keep your head up. Hit 'em hard. Chop your feet!"

Landon started stamping his feet on the floor in a quick staccato rhythm, the way he'd seen it done on YouTube. He got carried away until his mother shouted, "Stop that, Landon! Just stop."

They rode in silence again before his mother reminded Landon of the deal. "All we have to do is make sure the doctor will allow it. Football is okay with me, I said that, but we will have to make sure the doctor is all right with it. We'll see him the week after next."

Then she latched on to a new idea. "And what about a helmet? You might not be able to find one. Your head isn't as big as your father's, but the implants might be a problem, Landon. I didn't even think of that, and I'm sure you didn't either."

Landon nodded and grinned. Without speaking, he stroked his iPad a few times before handing it up to his father, who studied the page in front of him. "Actually, he has thought of it, Gina. Here's an article right here about an Ohio kid named Adam Strecker. They've got helmets for kids with implants. Football helmets. Look . . ."

His father held up the iPad for her to see, but she swatted it away. "I'm driving, Forrest."

Landon took the iPad back. He'd scored points and taken a big lead against his mother, but he knew it wasn't over. She would fight to the end. That was her nature. But Landon knew he could fight too, just as hard.

He tabbed open his book and pretended to read as if he hadn't a care in the world. He did have cares, though. Even though he'd spent his life pretending nothing bothered him, many things did. It bothered him that because of how he talked people thought he was special needs. It bothered him when people snickered at his clumsy size or whispered and pointed at the discs magnetically attached to his head. It bothered him that he had no friends, and it bothered him that there'd been no group outside of his family where he'd ever fit in.

That could all change now. The hope sent a shiver up his spine. He stared at the words on the screen without reading them. In his mind he was dressed in shoulder pads and a helmet, and he was marching out onto the field with his teammates, a band of brothers. They were tall and proud and ready for anything. When they all put their hands in for a common cheer, Landon's would be right there, one of the many.

That's all he wanted: to be, at long last, one of the many.

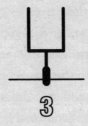

3

They'd stopped halfway to New York to sleep in a motel but were on the road again early the next day. That afternoon they drove through town and pulled up through a pair of gates and along a long driveway past a big front lawn bathed in sunshine. The house, huge and impressive sitting among a host of trees, had thick brown beams, white plaster, and a heavy slate stone roof.

"Wow." Genevieve pushed her face to the glass. "Are we rich?"

"No," their mother said in her fussy way. "We are comfortable. I wouldn't say rich."

"Okay." Genevieve's green eyes were alight as if she didn't believe it. "But we have a pool, right? You said there's a pool."

"It's out back!" Their mother couldn't hide her pride at bringing her family to such a great spot. She stopped the car

11

outside the triple garage door on the side of the house. The moving van was already there, backed up and unloading furniture.

"When you said 'Bronx' I didn't think it would be like this," Landon's sister said. "All these trees."

"It's Bronx*ville*," their father said, slipping out of the car and stretching as he assessed their new home.

"The Bronxville Broncos won the New York State Championship," Landon said, referring to the high school football team. He'd play with them when he was old enough.

"I need to keep an eye on these movers," their mother said. "Forrest, can you take the kids and get some lunch and some groceries?"

"What about you?" Landon's father asked.

"Bring back a salad, spinach if they have it. I'll take care of things here." Their mother walked away, already organizing the movers.

"Well . . ." Their dad looked at the Prius as if it were a dangerous dog, and Landon knew he didn't relish the thought of wedging himself back inside. "Let's take a walk. Good? We're not far from the center of town, and my legs could use it."

Landon tucked his iPad under one arm, tugged on his Cleveland Browns cap, and set off with his father and sister. They lived on Crow's Nest Road, which fed right into Pondfield, the main street of Bronxville. The sun warmed the tree-lined street, but it wasn't too hot. The big houses stood mostly silent. Only an occasional car cruised by. It was as if they had Bronxville mostly to themselves and the pleasant summer day was a greeting to them, a new beginning.

"Library." His dad pointed to a large brick building facing the street, and Landon felt a surge of pleasure because, even though he liked reading on the iPad, he preferred the feel and smell of a real book. The air on the sidewalk in the shadows of the maple trees lining the road was cool and heavy with fresh-cut grass. They only had to cross the street before his father pointed again. "There's the middle school."

That gave Landon the opposite sensation. His hands clenched and his throat went dry. He looked at Genevieve. She had small features and a sharp nose like his mom. She narrowed her green eyes the way a mountain climber might size up Mount Everest.

They continued on toward the center of town before Genevieve pointed out Womrath Book Shop. "A library *and* bookstore, Landon. This place is going to be heaven for you."

"And there's a famous deli across the street, Lange's." Their father consulted his phone "Five stars on TripAdvisor."

They crossed the street and made their way to the deli. Three bikes leaned against a lamppost on the sidewalk outside. They made Landon nervous because with bikes usually came boys. Sure enough, they walked in and Landon saw the three boys sitting near the back in a corner. Two had dark hair. One, with a pug face, wore his hair parted on the side and swept over the top, flopping down so it nearly covered one eye. The other's short hair, pointy stiff with gel, framed the elfin face of a TV character. The third had red hair in a buzz cut. He had freckles and big teeth. When they spotted Landon's father, they immediately began to chatter and point. They were too far for Landon to hear, but he read the pug-faced boy's lips as he laughed and said, "Hey, it's the Giant. Where's Jack?"

Landon knew he should turn away, knew he shouldn't look, shouldn't read their lips and see their words. Nothing good ever came from three boys laughing and gawking, but he felt drawn to it the way he might poke at a bruise to test how much it really hurt. He peeked around the edge of his father, who stood oblivious, looking up at the menu board.

"Dude," the spiky-haired boy said, pointing, "look. It's *got a baby giant from outer space.*" The boy made antennae with his fingers and clamped them on his ears. All three of them laughed, and Landon looked away now because they were staring at him. He tugged his cap down, horrified at what they might say if they could see the discs. All they were reacting to now were the battery packs and processors that fit over and behind his ears like giant hearing aids. If they saw the magnetic discs, which looked like fat quarters on the sides of his head, they'd go wild. They wouldn't even have to know that the discs covered implanted discs attached to wires that were tucked beneath his *brain* to get excited. He'd heard it before.

"Hey, Frank!" someone would say.

The first time it happened, Landon shook his head and pointed to himself. "My name is Landon."

"Franken*stein,* dude. Frank-n-stein!" And they'd point to their own heads with fingers in the spots where the moveable magnetic discs connected to the disc implants beneath his scalp. Sometimes they'd stick out their tongues, cross their eyes, or both.

Landon was nervous when a waitress took them to their table near the boys. He sat in the chair with his back to the three boys and focused on the menu. There were lots of choices. His father ordered a tuna melt, and Landon asked for the same. Genevieve got turkey on a croissant with brown mustard and Swiss cheese. She didn't eat like a kid, and it was just another way that she seemed more advanced than Landon, even though she was a year younger.

Landon couldn't understand the chatter behind him now. The sounds he heard with the implants weren't sharp enough for him to understand what was being said without the ability to also see a person's lips. He could read lips fairly well, but the best way for him to understand what was being said was to hear the fuzzy sounds and see the lips at the same time.

Landon tried not to stare at his sister, but he couldn't help feeling concerned each time she glanced past him to where he knew the boys were sitting. Then she put her croissant down without taking a last bite. Her face turned dark. Her eyes moved in a way that told Landon the boys were headed toward their table. Landon tapped Genevieve's arm, trying to get her to look at him. If he could draw her into a conversation, she might not do anything bad, but she swatted his hand away without moving her eyes.

The three boys moved past the table in a tight group. Landon heard one of them say something, but he had no idea what because the diner wasn't quiet and the boy didn't speak loudly. It must have been bad, though, because Genevieve sprang from her chair and darted at the biggest one of them like a terrier on a rat.

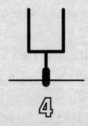

4

Genevieve gave the redhead a shove, pushing him back so that he stumbled into another table, upsetting the drinks of the four ladies who sat there. Landon heard a muffled shriek. Both he and his father jumped up. His father grabbed Genevieve by the shoulders, holding her back.

"What's your problem?" The redhead glared and clenched his fists. He stood nearly as tall as Landon, though half as wide.

"My problem is *you*!" Genevieve struggled to get free. "And you!" She kicked out at the pug-faced boy's shin. Thankfully she missed, but the three boys backed away toward the door.

"Come on, Skip." The spiky-haired one tugged the redhead's arm. He turned to the pug-faced kid with the floppy hair and said, "Xander, let's just go."

The entire diner stared in disbelief as Genevieve's eyes brimmed with tears.

"Genevieve, you can't act like this," their father scolded as he guided her back to her seat. He kept his voice even and calm, though, and then he turned to the ladies at the table of spilled drinks where a waitress was already at work with a towel. He produced his wallet and removed some bills. "I'm very sorry. I'll pay for those drink refills and any cleaning."

Landon took a quick look around. Everyone was staring and whispering. He wanted to disappear. He wanted to die. He shook his head and tapped Genevieve to get her attention. "You know I don't want people staring," he scolded.

"You can't let people disrespect you—here or when you're on the football field, Landon," Genevieve said. "You need to learn that."

"This isn't the football field. This is the diner."

Genevieve gave him a fiery look that quickly melted, and he was afraid she would burst into tears, but she bit her lip and put her hand on top of his and said, "I'm sorry, Landon. I just can't stand . . ."

"Don't worry so much about me, Genevieve," Landon said. "I'm gonna be fine here. This is a football town. When they see me play, no one's gonna laugh. I promise."

"You don't—"

Landon cut her off with his hand. "You have to *ignore* people like that, Genevieve."

Her eyes burned again and her nostrils flared. "Maybe you can ignore them, Landon. You didn't hear what they said, but I *did*."

Landon's mouth turned sour. He glared at his sister, removed his hat, and disconnected his electronic ears, the processors, the magnetic discs, and the wires that connected the two parts. The components dangled in his hand for a moment like small sea creatures, and he showed them to her before he stuffed them into his pockets and put the cap back on his head. Genevieve had humiliated them all. They'd just moved here and Genevieve was already getting in trouble. Whatever those boys had said, she should have ignored it, just like he did.

Removing the external equipment for his implants was the most powerful statement Landon could make. He was cutting off his sister, cutting off the entire world. Now, none of it mattered, and as long as he refused to read their lips, no one could bother him.

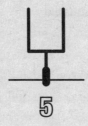

5

They walked home after lunch. Landon's mom was at the kitchen table surrounded by boxes, writing on a notepad and looking busy. She smiled when Landon's father set down her spinach salad. Landon didn't have to hear to know what his sister said as she threw her hands in the air. He snuck a look.

"Landon took off his ears!"

Landon cruised peacefully past them all, headed for the living room and his favorite reading chair, which the movers had positioned near the big window looking out over the pool and lawn. It was a heavenly place dappled with sun shining through the trees, and he took it, iPad already out. The smell of polished wood and the hint of warm dust filled his nose. He knew he'd be spending some serious time in this spot.

His mother usually gave him some space when he pulled the plug on his ears, so he jumped when someone tapped his shoulder. It was her. She motioned for him to reconnect. He stared at her for a moment to make sure she really meant it. She did. Moving slowly, he removed the gear they called his "ears" from his pocket and hooked it all up.

"What happened?" she asked.

"Genevieve is a maniac," he said.

"She's very protective of you."

"She knocked over everyone's drinks and made a big stink." Landon glared at his mom. "You and Dad teach us to walk away."

"It's harder to do that when it's against someone you love," his mother said. "It's easier to walk away when someone is making fun of you than of someone you're close to."

"Why?" Landon tilted his head.

"Because . . ." She threw her hands up. "I don't know, Landon, but it *is*. You just, you need to cut her some slack." She paused for a minute. "Do you want to see your room?"

"I like where they put my chair."

She swatted him playfully. "Who do you think had it put here?"

She sat down on the arm and hugged Landon to her. He hugged her back, but separated when it got too tight. She looked tired and sad.

"Are you okay, Mom?"

"I'm fine, Landon." She sighed. "I want you to be fine."

"I'm always fine, Mom. You know that." He got up. "So, where's my room?"

She studied him for a moment before rising and leading him into the front hall and up a big wooden staircase. Down at the end of a wide hall, they went right and into a long bedroom with its own bathroom. Part of the ceiling slanted at an angle and the whole room was paneled in wood. His desk and bookshelf stood empty on one side, and his bed lay on the other side beneath three rectangular windows. His computer sat on the desk. Boxes were everywhere.

"You like it?" his mom asked.

Landon climbed up on the bed and looked out the windows, smiling. "It's like the inside of a pirate ship."

"There's a park just a few streets away." His mom pointed out his window. "The school—did you see the school?—it's not far either."

"I did." Landon thought about the boys and the school, and then his face brightened. "I can walk to football practice! That'll make things easy for you guys."

"Landon . . ."

"Yes?"

She sat down on his bed and patted the spot beside her. He took it.

"I've been thinking about football."

"It's America's sport, Mom."

She stroked his hair and he made a big effort not to back away. "It's harder than it looks, Landon. You're not a violent person. You don't get angry very often, and when you do, you . . . you . . ." She pointed at his implants. "You unplug."

"Just because I don't push people into other people's tables doesn't mean I don't *want* to. In football, you're *supposed* to push the other guys. It's part of the game." He pulled away from her touch.

His mother stood up and went to one of the boxes. "I'll say this once and only once. Be careful what you wish for, Landon, because you just might get it."

From out of nowhere she produced a razor-blade box cutter and with one quick motion slit open the top of the biggest box. She began taking things out and setting them carefully on the bookshelf. He knew working calmed his mother's nerves. She placed several ceramic animals in a small cluster Landon could see—a lion, a tiger, a bear, an elephant. She stepped back to review them before fussing some more.

While she worked on arranging the cluster, Landon taped a Cleveland Browns poster to the wall.

His mother took a picture from the box, examined it, and smiled before showing him. "Remember this?"

It was a picture of the four of them—Landon, Genevieve, and his mom and dad—plummeting nearly straight down on Splash Mountain, the best ride in Disney World. His sister and his parents had their hands in the air and their mouths open, screaming with joy during that scary final plunge. Landon gripped the seat, ready to endure the fifty-foot drop. It wasn't his idea of fun, but he had wanted to prove to himself he could do it. He'd insisted they get the photo, to record the experience, and whenever he looked at it he was glad he'd taken the ride.

"That was a fun time." Landon glowed with pride.

She smiled warmly and set the picture on the shelf.

Landon removed his football from another box. It was his best present from his dad last Christmas, an official NFL ball, and he placed it next to the Disney World picture. His mom paused to study it.

"You know, I've been thinking . . . ," she said, "you can be part of a football *team* without actually having to be out there with people bashing your noggin where you've already got some sensitive equipment."

He tilted his head at her. "What do you mean?"

"Well . . ." She adjusted the picture. "You can help out the team and be a part of it. Every team has one of these . . . well, it's a manager, a team manager. All the big-time college programs have them, a student manager, and high schools do too. Lots of sports teams have managers, and they're very important, and I think it would be a super way for you to fit in."

She left the picture alone and stared hard at him.

Landon's mouth sagged open as he processed everything she was saying. She had actually devised a plan for him to be on a football team without *playing* football. It was diabolical. He shook his head violently and reached for his ears, ready to pull the plug again because . . . and he had to say this out loud.

"Mom, no. No way!"

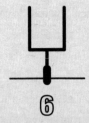

6

Ten days later, Landon was sitting on an exam table in a hospital gown and his boxer shorts while Dr. Davis, a cochlear implant specialist, studied his medical history.

The doctor set the folder down and then took Landon's head in his hands, squeezing like it was a melon in the grocery store. As his long, cool fingers searched around Landon's implants, circling the magnetic discs, he asked how Landon communicated.

Landon watched his mom clear her throat and explain. "His SIR . . . uh, Speech Intelligibility Rating—"

"Of course," said the doctor.

"He's a seven point two," his mom boasted. And Landon was proud of that score. He'd been going to speech therapy every week for years, and as a result, people nearly always understood what he was saying.

The doctor's pale green eyes stared at Landon's face. "What did you have for breakfast, Landon?"

"Uh, eggs and bacon. I had some cinnamon toast too. And juice." Landon knew from a lifetime of wrinkled brows or snickering grins that his speech didn't sound like most people's. "Garbled" was how it was mostly described—off base, not normal.

The doctor pressed his lips, looked at Landon's mom, and then turned back to him and said, "You've worked hard on your speech therapy, haven't you?"

Landon blushed and nodded. He couldn't help feeling proud, because here was a man who knew his business when it came to the way deaf people spoke.

"Yes, your impediment wouldn't keep anyone who's paying attention from understanding you." Dr. Davis looked back at his mom. "How does he understand others?"

"He gets a good deal from sounds, and he's good at lip-reading, but he does best with a combination of sounds and lipreading, unless you shout."

The doctor asked, "No sign language at all?"

Landon's mom's back stiffened. "We made a conscious decision to concentrate on auditory focus and lipreading."

"Also, coaches don't know sign language," Landon blurted. "So it's good to be able to read lips."

"Sports?" The doctor raised an eyebrow. "What do you play?"

"Football." Landon glowed with pride. "That's why I'm here."

"Okay, on your feet." The doctor took out a stethoscope

25

and began to look Landon all over, from head to toe.

Landon stood there in his boxers, his feet cold against the tile floor. A slight trickle of sweat escaped his armpits.

"But football . . . with the implants, how safe can that be?" Landon's mom seemed to sense the tide going against her.

"Most of that concussion business has to do with the pros, maybe college. And riding a bike can be more dangerous than junior league football. Breathe deep." The doctor speckled Landon's back with the chilly disc, listening to his lungs before he snapped the stethoscope off his neck, folded it, and tucked it away in his long white coat. "And this boy is healthy as an ox."

The doctor put a hand on Landon's shoulder. "He'll need a special helmet, of course, for the ear gear. And you need the skullcap under it."

Landon was ready for that one. He took his iPad off the chair where he'd set his clothes and showed the doctor what he planned to get.

"Yes! That's the best one."

"His . . . the implants?" Landon's mother worked her lips, maybe rehearsing arguments in her mind.

The doctor was a tall man with thick glasses, and authority had been chiseled on his granite face. "There's a risk to any sport, but with the helmets they make today . . ."

The doctor shook his head in amazement at modern technology as he scribbled some notes on Landon's chart. "Clean bill of health and ready to go. Just get that helmet before tackling."

"But . . . ," his mom got ready to protest. "Wouldn't something like soccer be safer?"

The doctor snorted. "Soccer? Mrs. Dorch, look at your son. He's built for football, not soccer. Anyway I'd have my kid in football with all that padding and a helmet any day before I'd have him running around full speed knocking heads or having a ball kicked in his face. Like I said, nothing is without risk, though."

"It's just that you hear so much about football . . ." Landon's mom was losing steam.

The doctor ignored her, stepped back, and surveyed Landon. "One thing's for sure: he could use the exercise."

Landon looked down at his gut and blushed. He was working on it, cutting back on the SmartChips, no matter how healthy they were, and on the second and third servings at meals despite his mother's urgings to eat more.

"Good luck in football, Landon. And remember that helmet!"

That night Landon waited until dinner had been cleaned up and his mom was locked in her home office, busily working away on her laptop, before he tiptoed past the doorway two down from his bedroom and sought out his dad. His father didn't need to lock himself away to do his work. His desk sat downstairs not far from Landon's chair, in the middle of the living room in front of the big window overlooking the backyard. His father kept the surface of the massive claw-foot desk clear except for the iMac he wrote on as well as two leather books held proudly upright by marble busts of William Shakespeare and Charles Dickens.

Landon's father declared that he liked to be in the center

of their home because it let him draw from the lifeblood of their lives for his own work. Landon wasn't exactly sure what lifeblood was, but he presumed it had something to do with the heart. He wondered also at the strategy since it hadn't earned his father anything for the first two books but a box full of rejection letters that he saved as a source of motivation.

He passed Genevieve's room. Ten days in and Genevieve already had friends like Megan Nickell. With a father who was president of the country club and a mother who was a partner at Latham & Watkins, SmartChips's law firm, Megan easily won the approval of Landon's mom. Genevieve was with Megan right now for a sleepover. The house was quiet. He could feel the cool air flowing through the vents—the weather outside had taken a hot turn. Landon's father sat slumped in front of his iMac, fingers on the keyboard, but idle.

"Dad?" Landon tapped him on shoulder to get his attention.

His dad turned and smiled like someone had sprung the lid on a treasure chest. "Hey, buddy. What are you doing? Finish your book?"

"No, but I wanted to talk to you."

"You got it. Want some ice cream?"

"Häagen-Dazs?"

His father wore a look of mock concern. "Is there another kind?"

Landon laughed and followed his dad into the kitchen area, which was separated from the living room only by the rectangular table where they ate. His father yanked open the freezer door and studied the shelves. "Hmm. When you don't know which one, choose both."

He removed a quart of butter pecan as well as one of vanilla, tucked them under his arm, and then grabbed two large spoons from the drawer. "I'd say let's sit out by the pool, but this stuff would be nothing but drool in five minutes flat."

They sat at the kitchen table, scooping out large hunks of ice cream and passing the quart containers back and forth in an easy rhythm until Landon held up both hands.

"Gotta go easy," he said. "Football."

"Ah, yes. The discipline of the Spartan." His father held up a giant scoop of butter pecan and inserted it into his mouth.

"What's that mean?" Landon asked.

"Well . . ." His father worked the ice cream around in his mouth and swallowed. "Discipline is you sacrificing—giving up something—for a greater cause. The Spartans were Greek warriors known for their harsh training. They were even crazy enough, I believe, to forgo butter pecan."

"I know Spartans."

"And now you've become one." His father bowed his head toward Landon.

"That's what I wanted to talk to you about." Landon glanced toward the hall, nervous that his mother might interrupt them. "Everything is going good. I passed my physical. The doctor said I could play. My implants are fine. Heck, he even told Mom playing football would be *good* for me." Landon patted his gut.

"Wonderful." His father took another big bite.

"But I need that helmet, and the special cap that goes under it," Landon said. "Football starts next Wednesday. The first five days it's just conditioning and running through plays, but helmets go on next week, and then the week after that we start to hit. But I need the helmet before so I can get used to it."

His father's eyes widened.

"I told Mom we gotta get my helmet and she keeps saying she'll work on it and how expensive it is, but next Wednesday will be here before you know it, and you can't just snap your fingers and have a helmet fall out of the sky. It's like she's trying to sabotage the whole thing by delaying, making it so I won't have enough practices to play in the first game and then I *will* end up as the manager."

His father put the spoon down and looked at it. "Yes, that's a problem, and I've seen this kind of strategy before. I wanted to see *Carmina Burana*. It was playing at the Cleveland Opera Theater, and your mom said she'd be happy to go and that she'd get the tickets through her office because they were sponsors. Well, I thought that sounded good because we could be in the pit or maybe even a box. Then the day before, when I asked, she snapped her fingers and said she was on it, but that night at dinner she announced that it had been sold out." Landon's father blinked at him. "Your mother hates the opera."

"Just like football." Landon looked down and rapped his knuckles on the table before looking back up. "Can you help me, Dad?"

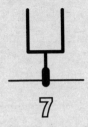

7

Landon peered over his father's shoulder. They were back at his desk, with the spoons rinsed and tucked away in the dishwasher. His father typed and then clicked, bringing up the website for Xenith Helmets, a company that made specialty sports helmets of every kind. They got to the football section and his father scanned the material quickly, his lips moving fast and silently, before he tapped the screen and leaned back.

"It's ingenious, really," he said. "There's a diaphragm in the lining, like a couple of mini beach rafts you can inflate. It says you can play football with the processors right behind your ears. I thought you'd have to take them out for sure, like you do for swimming."

Landon nodded because he already knew all this, but he didn't want to dampen his father's excitement. "That's awesome."

"Let's see . . ." His father tilted his head back for a better look. "We measure your head . . ."

"I can get the tape measure from the garage." Landon was already up and going. When he returned he was thrilled to see that his father had most of the order form already filled out. They wrapped the tape around Landon's head.

"Twenty-four," his father said. "I'm a twenty-*nine*. You believe that? Here, let me show you."

Landon's father wrapped the metal tape around his own head as proof, chuckling before he turned his attention back to the screen. "You know, I believe in this whole team thing. I mean, a marching band is like a team. An orchestra? How about that for working together, right? And those things . . ." Landon's father sat back in his chair and got a faraway look. "Those things are what I remember most. You're part of something."

Landon's dad looked at him and Landon let their eyes stay connected over the empty space. It wasn't something he and his father did very much, just look at each other, but it was as if this moment was one they'd both remember, and for some reason it didn't feel weird. His dad had dark brown eyes and a big forehead. His nose was slightly flattened and his mouth a bit too small for everything else. Looking at him, Landon felt like he was looking into a mirror, seeing himself in the future.

"There's real team spirit," his father said. "I want you to have that." Landon's dad turned back to the iMac and moved through to the purchase screen. He clicked the rush delivery icon, but the earliest delivery for the helmet and skullcap was

Saturday, a few days after the start of Landon's football career.

"Monday we'll get you football shoes—cleats," his dad said. They slapped a high five.

Neither of them had seen his mother creep up on them, so it startled them both when she barked, "What's going on here?"

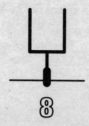

8

Landon's father jumped out of his seat, and the contrast between Landon's parents was staggering. His father towered, a giant of a man, but his body was soft and slouching like he was made of pillows. He blocked Landon's mom from the iMac. She glared up at him. Standing straight, her chin barely cleared his father's belt line, but her eyes fixed on his like a bird of prey.

"I was uh . . . helping." His father's fingers fluttered in front of him.

Landon sat and watched her peer around him and examine the iMac with growling hostility. Her lips curled away from her teeth. "I see." She took a deep breath and let it out. "Yes, I see."

She turned and marched away. Landon looked at his dad, who smiled, saying, "She'll come around. She's just worried about you."

By Tuesday night she had come around. Landon knew when his mom called his dad from the kitchen. "Forrest? I could use some help here. It turns out this football business is a family affair in Bronxville. I ran into Landon's coach's wife, Claire Furster, on the train into work this morning and found out that the mothers are expected to supply something for some sort of bake sale, so I was thinking oatmeal cookies with honey instead of white sugar—something partially healthy at least."

Landon looked at his dad.

"Of course." Landon's dad hurried off toward the kitchen.

"And Landon?" His mother pointed at him. "You better get some sleep. Tomorrow's a big day."

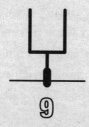

9

On Wednesday morning Landon's mother left for work on an early train. Her cookies rested in a Tupperware container with the doctor's clearance and a note taped to the cover for Landon's father in case she had to work late and couldn't talk to the football people herself. Genevieve was holed up in her room working at her online French class. She told Landon she wanted him to walk into town with her for lunch at the diner with two of her new friends. Later, she said, they'd all swim at the house.

Even though school was still over a week away from starting, football practice wasn't until the evening because the coaches had real jobs, and Landon was up for any distraction that would keep the voices of doubt at bay.

After Genevieve got acquainted with Megan Nickell, she had used Instagram and Snapchat to make friends with the other seventh-grade Bronxville girls as well. But Landon still wondered how she really did it, how she just barged into people's lives like a long-lost relative and found them happy to see her.

Landon tried to read a book, but he kept thinking about football. He put on his new cleats and took them off several times, worrying that they might give him blisters if they weren't broken in.

The morning was dragging on. He knew he shouldn't—because he could see his dad working feverishly—but he couldn't help it. He grabbed the football off his shelf, wandered into his father's space, and tapped his shoulder.

His father jumped. "Whaaa?"

Landon stepped back. He was used to startling people; it was just part of who he was. He needed to *see* them to know what they were saying. "Dad?"

"Landon. Son. I was far away."

"Sorry, Dad. Would you throw the football with me?" Landon turned the ball in his hands. "I feel like I need some practice. Even though I'm a lineman, I mean, everybody throws the ball around."

"Me? Throw? Uh . . ." His father gave the computer a sad look like it was a friend he'd hate to leave, but then he brightened. "Sure!" Standing and stretching he said, "I can throw you the football and you can help me with a problem."

"Okay." Landon followed his father through the kitchen and out the French doors to the pool area. They went through the gate and stood facing each other on the lawn. Overhead the sun shone brightly between fat white clouds and the tall trees that seemed to whisper. Landon tilted his head up at them and wondered how what he heard sounded different than what his father heard. He fluttered his fingers and pointed up at them.

His father smiled and fluttered his own fingers. "Yes, that's right. They're swishing." Seeing Landon's puzzlement, he added, "They sound like waves hitting the shore, but softer swishing."

Landon echoed, "Swishing," trying to fix the sound he heard and the word in his mind. Then he signaled his father to stay put. "You stand here."

Landon backed up, cocked his arm, and fired a wobbling pass. As the ball approached, his father brought his two hands together in a clapping motion, winced, and turned his head. The ball punched him in the gut and dropped to the grass. His father stared at it as if it were a bomb that might go off.

Then his father nodded and scooped it up. "Okay. I can get this," he shouted.

Landon thought about the band and the big tuba his father played. That must have taken some skill. Just a different kind of skill.

Landon jiggled his hands to create a target, and his father reared back with the ball. It flew sideways like a dizzy spaceship. Landon snatched at it, nearly catching hold before it plopped down in front of him.

His father shrugged. "We'll get it," he yelled. "This is why you practice, right? We're doing good."

They heaved the ball back and forth, sometimes getting hold of it, most times not.

"So," his father said after a halfway decent pass, "here's my big problem. Ready?"

Landon caught the ball, smiled, and nodded that he was ready.

10

His father's large face was flushed and he nodded merrily at Landon. "Okay, so—and this is really exciting, Landon—I was doing some research on names because my main character has an uncle on the planet Zovan and I wanted a name that also meant 'powerful,' and I dig and I dig and I find 'Bretwalda,' which is what they called the most powerful Saxon kings."

His father gave him a questioning look to see if he was following.

"Uh, okay, I get that." Landon heaved the ball, happy that his throw wasn't quite so wobbly. He wasn't sure where his dad was going with all this, but he was glad they were throwing around the football.

His father kind of swatted at the ball and ducked at the same time, and then he bent down to retrieve it from the grass. "So, I'm a writer—my mind wanders." His father waved his hands like magic wands, the football almost small in his huge grip. "And my creative curiosity asks a question: 'Forrest, what about Dorch? Where did *that* name come from?'"

Landon's dad paused with the ball cocked back. Landon could feel his father's excitement, and he had to admit that it made him curious too, a name like Dorch. He assumed it wasn't just a variation on "dork," which is what several kids in his Ohio school had called him.

His father threw the ball, a wayward lob, but Landon was able to get his hands on it and pull it proudly to his chest.

"Dorchester." His father stood up straight and saluted. "Yes, Dorchester. *And*, not just Dorchester, but the *guards* of Dorchester castle, the sons of the sons of the sons and so on . . . bred for what?"

Landon held the ball and waited.

His father flung his hands high in the air. "Stature."

Landon wrinkled his brow. "Stature? You mean a statue?"

"No: stature, size. Height." His father held a hand level with the top of his head. "Girth too." He patted the beach-ball bulge of his stomach and its impressive girth with both hands.

Landon looked down at his own hefty gut. In football his weight would be an advantage.

His father waved a hand to get his attention. His face grew serious and he said, "Enter the problem which I'd like you to help me solve."

"What's the problem?"

"*Return to Zovan* is nearly seven hundred pages long, probably halfway finished."

"Halfway?" Landon couldn't imagine anyone reading a

fourteen-hundred-page book. That would be like the Bible, or the dictionary, or . . . something.

"Yes," his father said. "A very good start with *tremendous* momentum. As I said, my main character is about to reach Zovan and meet his uncle, who we shall now name Bretwalda. *But*, a writer has to be *inspired*, and a writer has to be honest about whether he is truly inspired and . . . well, Dorch inspires me. Don't you get it?"

Landon didn't know what to say. He bought some time by turning the ball over in his hands, searching for just the right grip on the laces, like he'd seen Peyton Manning do on YouTube videos.

"I want to write a historical novel about Dorchester Castle. I can *see* it. I can *taste* it." His father paced the grass before he turned his attention back to Landon. "I am inspired, Landon, but will it sell? You read as much as anyone . . ."

"I read kids' stuff, Dad," Landon said, begging off and throwing the ball.

His father nodded excitedly as he muffed the catch, but he didn't bend down for the ball. "And that's what this would *be*—it's middle grade historical fiction based on our forefathers. Can you imagine the excitement of the librarians? You see, people love the past, but they love it when you can bring it into the future. It's like Percy Jackson. It's mythology, only *today*. Brilliant." His father paused and then asked, "So, yes or no?"

Landon looked pointedly at the ball. "Well, how would you bring the story about Dorchester into today?"

"Time travel, of course. You remember the Magic Tree House

42

books, right?" His father picked up the ball and cocked his arm.

"Sure," Landon said.

"More brilliance." His father didn't throw the ball but instead looked up at the clouds, contemplating the genius of a tree house for time travel.

When his father's eyes remained cast toward the sky, Landon looked up too, expecting to see a cloud in the shape of a dragon or a magic tree house or a castle.

Then he thought he heard something. A word?

Was it "catch"?

Landon looked toward his father the instant before the football hit him in the head and he collapsed on the grass.

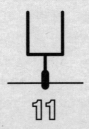

11

Landon's father was a ghost above him, a blurry and sobbing figure coming into focus. Landon read his lips. "Landon? Landon? Oh, God . . ."

His father's fingers scampered over his face and the right earpiece and the magnetic disc that had been knocked loose. "Landon? I'm sorry. I'm so sorry . . ."

Landon opened his mouth to say he was just fine. Nothing came out, or maybe it did. His father's panic and the bad sound and being on the grass disoriented him. One ear wasn't working, but otherwise, he was more embarrassed than hurt. He tried to get up.

His father's hands now pressed him down. "Are you okay? I don't know if you should move."

Landon shook his head and kept trying to sit up. "Dad, let me up. I'm *fine*."

"Okay. Okay." His father nodded, and with his knees buried in the grass, he gently helped Landon into a sitting position.

Landon felt for the apparatus on the right side of his head. The cochlear was crooked behind his ear. His father gently removed everything, checked it over with a frown, and then dangled the equipment in front of him. "It looks okay. Just unseated it."

Landon took it and put it back on.

"Is it okay?" His father's eyes were wet, his lips pulled into the frown of a sad clown.

Landon got everything reconnected and listened. "Say something."

His father looked confused. "Uh . . . one, two, three, four, five, six, seven—"

Landon cut off his counting with a nod and a smile. "Got it. All good, Dad."

His father scooped him up like a hundred-and-seventy-pound doll. He hugged him and spun him around before placing him down. "Oh, thank God. I thought I'd hurt you."

Landon laughed. "I'm okay. You threw it and I wasn't looking."

"I know. I know. Stupid, stupid, stupid." His father shook his head. "I wasn't thinking. I mean, I was thinking—about the book—I mean, I can't use time travel, right? And then I remembered I was supposed to be throwing to you and my arm just launched it and . . ."

"I'm okay. I'm okay." Landon couldn't stand when his parents fussed over him.

"Really okay?" his father asked.

"Good thing you don't have a very good throwing arm." Landon smiled and his father mussed his hair.

"And . . ." His father looked around. ". . . I don't see any reason why we need to say anything to . . . Well, this is one of those little things you just forget about because they're so unimportant."

"Absolutely." Landon didn't want to give his mother another reason to freak out about football. He hadn't even gotten the pads on yet. When his father's eyes widened, he turned to see Genevieve staring at them with her hands on her hips. Her frizzy red hair was gathered in a kind of crazed ponytail.

"What happened?"

"Playing football," Landon said.

"Are you okay?" Genevieve eyed them suspiciously.

"Great," his father said. Then his eyes narrowed and he pointed at Genevieve's hand. "And what is that, young lady?"

Genevieve didn't try to hide her nails; instead she splayed the fingers on her free hand to show off the purple paint. "Polish."

"I don't think so." Their father shook his head. "You do something like that and *I'll* catch the blame."

Genevieve pointed to her face. "No lipstick. No eyeliner. That's what you can tell Mom. I will too."

Genevieve had the strong-minded look of their mother, and she jutted out her chin. "I can get by without makeup, but you don't show up at the deli or the park without nail polish. Not in this town anyway."

"What do you mean, 'this town'?" their father asked.

"Bronxville." Genevieve tightened her jaw. "This isn't like Cleveland."

46

Landon looked back and forth between them like it was a Ping-Pong match.

"Meaning?"

"Certain things are expected here, Dad."

"Like what?"

"Like nail polish. Tevas instead of Crocs." Genevieve wiggled her toes at them. "Nothing too crazy, but it's different. Oh, and Tuckahoe are our mortal enemies."

"Tuckahoe?" Their father wrinkled his brow.

"Arch rivals in all sports, especially football." Genevieve handed Landon the shirt she'd been holding. "Here, put this on."

"I have a shirt on." Landon pointed to his dark gray *Minecraft Eye of Ender* T-shirt.

"Izod. Put it on," Genevieve said. It was an order.

Landon looked at his father and shrugged. "She's good at this stuff."

Genevieve looked away as he tugged the blue collared shirt with its little alligator patch down over his jiggling belly.

"Good." Genevieve turned from Landon to their father. "Now we're off to lunch."

"What do you mean, 'off to lunch'?" he asked.

Genevieve sighed. "It's what kids do here, Dad. They meet at the diner or the club or the pizza place."

"And how do kids *pay* for that lunch?" He scratched his jaw.

"Mom gave me a credit card," Genevieve said. "She said if you had a problem to say it's this or join the country club. Lots of kids eat there."

"I don't golf." Their father blinked.

"I know," Genevieve said.

"Guess I'll make a sandwich and get back to work." He gave Landon a knowing look. "I think I had a breakthrough."

Landon retrieved his Cleveland Browns cap and followed his sister.

"Don't walk behind me, Landon." She waved her hand. "Walk beside me."

Landon hustled up. "Well, you walk so fast. It's always like a death march or something with you. You and Mom."

"We have places to go," she said.

They were passing the library when she tapped him and asked, "What's Dad's breakthrough?"

Landon explained as best he could. Genevieve shook her head. "He's something."

"*I* like it." Landon didn't want to trample his father. In fact, he wanted to look up to him, but sometimes it was hard. Whenever anyone asked what his father did and Landon told them he was a writer, the next question always hurt. He tapped Genevieve's shoulder. "Do you have to have a book *published* to be a writer? Technically, I mean?"

Genevieve frowned. "Of course not. Did you ever hear of *A Confederacy of Dunces?*"

"You saying Dad's stupid?"

"No." Genevieve swatted him. "It was a book no one wanted. Dad told me about it. The author was John Kennedy Toole, and he never published anything. He died . . . actually, he killed himself."

Landon's stomach clenched. "Geez, Genevieve."

"Yeah, but then his mom *forces* some writing professor

48

to read her son's manuscript and *bam*, it not only gets published, it wins the Pulitzer Prize."

"Gosh." Landon thought about that all the way to the diner.

When they arrived, there were no bikes outside, and that relaxed Landon a bit. They went inside, and Genevieve waved to a table where two girls sat holding two empty places.

"Guys, this is my brother, Landon." Genevieve presented him with a flourish. "Landon, this is Katy Buford and this is Megan Nickell. We'll all be in seventh grade together."

Katy's short hair was straight with bangs and so blond it was nearly white. Megan had dark, wavy hair pulled back by a band across the top of her head. They both wore shorts and colorful Polo shirts with Tevas on their feet. Landon blushed and said hello. As he shook hands he noticed that they not only had painted nails, but also a touch of lipstick and maybe something on their eyelashes.

They all sat down. Katy launched into an excited discussion with Genevieve and Megan about the new middle school girls' soccer coach.

Katy rolled her eyes. "Wait till you see how cute he is! But my mother said he grew up in New Haven, so he's probably poor as a church mouse. Can you believe people *live* in places like New Haven? I bet there are some pretty bad places in Cleveland, huh?"

When Landon looked over, Megan was staring at him with large, pale blue eyes. He was afraid she'd ask about his ears, but she smiled. There was a gap between her front teeth, and they were all strapped together with bright orange braces.

He looked back at her eyes. She was beautiful.

They ordered Cokes and iced tea. While the girls looked at the menu and Katy babbled on about boys and clothes and makeup and money, Landon stole glimpses of Megan. He couldn't take his eyes off her. When the waitress returned with their drinks, Landon reached for his soda too fast and knocked it over, and some spilled on Megan's white shorts. She gave a little shriek and jumped up, her face reddening at the attention from everyone around them. Landon struggled up out of his seat and dabbed at her shorts with his napkin.

"Sorry, sorry, sorry," he said.

Megan laughed nervously and gently pushed him away. "No, I'm okay. Please, Landon. Stop."

Landon stood, his shoulders slouched, a tower of shame. "I . . . I am just so sorry."

"It's okay. It's no big deal." Genevieve patted his shoulder and they all sat down.

Landon could see Megan was still embarrassed by the incident and blotting her shorts with water under the table. He suspected Katy's now-deadpan face was her way of showing contempt. Landon felt his own face burning. To rebuild their image of him, he forced a chuckle and blurted out, "I'm good at knocking things over. That's why I'm going to play football."

"What?" Katy's face morphed into disbelief. "How?"

"Well, he's getting—" Genevieve started to explain.

Megan's face brightened, though. "That's *great*, Landon."

"Is it?" Landon thought so, but her enthusiasm puzzled him.

"Yes." She nodded, smiling.

He had to ask. "Why?"

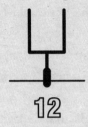

12

Landon leaned toward Megan's face, intent on her lips. The diner around them created a buzzing hum that made hearing even more difficult for him. Crowded places were always a nightmare.

"Well," she said, still bright, "my boyfriend is the quarterback."

"Your . . . wait, what?"

"My boyfriend."

Landon didn't think things could get worse. Then they did.

"His name is Skip," Megan said.

Landon knew of only one Skip, the redheaded boy from their first lunch at the deli, and something told him that was exactly who Megan was talking about.

"He's super nice." Megan spoke very directly to Landon, and he now noticed that her voice was funny, loud and slow, like he was four years old instead of twelve. "He's tall and he's cute and he can help you fit in." Megan reached out and patted Landon's arm and then sat back, proud of her ability to communicate with him.

"You talk like you think I'm stupid." Landon's mood plummeted.

Genevieve poked his arm. "Landon, be nice."

Landon glared at his sister. "I can hear, you know." He pointed to his cochlears.

The waitress appeared, and Genevieve took advantage of the opportunity to change the subject. "Let's order! I'll have prosciutto on toast with a side salad and balsamic vinaigrette, please. Landon, how about you?"

"Pastrami." Landon folded his arms across his chest and slumped in his chair. His brain felt like mud, wet and gooey, a real mess. Katy looked at him like he was some kind of toad. When he felt a tap on his arm, he turned to see Megan, not sulking back or mad or babying him, but with a bright smile.

"I'm sorry, Landon," she said. "I never knew a deaf person before. I'll get it right. Just be patient with me, okay?"

Landon's mouth fell open. He wanted to cry, but knew he had to choke back his emotions. He hadn't really known how he wanted people to treat him before, only that they all either treated him with syrupy kindness that felt fake or, worse, with cruelty for being so big and clumsy and hard to understand and deaf.

Now, here was this beautiful girl who made his heart whirr, and she'd done what he wanted everyone to do: be honest and understanding, offering kindness without pity.

"Yes," he said, "I can be patient. Thank you."

"My pleasure," she said to him before turning to the waitress. "I'll have a grilled cheese with fries, extra pickles, and can you bring my friend another Coke, please?"

Megan nodded at Landon's nearly empty drink, and it was only then he realized she was talking about *him*.

Landon took a breath and held it, savoring the fizz and the flavor, not of the Coke, but of maybe, finally, having a friend.

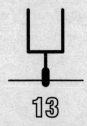

13

Landon stayed busy with his sandwich and then explained to Megan that he could hear, just not like most people. He pointed to the metal disc attached to the back of the right side of his head. "I had surgery. There's an implant under here. A wire goes from the implant into my inner ear, where they put a computer chip. The disc transmits sound impulses to my inner ear."

Landon pointed behind his ear. "You might think this is a big hearing aid. Actually, it's the processor and also the battery, and it picks up sound waves and sends them to the metal disc, which sends them to my inner ear. I've got the same things on the left side. My mom just calls the whole setup my 'ears.'"

Megan nodded, clearly interested. But Katy just looked on, more in bewilderment than anything, like she couldn't believe Megan was bothering with him.

"So, I hear," Landon explained to Megan, "but it's not like what you hear. Nothing is ever really clear, and I need to see people's faces."

"Like lipreading?" Megan asked.

"Yeah, but really the whole face is important," Landon said. "I put it all together, what I hear and what I see, and I guess I can understand people pretty well, but . . ."

Megan tilted her head. "What?"

"With my family, I tap them to get them to look at me so I can see them. It's a habit," he said.

"So?"

Landon shrugged. "Other people don't always like it."

Megan shrugged back. "Too bad for them." She popped the last of her fries into her mouth. "Hey, are we going swimming or what?"

Genevieve paid with the credit card, and when the other girls tried to give her money she told them they could take her out next time. Landon just watched and felt like a goof, but that didn't stop him from feeling proud of her and mystified at this new world they lived in: his little sister buying lunches on a credit card, ordering iced tea and prosciutto like grownups. On their way out of the diner, Landon tapped Genevieve on the shoulder and spoke low. "You're awesome, you know that?"

"You are, too." She hugged his middle and stood on her tippy toes to kiss his cheek.

Landon walked behind Genevieve and Katy, right along-side Megan.

Landon learned that Katy's father was the richest man in Bronxville, and he supposed that was why Genevieve tolerated her eye-rolling and rude attitude. Megan was confident. She described her father, the president of the country club, as a "climber"—which made Landon think of his mother, although he didn't say so.

Megan was careful to look at him when she spoke, and they talked about *Bridge to Terabithia*, which was her favorite book. Landon mostly listened and felt a little foolish when he told her it was too sad for his taste.

Megan looked disappointed. "Lots of the best books are sad."

Landon wiped the beads of sweat from his upper lip, aware that his bulk was making him feel hotter still. "I know. But life is sad. Why should books be sad, too? I want books to be happy. I like heroes, and adventures."

She brightened. "Do you like *Ella Enchanted*?" Then she scowled. "Did you read *Ella Enchanted*?"

"I did." Landon nodded hard and fast.

Katy laughed, and it seemed to Landon from the flick of her eyes that she was laughing *at* him, but he ignored her and continued. "See? That's a happy ending. How about the Chronicles of Narnia? Have you read those?"

Megan shook her head. "No."

"Oh, well, you have to." Landon trudged on, feeling the solid sidewalk beneath his feet and standing tall so that he easily looked over the top of his sister's head as they walked past the gate posts into their driveway. Now that he saw the house through the eyes of the richest girl in town, it seemed more like a cottage than a mansion, and Landon was sharply aware of the untrimmed hedges and a shutter that needed fixing on one of the upper windows.

As they reached the side door, he wondered if he should have even admitted to reading *Ella Enchanted,* because he doubted that was the kind of book a real football player would read. He felt certain Megan's boyfriend, Skip, wouldn't read such a thing. In a storm of self-doubt and discomfort, he went upstairs to his room to get changed into his bathing suit.

When he arrived at the pool, the girls had already put out their towels on the lounge chairs. Landon claimed a chair, and then he pulled Genevieve aside. "Should I wear my shirt or take it off?"

Genevieve studied his face. "Why would you leave it on?"

Landon lifted his shirt and pointed to the pale roll of blubber spilling over the band of his red bathing suit. "This."

Genevieve frowned and swatted the air. "No one cares, Landon. You're not posing for a magazine." She said louder, "How about a cannonball contest?"

Landon raised his eyebrows.

Katy frowned.

Megan studied Landon's face and seemed to read his mind. "That's a great idea. I love cannonballs."

Landon grinned and disconnected his "ears" without hesitation, wrapping them in his towel and setting them on the table next to his chair beneath a wide green umbrella. He was bursting with pride as he stepped up to the board. He remembered his manners and invited the girls to go first. When they said no, he dove right in, showering them in a geyser of water. They all declared him the clear winner. After that, he sprang off the end of the diving board—time after time—sending up fountains of spray that reached for the sky and waves that had the girls giddy, laughing and rocking like ships in a storm on inflatable rafts.

He didn't have to hear to know they were bubbling with joy, even Katy. It was one of those summer days that were never meant to end. He'd even forgotten about football, until his father called them in for an early dinner. Landon saw the joy drain from everyone's faces. He dried his head and then reattached his ears, nerves already back on edge.

"Your friends are welcome to stay, Genevieve." Their father stood in the kitchen doorway with an apron on and a spatula in his hand.

The girls seemed shaken by his presence. They toweled off and said they had to get home.

"But thank you, Mr. Dorch." Megan gave a happy wave as she and Katy made a fast exit through the gate that led to a path through the bushes to the driveway.

Dripping on the red brick terrace surrounding the pool, Landon said, "That was fun, Genevieve."

"You were great." Genevieve reached up and put a hand on his shoulder. "Landon, they really like you."

Landon blushed. "Well, I think it's you they like and they were just being nice."

She shook her head. "No, Landon, they liked *you*. Especially Megan."

Landon felt a jolt of pleasure at the sound of her name, and he stared at the gate through which she'd departed. "But she has a boyfriend. It's gotta be that Skip kid you shoved."

Genevieve bit her lip. "It is him, but sometimes people make mistakes. Maybe he'll turn out all right. Maybe when she tells him we're all friends, he'll be nice to you. Heck, you're going to be teammates. That counts for a lot, right?"

Landon studied her face. He wanted her to be right, but when he remembered the shove she'd given Skip, knocking him back into that table full of women and spilling their drinks and embarrassing him in front of everyone, he said, "I don't know, Genevieve. Does it?"

They both knew that as soon as dinner was over, he was going to find out.

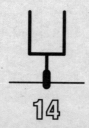

14

A handful of signs taped to broomsticks and stuck into orange highway cones directed Landon and his father to the Westchester Youth Football League weigh-ins. They could have just as easily followed the crowd of parents and their sons ranging in age from four to fourteen.

People were putting baked goods on the check-in table as if they were making an offering to the gods of football. Landon's mom had had to work late, so his father set the oatmeal cookies made with honey down beside a plate of brownies. Landon's father also had the list of things she wanted him to tell the officials, including the doctor's clearance. Under an overhang outside the middle school gym, they got in line in front of the seventh-grade team check-in table. Landon mostly kept his eyes ahead, but stole secret glances all around and tugged his Browns cap down snug on his head. The man behind the desk wore stylish metal-framed glasses. When he saw Landon he reared back. "Whoa! Heh, heh. Guys, this is the seventh-grade line. Eighth is over there."

"No," Landon's dad said, getting out his checkbook. "He's in seventh grade."

The man with glasses turned and nudged the tall man sitting next to him. "Bob, we got a bison here, for sure a Double X."

"What's your name?" the man with glasses asked.

"He's Landon Dorch," Landon's father answered for him. "What's that mean? Double X?"

"Dorch, I got it." The man with the glasses drew a line through Landon's name on his list of registrants from the league's website. "Uh, it means he can only play right tackle on offense and left end on defense. No big deal. A kid his size is a hog anyway, right?"

Landon's father frowned and he straightened his back. "Hog?"

The man with the glasses laughed in a friendly way. "A line-man. A hog. It's a good thing. A football term. We love a kid as big as yours. Coach Bell was a hog, right, Coach?" He turned to the man standing at the scale with a clipboard. Beside him was a boy nearly as big as Landon, but harder looking, like a big sack of rocks.

"Yes, and so is my boy." Coach Bell clapped the big bruiser on the shoulder. "You and Brett will be on the line together."

"Hi, I'm Brett." Brett Bell stepped forward without hesitation and gave Landon a firm handshake and a smile. "See you out there."

Landon watched Brett march off toward the exit before turning toward the coach. Coach Bell was about six feet tall and easily three hundred pounds. He wore a bright green T-shirt, a Bronxville Football cap, and a whistle around his neck.

"Coach Bell was a Division III All-American at Union, and his wife's little brother plays for the Giants. You know, Jonathan Wagner? He's the right tackle." The man with glasses gazed at Coach Bell with respect. "Here, let's get Landon on that scale, and Mr. Dorch, you'll need to sign up for at least two volunteer jobs with Bob, but we'd be happy if you took three or four, depending on your work schedule."

"Let's get Landon weighed," Coach Bell said.

"Should I take off my shoes?" Landon asked Coach Bell, awed by the coach's All-American status and relationship to a real NFL player.

At the sound of Landon's garbled voice, all three men from the league looked at each other with alarm. The man with the glasses turned to Landon's dad and spoke in a low voice so that it was hard for Landon to make out what he was saying. But if Landon read his lips right, he said, "Uh, Mr. Dorch. Is your son . . . uh, does he have a problem we should know about?"

Landon's dad gave Landon a nervous glance, then shook his head at the man with glasses. "Landon has a slight difficulty speaking, but he's a B-plus student. He has cochlear implants to help him hear, so we've got a special helmet on order and a doctor's clearance for him to play."

"Wait a minute," the man said. "I need more than that."

Standing by the scale, Landon swallowed hard and bit his lip. This wasn't how he wanted to begin his football career.

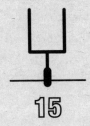

15

Landon's dad went into his speech. "Landon is deaf. When he was four he got cochlear implants, so he hears sound and he can read lips. But to really understand speech it's best if he hears and sees what's said."

"He reads lips?" The man shot what looked like a nervous glance at Landon.

"He uses a combination of sight and sound to understand," Landon's dad said.

"But he can't wear those things with a football helmet," the man said.

Landon's dad nodded. "Yes, he can. There's actually a company that makes custom helmets. Landon isn't the first, either, and we have a doctor's note."

"Okay, okay. That's great. Really." The man with glasses threw his hands up in the air in total surrender. "I'm sorry. I didn't mean any offense at all, and if he has special needs we can work with that, but we just have to know."

Landon's father gritted his teeth and shook his head. "No, he isn't special needs. He just needs to see you speak." He showed them all the doctor's clearance.

The men looked at the paper, and then Coach Bell said, "Super. Okay, let's go. On the scale, Landon. Here we go."

"So, should I take off my shoes?" It seemed like years since Landon first asked this.

Coach Bell looked down. "Yeah, it's the rules."

Landon bent down and took his shoes off. He tugged his T-shirt over his gut before he stepped onto the scale.

"I knew it!" Coach Bell craned his neck to read the digital number. "Yup. Double X. You'll be great on the line."

Landon's father said, "But he can only play certain positions?"

"Yes," Coach Bell explained. "For safety these really big boys—the Double X's—can only play right tackle on offense and left end on defense."

Landon didn't know whether to feel proud or humiliated. The man with glasses gave him a mouth guard in a plastic bag and instructed him to go out on the football field and look for the coaches with the bright green T-shirts. Landon's dad put a hand on his shoulder and guided him toward the field.

When they got there, Landon's dad pointed to one end where two fathers wore bright green T-shirts with matching caps and whistles around their necks, just the same as Coach Bell at the weigh-in. There were blocking dummies and small, bright orange cones set out in some kind of order Landon didn't recognize from his YouTube study of the game. Some of the dummies, big yellow cylinders standing tall, were for blocking and tackling. Others, blue rectangles lying flat in the grass, were used for soft boundary markers. Beyond the end zone was a metal sled with five football-player-shaped pads whose single purpose he knew: blocking.

"Okay." His father stopped at the sideline and pointed. "There's your group—your team. Good luck, son."

Landon looked up at his father, who studied the team from beneath the shade of his hand. When he realized Landon wasn't moving, he gave him a little push. "Go ahead. You can do this, Landon. Everything new is always a little scary."

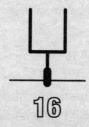

16

He nodded. "Okay, Dad." Landon put one foot in front of the other and headed toward the growing group of kids wearing shorts and T-shirts and cleats who milled around the coaches in green. Skip was throwing a ball to his spiky-haired friend, and when he saw Landon he called out, "Hey, Mike, the baby giant came back." Landon moved toward the other side of the field where two other boys huddled together on a tipped-over blocking dummy, whispering. Landon sat down on the dummy directly across from them. He looked intently at them until they suddenly stopped talking.

The two boys looked at Landon like he was crazy, then at each other, and simply got up and walked away without a word.

Landon scanned the area and picked some grass. He knew he should have just said hello, but he wasn't comfortable doing it. He knew his speech sounded off. The other kids were fooling around, pushing each other with foam shields or tossing foot-balls.

That outsider feeling he'd lived with his whole life tight-ened its grip on Landon's heart, threatening to turn him into a mound of jelly. It felt like the drop at Splash Mountain all over again, so Landon clenched his teeth and dug deep. This was his chance to be a football player, and if he did what he thought he could do, they'd all respect him—and maybe out-right *like* him. One coach noticed him and headed his way with a bright white smile that made him feel much, much better.

The coach smelled of citrus cologne, but he looked like a tri-athlete. His cabled muscles were tan and his close-set, dark eyes intense without effort. Up close, Landon could see a dusting of gray at the edges of his dark, short hair. The coach stopped in front of Landon and extended a hand weighed down by some kind of championship ring. "Hey, buddy, I'm Coach Furster, the head coach. Look, you don't want to sit on the bags like that."

Landon popped right up. "Sorry, Coach. I . . . the other guys . . ." Landon stopped because he didn't want to seem like a rat.

"And lose the hat, buddy." Coach Furster glowered so that his eyes almost appeared to have crossed, and Landon wondered if he had some deep-seated hatred of the Cleveland Browns. "You see anybody else wearing a *hat*?"

"Oh, um," he started, but with Coach glaring at him, Landon reluctantly tugged off his hat. Coach Furster's jaw fell. "What? Whoa. Hey, what the . . ."

"It's . . . it's just my hearing stuff, Coach. My mom calls them my 'ears.' They help me hear."

Coach Furster waved a hand. "No worries, buddy. Hey, you're okay with the hat. That's fine. I had no idea. I know you're new and I was just thinking you'd want to fit in. That's always what you want, but you're fine with the hat."

Landon replaced the hat and studied the coach intently. Coach Furster stood straight and wiped his mouth like there was food on it. "What? What are you looking at?"

"Just . . . your face, Coach."

"Why?" Coach Furster wrinkled his thick brow so that his eyebrows sank and his eyes nearly crossed again.

"Just"—Landon pointed in the general direction of his ears—"so I can hear what you're saying, or know what you're saying."

Coach Furster only blinked at him.

"It's easier to understand when I can see your lips," Landon explained.

"Well, you're apt to miss a lot that way." Coach Furster twirled his whistle and the tattoo on the side of his biceps—some Chinese symbol—jumped and quivered. "But don't worry. We can bring you along slow. Was Coach Bell at your check-in?"

"Yes," Landon said. "He told me I was a Double X player."

"Coach West and I will have to talk to him," Coach Furster said. "Meanwhile, you just watch how we do things and then we can see how you do."

"I'll watch everything, Coach." Landon nodded vigorously. "For sure. I watch drills on YouTube all the time."

"Great." Coach Furster put a hand on Landon's shoulder and escorted him over to the sideline in a cloud of that citrus cologne. "You know what? Heck, who cares?" Coach Furster knocked over a blocking dummy and dragged it ten feet off the field. "You can sit right there. That's fine. You sit and watch and you'll pick up a lot, right? You're a careful observer, I bet." Coach Furster pointed at him and winked.

"For sure, Coach." Landon took a seat and beamed up at his new coach.

"That's great, Landon." Coach Furster patted his shoulder. "This is gonna work out just great. Glad to have you on the team."

Landon followed the coach with his eyes, the smell fading into the grass. Coach Furster returned to the other coach—Coach West—a tall, thin man who made Landon think of an undertaker. They were soon joined by big Coach Bell. They had a short, animated discussion. Landon couldn't make it all out, but he knew by the way they kept looking at him that he—or really his ears—was the topic.

Then he caught a full view of Coach Bell's red face and could clearly see what he was saying. "—not mentally challenged. He talks funny because he's *deaf.* He's huge, and he's got a doctor's clearance and a custom helmet and his dad says he can read lips."

At that, all three coaches looked his way and Landon quickly averted his eyes, studying the grass. The blast of whistles got his attention and he saw that the coaches had moved on. The team fell into five lines, creating a rigid order where before it had been mayhem. Skip and his two friends, floppy-haired Xander and

69

spiky-haired Mike, headed up three of the five lines. Another was headed by Coach Bell's son, Brett.

Whistles tooted and players took off from their lines, running with high knees from the goal line to the thirty-yard line and then stopping and reforming the lines, only to return some other way. They went back and forth with a backward run, a sideways shuffle, cross-over steps, butt kickers, and some runs Landon couldn't even describe.

After about ten minutes of that, everyone spread out and they did some more stretching. Five minutes later they were broken into three equal groups and running through agility drills overseen by the coaches. On the whistle, the players would sprint from one station to the next, with the coaches issuing an occasional bark—it seemed to Landon a mixture of criticism and praise.

After that they worked on form tackling drills, just going through the precise movements of a tackle in slow motion since no one had pads on. Then the team split up into skill players—mostly the smaller guys like Skip and Mike and a kid named Layne Guerrero—who went with Coach Bell, and the lineman, or hogs, like Brett Bell, who went with Coach Furster and Coach West.

When the lineman began getting into stances and firing out into the blocking dummies held by their teammates, Landon stood up.

He felt silly just sitting and was pretty certain he could do what they were doing. There was one guy without a partner, a kid not as big as Landon but with even more girth around the belly and big Band-Aids on each knee. Landon grabbed the dummy he'd been sitting on and dragged it over to him.

"Hey," Landon said cheerfully. The kid looked at him like he was nuts, but Landon pressed on. "I can be your partner. Here, you go first."

Landon hefted the bag between the two of them, grabbed the handles on both sides, and leaned into it just the way the others were doing. The kid got down, and on the coach's cadence, he fired out into the dummy, jarring Landon, who fought to keep his feet.

"Hey! Hey!" Coach West was shouting, and he flew over to Landon's new partner and got right in his face. "Did anyone tell you to pair off with this kid, Timmy?"

The boy named Timmy shook his head with a terrified look.

A whistle shrieked and all motions stopped. Coach Furster marched over in a cloud of cologne. "Whoa, whoa, whoa. Landon, what are you doing, buddy?"

"I just . . ." Landon hefted the bag. "I can do this, Coach. It's easy."

The word "easy" set Coach Furster off. He was suddenly furious. "Easy, Landon? Glad you think it's easy. Okay, let's give you a shot and see how *easy* it is. Ready?"

Coach Furster jammed the whistle in the corner of his mouth and snatched the dummy from Landon, spinning it around without any regard for the fine gold watch on his wrist. "Down!"

Landon looked all around. The kids were all smirking, and some were giggling.

"I said, 'Down!' Come on, you been watching." Coach

Furster's face was turning red. "You know what to do. Down!"

A light went off in Landon's head and he put his hand down in the grass, just one, palm flat in a three-point stance.

"Set . . . Hut!"

Landon stumbled into the dummy with his shoulder and started pumping his feet up and down the way he'd seen the others do, pushing with all his might. Coach Furster dragged the dummy backward and Landon felt it slipping away. He churned his feet, grabbed for the handles on the bag but missed, caught the coach's fine watch, let go with a gasp, tripped, and fell flat on his face. Landon could taste the grass and feel the vibration of laughter all around him. He didn't have to see it.

He didn't have to hear it.

In his ears rang his mother's words: "Be careful what you wish for, Landon, because you just might get it."

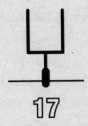

17

"How was practice?" Landon's mom looked up from her cup of tea as he and his dad walked in through the garage door. Her eyes were red-rimmed and drooping with exhaustion. She had her shoes off and her feet up on an ottoman, stretching her toes. Beside her, a briefcase bulged with papers, and her dress was wrinkled.

Landon didn't want to alarm her, or anyone. "Fine."

"Just fine?" She arched an eyebrow and studied his face.

His father stepped into the scene from the kitchen. "He has lots to learn, is all. They don't give the babies rattles in this town; they give them footballs."

Landon shook his head. "We had to run about a million sprints at the end of practice. I'm tired."

He thought she might have said, "Me too," as he walked on past, heading for the stairs and a shower.

It was under the safety of the pounding water, without his ears and in the silence of his own world, that he let himself sob. Football practice was nothing like he had expected. Instead of being glorious and uplifting, it had confused and belittled him. He felt like an orange with all its juice squeezed out. When he got out of the shower his eyes were so red that he decided to get in bed with his book and the clip-on reading light that wouldn't let his parents get a good look at him when they came in to kiss him good-night.

After a short time, his mother appeared. She gave him a kiss and a hug, and he could tell she was exhausted because it was a rare thing to see her shoulders slump.

His father came in a few minutes later, sat on the edge of the bed, and patted his leg to get his attention.

Landon sighed and looked up. "Tired."

His father looked at the ears Landon had placed on the nightstand beside his bed, and then he made a fist with his thumb sticking out. Even though they didn't use sign language, there were a few signs they all knew, and when his father kept his fist tight, put the thumb into the right side of his stomach, and drew a straight line up toward his face, Landon knew what it meant.

Proud.

Landon bit the inside of his lip and hugged his dad. He tried not to cry again, but it hit him like a tidal wave.

"I don't want to be deaf, Dad," he cried out, painfully aware that he couldn't hear his own words. "I don't want to be different." His whole body lurched and shook, and he squeezed his father tight.

His dad simply hugged him tighter as they sat together in the dim light.

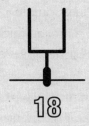

18

Landon spent the next day studying football drills and stances on YouTube. And that evening at practice, he refused to sit out and just watch. Instead, he joined everyone and fell into a line for stretching. The coaches had to have noticed him but didn't say anything, and Landon's apprehension began to fade as he jogged around with the other big guys, running through agility drills. He had watched closely the day before, so he knew what to do in the drills, even though his feet weren't as nimble as his brain. He wasn't expected to look as graceful as the quarterbacks, Skip Dreyfus and his backup, Bryce Rinehart, but he hoped he could match a fireplug like Travis Tinnin or Timmy Nichols. It wasn't pretty, though. Landon stumbled regularly on the bags as he wove in and out or high-stepped over them. He got through it, though, sweating and huffing but proud.

When they began hitting bags, Landon stood back to

watch. He didn't want a repeat of the night before when he'd made a fool out of himself, falling on his face. His plan was to watch until he was confident about exactly what to do. Gunner Miller was the right tackle, the only position Landon could play, so he watched him most carefully. Still, Brett Bell stood out, as did the center, the short and thick Travis Tinnin.

After a while Coach Furster gave his whistle a blast and shouted, "Sled time, boys!"

They all jogged over to the rough patch of grass beyond the end zone where the blocking sled waited with its thick metal skeleton and five firmly padded blocking dummies in a row. Landon thought he might be able to do this drill, but he hesitated and stood back as five players jumped in front of the pads, blasting them on the sound of Coach Furster's whistle. The next group replaced them immediately, striking the bags on the whistle and driving their feet like they were pushing a boulder up a hill.

It didn't look easy. The sled lurched reluctantly across the grass on the thick metal skids. If one of the players on either end didn't do his part, the entire sled would rotate like the spoke of a wheel, with the deficient player stuck in one spot, exposed for all to see.

"We're only as strong as our weakest link," Coach Furster— who rode atop the sled like a rodeo cowboy—growled. Two out of three times that happened, the offender was Timmy Nichols. "Come on, Nichols! Is that all you got? My grandmother could do better than that!"

Landon felt like he could do at least as good as Coach Furster's grandmother, but it was time for the next drill before he had a chance to try.

Sprints at the end were awful. Landon quickly lost his breath. Sweat poured from his skin. He was slick and hurting as he stumbled across the finish line, dead last every time. No one was in as bad a shape as Landon, not even Timmy Nichols, but Landon knew that football was a game of getting up. You had to keep going, again and again. That's how you got better, and that's what he meant to do.

The next day at practice, Landon spotted Timmy Nichols off by himself before the start. Apparently, Timmy arrived early to improve his sled skills by firing out low and hard against his nemesis time after time before practice began. Landon knew what Timmy was trying to do—he'd studied over a dozen YouTube videos on sled work earlier that day. Landon reached the sled without Timmy's notice. He watched the chunky player line up in his three-point stance, fire his shoulder into the sled, chop his feet up and down like engine pistons, and then stop and do it all over again. Landon stood watching several times before he stepped forward and spoke. "Hey, want some help?"

Timmy looked up in disgust. "Get away from me. I don't need any help. I'm not some moron."

Landon scowled and shook his head. "I'm not either. And I watched—"

Timmy let his hands hang uselessly in praying mantis form and turned his toes inward like a pigeon. His mouth hung open

77

and his tongue slid sideways as he mocked Landon. *"I'm not a moron."*

"I'm not." Landon swallowed. He felt like he was falling through space. "I've got a B-plus average."

But Timmy wasn't listening. He'd already turned away, back toward the blocking sled, and Landon didn't catch what he'd said. Determined to get Timmy's attention, Landon moved close and tapped his shoulder. Timmy spun violently and glared up at Landon with the hatred of a small, trapped animal. "Don't touch me!"

Startled by Timmy's poisonous look, Landon only wanted to explain. "I didn't mean to scare you. I just didn't know what you said. I need to see."

"Get out of here!" Timmy gave Landon a shove that barely moved him.

Landon stood still as fury engulfed him. In his mind, he saw himself grabbing Timmy and slamming him into the dirt. "What is your problem? I said I'd help you!"

"Oh?" Timmy acted like he could read Landon's mind. "You think you're tough? Go ahead, if you're so tough; hit me!"

Timmy stuck his chin out and pointed to the sweet spot, jabbing his finger, just off center to the right where his small chin made a dimple in the rolls of neck fat.

Landon's fists balled into tight hammers of war and he reared back, ready to throw the punch of a lifetime.

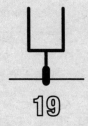

19

The shriek of a whistle shocked Landon like a wet wire.

Timmy jumped and took off.

Landon dropped his fists to his side. He stood, shoulders slumped, as he watched Timmy disappear into the swirling throng of football players who quickly assembled with the precision of a well-trained army.

Still enraged, Landon folded his arms tightly across his chest and marched defiantly to the end of a line. He had to force himself to do the warm-ups correctly, and when the blocking drills began, instead of sitting on a dummy off to the side, he stood scowling and trying to work up his nerve to try. He shadowed the linemen, following them closely so the coaches would know he was watching carefully, even though he never could quite bring himself to enter the drills. He wore an

79

unending frown and muttered to himself, wanting everyone to see how angry he was.

But practice went on as normal, and no one seemed to notice him. When it was time to run, Landon set himself up on the line along with the others, determined to show them something. He ran like his life depended upon it, beating Timmy and several of the other slower kids on the first sprint, and then turned, ready to go again on the whistle. For the first ten sprints, he stayed ahead of Timmy, but then his stomach clenched. Timmy tied him on the next sprint. After that, even Timmy began to pull away. Still Landon labored on. He was going to do better. He wasn't going to let them mock him.

He chased the sluggish Timmy and kept at his heels. On the last sprint, when the rest of the team turned to cheer him over the finish line, he could only hear Timmy's insult crackle in his head over and over. The jolts made his legs pump just a bit faster and just a bit more true. With hatred fueling him, Landon pushed past the pain. Halfway across the width of the field, Landon caught up to Timmy. The rest of the team went wild, cheering now for sure, delighted by the contest between two chubby boys for last place.

Landon felt like if he could only beat Timmy, he'd stop being the biggest loser on the team. He'd have someone beneath him. With an agonizing groan, he flung his arms and legs forward. That's when Timmy made the mistake of looking back. When he turned his head, his tired legs tangled. He tripped and fell and Landon slogged past, pumping his arms and legs for all he was worth, the team now going wild.

"Lan-don! Lan-don! Lan-don!" they all chanted.

When Landon crossed the line, he staggered and collapsed. He rolled to his side and wretched, vomiting the remains of his father's tuna and string bean casserole onto the grass. The entire team roared with laughter, and as Landon lay there, doubled in pain, he was suddenly not so sure that he'd made things any better for himself at all.

Laughter swirled around him like smoke, and his vision was blurred by sweat and maybe a tear, but he tried to think not. Someone was saying something to him. He could hear it amid the other noise. He wasn't sure what they were saying. He thought it was, "Come on, Landon, get up."

Then he felt a hand grip his arm, and he turned his head to see who had reached down to help him. When he saw who it was, Landon got so emotional that he almost lost it.

20

Landon didn't break down. He fought his twisted face back into a mask of toughness and let Skip Dreyfus help him up. Everyone else was still laughing, but Dreyfus was all business.

"Let's go!" Coach Furster hollered. "Bring it in on me!"

Everyone reached his hand in toward Coach Furster's fist, carefully avoiding contact with the watch Landon had learned was a Cartier Panther. Landon concentrated on the coach's face.

"You gonna be ready to beat Tuckahoe?" Coach Furster bellowed.

"Yes!" the team answered.

"You sure?" Coach Furster's face turned red and his eyes turned dangerously close to his nose.

"Yes!" they screamed.

"All right, 'Hit, Hustle, Win' on three," the coach barked. "One, two, three . . ."

"HIT, HUSTLE, WIN!" The whole team shouted, raising their hands straight into the air before breaking apart like a wave on the beach.

Landon found himself next to Timmy, with Skip's spiky-haired friend, Mike, who was Coach Furster's son, on the other side. Landon thought he heard Mike Furster talking to him, so he looked, but Mike was talking to Timmy.

". . . careful or he'll take your position."

"My position?" Timmy wrinkled his face.

"Yeah, left out." Mike busted out laughing like a maniac at his own joke. Landon looked away and kept going. He was aware of the joke. Some people played right tackle or left guard or right end, but if someone wasn't even worth being on the field, their position was left out.

Landon trudged uphill toward the parking lot where his dad stood just like the other dads, looking down onto the field.

"Are you okay?" His father kept his voice down, but Landon could see what he'd said and also the alarm on his face.

"I'm fine."

"Fine? It looked like you collapsed. Did you get *sick*?" His father spoke in a hushed tone and he looked around.

"I'm fine." Landon waved his hand dismissively, feeling a bit proud. "It happens, Dad. That's football. You gotta get up. You gotta keep going."

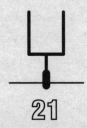

21

Saturday, the FedEx man delivered Landon's helmet. Landon and his father unwrapped it together, and his father helped him put on the skullcap and adjust the chin strap according to the instructions. As promised, the helmet went nicely around his cochlear, and with a rubber bulb pump, his father inflated the inner bladder, making everything good and snug for a safe fit. Landon attached the mouthpiece to the face mask cage and wore the helmet around the house for the rest of the morning.

After lunch, Landon's dad reminded him he had to cut the lawn. Landon got that job done—riding around on their John Deere and sweating beneath the helmet in the hot sun. After a splash in the pool to cool down, he changed into shorts and cleats for football practice. He swapped out the new helmet for his Browns cap, leaving the helmet on his bedpost.

"You don't have to drive me," he said to his father as they

backed out of the driveway. "I could walk to the school—it's close enough."

His dad angled his mouth toward him while keeping his eyes in the mirror as he maneuvered the Prius. "Don't want you wearing out your cleats on the sidewalk. Besides, everyone else gets dropped off."

"Well, thanks." Landon's mind quickly turned to practice—which drills he'd participate in and those he knew he wasn't ready for.

Landon felt the thrill of being on a team as he ran onto the field and looked around from his spot in the back of a line. Stretching was a breeze, even though no one spoke to him, and doing bag drills was easier, but he still hesitated when it came to blocking the sled. He stood close, hoping maybe Coach Furster might invite him to join, but the coach was intent on the players in front of him and his whistle, and sweat flew from his face and arms like insects taking flight. Landon told himself that not this practice, but the next would be the day he would participate fully.

After the first three drills, the whistle blew for their lone water break. The team had water bottles that Coach West seemed to be in charge of, and Landon stayed far away from them. There were two metal-framed carriers that held six bottles each, and Landon didn't want someone asking him to give them one even once, afraid that it could set a pattern for him to be the water boy.

Each plastic bottle had a screw-on cap with a nozzle that looked like a bent straw, and the players would grab them and squirt water into their mouths. This way, Coach Furster explained to the team, they could constantly re-hydrate without having to waste precious practice time on multiple water breaks.

"I'm greedy." Coach Furster looked around at his players with a crooked smile. "The league says we can only practice two hours a day, and I don't want to waste a second of it. It's like an Ironman, boys. When I do one, they run alongside you and squirt fluids into your mouth. You don't even break stride."

At the end of practice, after the first few sprints, Landon lost his steam. By the time they reached the twentieth sprint across the field, he could barely make it. The whole team cheered—or jeered, Landon wasn't exactly sure of the sound—as he dragged himself, gasping, in an agonizing shuffle across the final finish line.

Coach Furster looked at him with something between amazement and disgust and said, "Well, kid, you don't quit. I'll give you that."

Landon blushed and tugged his Cleveland Browns cap low on his head as he fought back the urge to puke up the churning liquid in his stomach.

He didn't know how the other linemen did it. Travis looked so blocky. Gunner and Brett Bell were both big guys too, but they ran right alongside the team's running back, Guerrero, and Rinehart, the backup quarterback. Skip Dreyfus, the starting quarterback, was in a league of his own. He led the team in every sprint, from start to finish. If Skip ever got tired, he never showed it.

Even though he was kind of scary with his burning green

eyes, red hair, and angry freckles, Landon couldn't help but admire Skip. First in everything, he snapped from one place to another like a gear in some kind of machine. As quarterback, he barked out the cadence with command, executed handoffs with precision, and delivered whistling passes that sometimes left the receivers wiggling their fingers to ease the sting. Everyone admired Skip, even the coaches.

Landon wondered if he'd ever get respect like that. Or any respect at all.

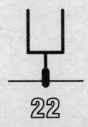

22

After practice he climbed into the Prius without speaking. And even though the drive wasn't more than a few blocks, Landon left a puddle of sweat in the front seat when he got out.

"Landon." His father pointed to the puddle. "Get a towel, please."

"Sorry. We ran super hard." Landon grabbed a rag from the bucket in the garage that his father used when he washed the car, and he mopped up the sweat.

"I know." His father watched him closely and gave a nod of approval before they headed into the house. "I saw you. You worked really hard, and you'll get there someday."

His father's words somehow made Landon feel worse.

Inside, Landon headed upstairs to take a shower. Minutes later, from his bedroom window, dripping and wrapped in a towel, he saw his sister and her two new best friends splashing about in the pool in the evening shadows. Already there was a star in the sky, but he could still make out Megan's skinny figure as she bounced high and did a flip off the diving board. Katy and Genevieve shrieked and clapped from the shallow end. Landon turned away from the window. It felt wrong to spy on them.

When he came back down in clean shorts and a T-shirt, his father was busy in the dusky shadows of the living room, writing feverishly at his desk. Landon wandered over and stood until his father looked up.

"Where's Mom?" Landon asked.

"Oh." His father scratched his neck. "This is a big job she's got now, Landon. Really big. So it's hard for her not to work, even on a Saturday. I think it'll be a while before she gets settled into more regular hours."

"Like days?" Landon asked.

"Maybe weeks. Maybe months." His father glanced at the glowing computer screen, the bluish light spilling over his face. "I'm not sure, really, but my book is coming along well. I'm calling it *Dragon Hunt*. Um . . . my main character is kind of modeled after you."

"Me?" Landon looked suspiciously at the screen. "Why?"

"Well, a good main character has to overcome obstacles, and you want him to be a nice person, and that sounds like you to me." Landon's father smiled and pointed at him before glancing toward the screen. "I thought I'd maybe name him 'Landon' too."

Landon felt a chill. If his father *did* ever get his book published, the last thing Landon needed was another thing people could make fun of—Landon, the oversized guard of Dorchester. "No, that's okay. I don't think so."

"What do you mean?" Landon's dad laughed and offered a puzzled smile. "Why wouldn't you want a character named after you?"

"I just . . . I don't know, Dad. Do I have to have a reason?" Landon backed away toward the kitchen. "Can I get something to eat?"

"Sure, there's plenty of casserole left." His father looked at him but remained seated in front of the computer. "Or you could make yourself a cheese sandwich. There are tomatoes in the crisper."

The thought of the casserole he'd spilled onto the football field the day before turned his empty stomach. "I'll make a sandwich."

Landon had everything out and had just finished construction of his sandwich, with thick wedges of cheddar and juicy, ripe tomato slices on fresh-cut Italian bread, when his father wandered into the kitchen. "What about the name Nodnal?"

"Nodnal?" Landon stopped with the sandwich halfway to his mouth. "Is that even a name?"

"Well, we're talking about the Middle Ages, so . . ." His father's face went from thoughtful to happy. "It's 'Landon' spelled backward."

Landon set the cheese sandwich down in front of him on the kitchen table. "Dad, no. Please."

"Oh, okay. I'm just trying to be creative here."

Landon rolled his eyes and felt a tap on his shoulder. Genevieve and her friends had come in behind him.

"Creative about what?" Genevieve asked.

Landon glanced at Megan and blushed, horrified. "Nothing. Dad's just writing his new book."

"Hi, Landon." Megan stood wrapped in a towel, her long hair dark and damp, her pale blue eyes aglow.

Landon looked down at his sandwich before looking back at them with a wave. "Hi."

"Yeah, hi," said Katy, also waving, but all business.

"Do you guys want a sandwich?" he asked, unable to think of anything else. He pointed at the supplies on the table.

Katy laughed, but Megan shook her head and said, "No, thanks."

"C'mon guys." Genevieve headed for her room.

"How was football, Landon?" Megan hung back and looked at him like she really cared. "What position are you gonna play?"

Landon thought of Mike Furster's words, "Left out."

He cleared his throat. "I won a race yesterday."

"Really? Wow," Megan said. "That's great."

"Yeah, then I, like, collapsed and Skip helped me up."

Megan pinched her lips together but couldn't hold back a smile. "Good. I'm glad he did. I told him we were friends. He already texted Genevieve that he was sorry for what happened at the diner."

"He did?"

"She didn't tell you?" Megan frowned. "I wonder why."

Landon just stared at Megan, unable to take his eyes off her face.

Finally, she shrugged and said, "Okay, well . . . gotta change."

Then she was gone. Landon hadn't even realized that his father had returned to his writing desk, but he found himself alone in the kitchen with his big, thick cheese sandwich. He picked up the sandwich and looked down. He poked at his bulging stomach and then got up and dumped his snack in the trash. It was only one sandwich, but it was a start.

He'd seen Coach Furster tell the team that's how he'd built his half-billion-dollar equity fund—one investor at a time, one deal at a time. He told them one mile at a time was how he qualified for the Ironman in Hawaii. Coach Furster then said you built a champion the same way, one practice at a time. And that's what Landon intended to be.

A champion.

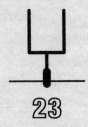

23

Sunday was a day off from football, but Landon's mom had plenty for them all to do around the house.

"Okay, guys. We've got to get settled in for real," she said.

Evidently that meant a lot of cleaning and moving and straightening and throwing things away followed by a mess of yard work that continued for Landon into Monday afternoon. By the time football practice came around that evening, Landon was already exhausted, but he was determined to get more involved. This time, after stretching and agilities and bag work, he got in the back of the line for blocking drills. Watching carefully and visualizing himself doing exactly what Brett Bell did, Landon heard a whistle blast signaling his turn before he knew it. He stepped up, got in his three-point stance, faintly heard the cadence barked out by Coach Furster, and fired into the bag.

It felt more like shoving someone in the aisle of a crowded bus than the blocking he'd seen the others do, but Landon chugged his feet and the bag moved a bit before the blast of a whistle told him to stop. He dashed back to the end of the line, out of breath and beaming to himself. Everything went on as it had before. He hadn't impressed anyone, but he hadn't made a laughingstock of himself either. It was a victory.

Twice more he did the blocking drill on a bag held up by Coach West, and then it was time for the sled.

Landon fretted to himself and tried to get in one of the lines on the inside of the sled, but when he stepped up at the center position, Coach Furster stopped everything.

"Landon! Landon?"

"Yes, Coach?"

"You're a Double X player. You play right tackle on offense, left end on defense, son. You're not a center. Travis is a center. Jones is a center. Not you."

Landon nodded and followed the direction of Coach Furster's finger. Timmy, wearing an impish grin, stepped back to allow Landon a turn.

Landon got in place and hunkered down into his stance, knowing all eyes were on him. On the count, he fired out into the sled. The rigid pad was on a spring-loaded arm, and it bounced him right back. The other linemen were already moving the sled. Landon panicked and hugged the dummy, leaning and pushing, determined not to let it spin on him. With a great roar, he got his end of the sled going. He knew he looked like a dancing bear and his technique wasn't close to the other guys, but the sled didn't spin, even though it wasn't exactly straight.

Finally the whistle blew, and he realized Coach Furster had paused to stare at him.

"Well, that's one way to do it." Coach Furster shook his head and then got back to business. "Okay! Let's go! This isn't a puppet show! Get me that next group up here!"

The next two times on the sled, Landon took his turn and did his thing without comment or reaction from Coach Furster. When it came time to work on plays, Landon took a deep breath and jogged into the huddle with a handful of reserve players, who were a mixture of third- and fourth-stringers, when he felt a tap on his shoulder.

It was Coach Furster. "Let's get a little better at the individual stuff before you jump into running plays, okay, Landon? Just so you don't mess up the timing."

Landon nodded. Happy to be talked to, happy to obey the orders of his coach, he stepped to the back to watch until it came time for sprints.

Sprints went a bit better for him. He beat Timmy for the first seven and then dropped behind before he got a second wind. Landon finished the final sprint second to last and joined the team that was already gathered around a glowering Coach Furster.

"Everything changes tomorrow night," Coach Furster snarled at them, looking all around. "Tomorrow night, it's live. The pads go on and you better remember that football is not a contact sport. Football is a *collision* sport, so you better be ready to *hit*."

The team roared its approval, and even Landon found himself growling, excited for tomorrow.

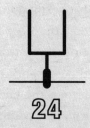

24

The next afternoon Landon attacked the bag of equipment the league had given to all the players. He pulled it out onto the living room floor and began stuffing his pants and the girdle with pads. It was like a puzzle, figuring out which pad went in which pocket and then getting into everything, since the uniform also included rib pads, shoulder pads, elbow pads, and hand pads for the hogs.

"I think the rib pads are supposed to go on first." Genevieve was paying more attention to her phone than him, but after struggling a bit, Landon knew she was right.

Landon figured it all out with Genevieve looking on while their dad flooded the house with the smell of roasting lamb chops and sautéed spinach. He was boiling potatoes that he'd mash to become delicious volcanoes filled with meat gravy.

Genevieve stuck out her tongue, tilted her head, and snapped a selfie with Landon in the background.

"Don't post that!" Landon scolded her.

"Why?" she said. "You look cute."

"I'm not supposed to be *cute*, Genevieve. It's *football*." Landon gritted his teeth.

Genevieve laughed and put her phone down. "Okay, already. Grumpy."

In truth, Landon wasn't grumpy. He was excited because if what the coaches and players had been saying for the last few days was true, then today everything changed. When the pads went on, the real players were supposed to rise to the top like cream.

"Football is not a contact sport. Football is a collision *sport, so you better be ready to* hit.*"*

Landon heard the coach's words in his mind on a closed loop as he stood in front of the full-length hallway mirror, dressed in full uniform, with Genevieve beside him. He bent down in a sort of frog-like, upright three-point stance so she could reach him but he could still see her face. "Go ahead. Hit my shoulders."

Genevieve slapped the pad on his right shoulder.

"Ha-ha. Harder than that," he said.

She made a fist and bopped him.

"Harder!" Landon was feeling bold and unbreakable. "Seriously, hit me with everything you've got."

Genevieve tightened her lips, reared back with a fist, and slammed his shoulder.

97

POP.

Landon smiled wide. "This is so cool. I can't even *feel* that."

With the pads and helmet and his huge size, Landon felt certain that everything—not just with the football team, but his whole life—was about to change.

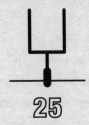

25

Sunshine had grilled the grass, trees, rooftops, and pavement all day long. Even fresh from its shaded harbor in the garage, the Prius felt like a sauna. Landon's palms and feet burst into sweat, and a bead of it scampered down his cheek like a roach. He swiped at it with a padded hand and glanced at his father, hunched over the wheel like a big kid on his little brother's tricycle.

As his father pulled into the school parking lot that over-looked the football field, he glanced Landon's way. "You'll be okay. Your whole team is nervous, I'm sure."

They pulled up to the end of the lot, and Landon craned his neck to look down on the field. Only a handful of guys were there, including Coach Bell and Brett. Skip was rifling footballs to Xander and Mike.

"Skip Dreyfus isn't nervous," Landon declared. "Neither is Brett Bell."

"Well, they're the best two players on the team, and Brett's uncle plays for the *Giants*." His dad stopped the car. "Everyone else is sweating bullets, I bet."

Landon wasn't so sure, but he opened the door and said good-bye to his father. Heat from the parking lot swallowed him, and he wondered if there was a chance that practice might be canceled. He'd seen on his phone app that the heat index was up over ninety. People with asthma were being advised to stay indoors, but Landon didn't have asthma. He took several deep breaths, almost eager for a sudden attack of that ailment, but the air swept in and out of his lungs, filling his nose with the harsh scent of bubbling tar and plastic football pads.

The grass crackled beneath his feet and he could smell the cooked dirt as he slogged down the hillside. Timmy Nichols appeared and went straight for the sled. Landon was sweating from every available pore by the time he reached the sideline, but when he looked around he saw the rest of the team— which was arriving quickly now—frolicking like they were at a pool party. Could such a disregard of the elements be part of this football mania? From his living room couch, he'd never considered the Cleveland Browns baking like potatoes when they had to play down in Houston or Jacksonville early in the season.

Someone smacked his shoulder pad and he turned, smelling the cologne at the same time so that he wasn't surprised to see Coach Furster's black eyes and white smile. "Landon? You've got your pads on."

"I'm supposed to have 'em on, right, Coach?" Panic flashed across Landon's brain like the shadow of a hawk.

"Oh, sure. You'll look good gettin' off the bus. Scare the heck out of Tuckahoe when they see you. Ha-ha. You'll be like our El Cid." Coach chucked Landon's shoulder pad again.

"What do you mean?" Landon shifted the shoulder pads, which now felt too tight.

"El Cid? Famous Spanish knight." Coach Furster's eyes grew close enough to make Landon uncomfortable. "Just the sight of him terrified the enemy. Made them turn and run."

Coach Furster grinned like he owned the memory. "When he died, they sewed open his eyes and let his horse carry him into battle. The enemy fled. He couldn't fight a lick—being dead and all—but he scared the heck out of people."

"Oh." Landon had no idea what else to say.

"Yup. El Cid." Coach Furster shucked a piece of gum, gobbled it up, and marched away, trailing an invisible cloud of citrus cologne toward his son, Mike, and Skip. "Ready to hit, boys?"

The football equipment made Landon feel like he was wrapped in bubble paper. There was comfort in the protection it would provide, but it made him feel even more awkward than normal. He wished he'd had time to practice wearing it, like he'd done with the helmet. Most of the other players had been wearing football pads since they were eight or nine, so for them it was almost second nature. Twice he tripped and fell during agility drills, but no one stopped to laugh. Such was the intensity of the boys around him. Everyone seemed to be in a trance, moving with quick concentration. They alternated between high-knee running, darting around cones placed a few feet apart, and jumping around the rungs of rope ladders stretched out on the practice field. It was organized chaos that almost everyone but Landon and Timmy seemed to ace.

When the last agility drill was complete, Coach Furster gave his whistle three blasts and they all crowded around him. Landon glanced at his teammates' faces, wondering if anyone else's stomach was twisting under the sour smell of their coach's cologne.

"All right." Coach Furster crossed his arms. His Chinese calligraphy tattoo bulged. He stared all around. "You all know what comes now. Tackling drills. Live!"

Everyone let out a roar. Landon joined in.

"Two lines!" Coach Furster broke free and sprinted toward the end zone, where Coach Bell and Coach West had created a narrow column of grass bordered by tipped-over blocking dummies. The team split like geese in a November sky, some breaking to one end of the bags, some breaking the other way, without rhyme or reason. Landon found himself in the line of tacklers in back of Timmy, a loose string of players in the end zone. The runners were at the other end of the dummies, on the ten-yard line. The grass stretched between them was their battlefield.

The first tackler was Skip. The first runner was Brett Bell, looking like a rhinoceros with a football.

Coach Furster howled, "Here we go, boys!"

Then he blasted his whistle. Brett and Skip went at each other like locomotives racing toward a collision on the same track. The crack of pads was thrilling. When they collided, the smaller player, Skip, was able to stop Brett in his tracks, standing him upright with the ball cradled in his arms. Nonetheless, Brett's churning legs carried Skip backward two yards before they went down in a heap.

Both players bounced up unscathed, screaming with excitement, and slapping each other's shoulder pads and helmets with respect.

"Good hit! Good hit!" Coach Furster bellowed as they swapped lines. "Next two!"

Miller, playing defense, and Rinehart, as the runner, fired off like mortal enemies, blasting each other with all the bone-crunching intensity of Brett and Skip. Miller dropped Rinehart like a bag of groceries before they popped up too, howling at the white-hot sun like it was a new moon before they swapped lines, Miller heading to the end of the runner's line while Rinehart fell in the tackler's line behind Landon and Brett.

Players cheered. The coaches laughed and yelled, "Next up!"

And so it went, with Landon's line melting away in front of him. Counting bodies in the opposite line, he saw that his line had an odd number, which would leave him matched up with Skip.

Landon's stomach flipped at the sight of their starting quarterback. His mouth got sticky and then went desert dry. He had no idea what to do, really. He'd seen NFL highlights of the Browns' middle linebacker, Karlos Dansby, on YouTube. He saw right in front of him how his teammates did it—the tacklers lowering their shoulders into the runners' midriffs, exploding, wrapping them up with their arms, and then driving them back if possible. But he didn't see how he could even hope to complete the first step, let alone the last three.

Timmy Nichols was up, and he was blasted apart by the runner like a puff of smoke in a stiff breeze. Nichols rolled over and hopped up, though, jogging to join the runners. When Landon stepped to the goal line, Skip accepted the football from Coach Bell, snorting like a maniac. His feet pawed the earth like a bloodthirsty bull's.

He crouched into a stance and leveled his eyes at Landon, who stood stiff as a tree trunk.

Every fiber in Landon's body begged him to just run far away.

And then the whistle shrieked.

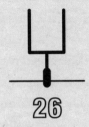

26

Skip paused and stood up.

"Coach?" Skip's killer expression faded and he angled his head at Landon.

Bent over with his hands on his knees to watch the action, Coach Furster looked like a man awakened from a pleasant dream. His mouth tilted open in confusion, and it looked like the whistle might slip loose from his lips as he considered Landon. "Yeah. No."

Coach Furster looked around for someone else, his lips dragged down by a frown and the whistle dropping to the end of the lanyard around his neck before he pointed to the back of Skip's line. "Nichols! You're the runner!"

"Coach?" Landon said. "What's wrong?"

Coach Furster ignored him as Nichols looked confused and said, "Huh?"

"Nichols! You jump to the front of the line. Now!"

Nichols shrugged, waddled up to the front of the line, and accepted the football from Skip. Before Landon could think, Nichols crouched in a much less ferocious manner than Skip, Coach Furster blasted his whistle, and Nichols barreled right toward Landon.

Landon's feet did a little dance in place. He took half a step forward and opened his arms before Nichols punched a shoulder pad into his midriff. The air left his body in a great gust. He staggered sideways, shocked by the impact, but aware of Nichols slipping past him. Landon couldn't let that happen. He grabbed for anything to hold. His hands locked onto Nichols's jersey. Like a great felled tree, Landon tipped and went down, dragging Nichols with him.

Nichols collapsed without a fight in the end zone. Landon lay on the grass, looking up at the blazing hot sun. A beam of light cut through the cage of his face mask like a gleaming sword. Coach Furster appeared standing over him in a nauseating funk of cologne and baked dirt.

"Okay, Landon." Coach Furster seemed like he was talking to a kindergartner. "You did it. You got him down. Your first tackle."

Coach Furster turned away, his face cast into darkness by the shadow of the sun, and returned to normal. "Next! Let's go, ladies! This isn't a fashion show! This isn't a candy store!"

Landon scrabbled to his feet and Nichols bumped him with a shoulder that seemed intentional before Landon jogged to the end of the line of runners. No one looked at him. No one celebrated his tackle, and as he watched the backs of his teammates' helmets queuing up in front of him, he realized it wasn't much of a tackle, if it was a tackle at all, because Nichols had made it into the end zone.

Landon stood still at the back of the line, his teammates jumping in front of him without so much as a glance. He was frozen with disappointment. The glorious tackles he had imagined himself making, blowing people up like Karlos Danby did, now seemed utterly impossible. He had barely brought down Timmy. What would Guerrero do to him? Or Brett Bell? It wasn't fear that froze him, but bewilderment. He felt like he was suddenly walking on the moon without gravity.

Because he stood still, people moved in front of him to get their turn to run the ball. Soon a pattern was established, and although no one said anything to him, he found himself standing at the end of the line and watching the tackling drill, big and hot and sweaty and forlorn.

It made him sick to just stand there, but the idea of taking the ball and having someone blast into him full speed suddenly seemed ridiculous. He'd never be a running back anyway. He was too timid to cross the open grass and go back to the line of tacklers in the end zone, so he stood there, and no one said a word, including the coaches. They must have been thinking the same thing he was thinking. Everyone on the same page. A-okay.

Landon grew slowly more comfortable, and he began to entertain the idea that when they got to the blocking drills, that's where he'd prove himself. That's where he belonged.

"I'm a hog," he whispered to himself, and straightened his spine. "Hogs are made for blocking."

Everything seemed just fine, until Coach West looked around as if he'd dropped his keys. When he spotted what he was looking for, it was halfway across the field. Coach West pointed to the water bottle carrier and looked toward Landon from behind a pair of mirrored aviator sunglasses. "Hey, Dorch! Don't just stand there. Make yourself useful and go get me that water, will you?"

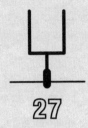

27

Coach Bell stepped up beside Coach West, and Landon could tell by the expression on his face that he understood the situation instantly. Even though Coach Bell coached the skill players, he was an old hog himself, an All-American, so he'd instinctively understand the value of a big guy like Landon. He'd know that Landon wasn't just some water boy, and Coach Bell was the gentlest coach they had. He spoke so softly Landon barely made out what he was saying, but when he did, he saw nothing but words of praise and encouragement. He saw smiles of appreciation and concern. So when Coach Bell opened his mouth to speak, Landon was filled with hope.

"Get the other one too, will you, Landon?" Coach Bell pointed a sausage finger beyond the first water bottle carrier to a second resting alone on the bench. "Please."

When Landon saw the word "please" coming from the kind

face of Coach Bell, a man whose own brother-in-law was an NFL player, he went into action without thinking. He knew about manners and he knew about the order of things: obeying parents and teachers and coaches. He jogged toward the bench, got the water there, and then scooped up the carrier in the grass, trying to look as cool and casual as one could when retrieving water.

Before he could set the water down, he was swarmed by teammates like bees on sticky fruit. They grabbed at the bottles, their sweat sprinkling his forearms, and sucked greedily at their contents. Then they replaced the bottles back in the carriers. Landon set one carrier down and went to work with the second, passing out water.

"Thanks, Landon."

"Thanks."

"Yeah, thanks."

His teammates' words showered down all around him, cooling the boil in his brain in a way he hadn't thought possible. He remembered his mom's words, about being part of a team without actually playing and how the manager was an important role.

"My pleasure," he said. "Sure, Skip."

"Here you go Brett, here's one."

"I'll take that."

"Yup, right here."

He remembered the peanut seller at an Indians baseball game his father had taken him to in Cleveland, the vendor's hands working like an octopus, slinging bags and accepting money in an economy of motion—a circus juggler of sorts.

110

Finally, Coach Furster blew his whistle three times and shouted, "Hogs with me and Coach West! Skill guys with Coach Bell! On the hop!"

As everyone scattered, Coach Furster stepped up to Landon and nodded at the carrier. Landon hesitated before he understood and handed a bottle to Coach Furster. Coach held the bottle up high and squirted a sparkling silver stream into his mouth, his Adam's apple bobbing like a cork, before he lowered it, smacked and wiped his lips, and released a sigh of pure pleasure.

"Good." He handed the bottle back to Landon. "You know, you don't *have* to help out with the water, Landon."

Landon studied Coach Furster's sweat-drenched face and knew with the confidence of someone who read faces every hour of every day that what Coach really meant was the exact opposite of what he said. Helping with the water was *exactly* what Coach Furster wanted him to do. For a brief moment Landon doubted himself. Maybe that wasn't his coach's intention. Maybe it was just mixed signals . . . but then he figured the coach knew exactly what he was doing.

"I can help out." The words escaped him like doves from a magician's sleeve.

Coach Furster put on a full display of porcelain-white teeth. "Nice, Landon. That's real nice."

And just like that, Landon Dorch got the starting job at a position he'd sworn he'd never play.

Left out.

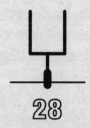

28

At home, Landon showered and changed into his pajamas.

He peeked down through the stair railing at his father, a hulking form aglow in the blue light of the computer, fingers skipping across the keyboard.

All was well, so he retreated to his room. He sighed and flipped open the hardback copy of *The Three Musketeers* his father had found for him at a garage sale in Cleveland. The scratch of his fingers on the pages made no sound. He'd removed his ears when he got back from practice and put them in their dryer case. But even in the total silence, he had a memory of the sound of turning pages, dull and faint, and he flipped through several random pages to feel their snap before settling back into the pillows to read.

In his own mind, Landon was, of course, d'Artagnan, the outsider who must prove his worth as a musketeer. As he read, a part of his mind danced with the idea that d'Artagnan had to serve the musketeers before he could become one. Hadn't d'Artagnan been left out too before becoming the most famous musketeer of all? Landon pursed his lips and set the book in his lap, nodding to himself before he continued. Halfway through the next chapter, when d'Artagnan was about to fight a duel, the overhead light in Landon's bedroom flickered.

He looked up, expecting his mother. She'd yet to return from her office and it was already past nine. Instead, Genevieve gave him a wave and sat on the edge of his bed. She pointed to his ears in their drier on the nightstand and then motioned for him to put them on.

He huffed and mouthed a word he could only sense through the movement of his lips. "Really?"

She nodded yes and motioned again.

Landon sighed, set down his book, and put on his ears. Genevieve waited patiently and didn't speak until he had them on and asked her, "What?"

She gripped his leg through the covers and leaned toward him. "I don't want you to quit."

Landon jerked his head back and lowered his chin. "You mean football? Who said I quit? I didn't quit."

Genevieve held up her iPhone as evidence. "Megan said you did one tackling drill and carried the water bottles around for the rest of practice. Landon, you can't quit. I know you can do this!"

Landon stuttered, the words piling up in his mind, unable to get them out through his mouth fast enough to explain everything. It wasn't as easy as it looked. A manager was a valuable part of a team. Coach Furster *wanted* him to do it. He'd felt joy hearing and seeing people *thank* him. And d'Artagnan! D'Artagnan had served the other musketeers before he could become one.

It all got garbled.

Genevieve scowled and shook her head, showing him her phone. "Look, Skip texted Megan that you're a big powder puff. I want you to *smash* that jerk, and I know you *can*."

Landon looked at the whole text. "Yeah, but see? He says, 'Landon is a great kid.' He says that first, before anything about being a powder puff, so . . ." He looked at her weakly. "Skip's my friend."

Genevieve grabbed the front of Landon's pajamas and yanked him close. Her creamy face was blotched with red and her eyes burned like gas flames. "He's not your *friend*, Landon."

"He's not mean," Landon shot back.

"That's not a *friend*. A friend isn't someone who's just *not mean*. A friend is someone who's *nice*. *'Hey, Landon. How you doing, Landon? Come hang out with us, Landon.'* When are you gonna get that?"

She released him, jumped up, and paced the floor. "You are not a powder puff. I know you're not. Now you have to show people you're not. Landon, you're a *giant* and you're strong."

Genevieve stood in the middle of his room, hunched over, and smacked a fist into her open hand. "You have to smash them and *smash* them, over and over, until they *respect* you!"

Landon's head got warm and his stomach complained. He reached for his ears before Genevieve saw him and shrieked, "*Don't* you unplug! You *listen* to me!"

She threw her eyes and her hands toward the ceiling and started to move around the room like a wild thing in a cage. Then she turned on him, glaring. "If I could be you for a *week*, for a *day*, for an *hour*! I'd *crush* them! If I had what you have they'd *run* from me! They'd *whimper*! They'd hide."

He thought she was going to come at him again, but she stopped at the edge of his bed, her face mottled and contorted with pain. Tears coursed down her cheeks, glittering in the yellow light that seeped through the shade from his nightstand lamp. They dropped onto his blanket, and he knew that if he weren't deaf, they would make a sound he could hear.

And then Genevieve held up something from when they were little.

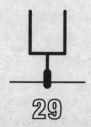

29

From her shorts pocket, Genevieve removed a gold medallion strung from a red, white, and blue ribbon. She sniffed and let the medal dangle from the ribbon so that it wobbled back and forth, and even in the yellow light of his reading lamp, it flashed brightly. "Remember this?"

Landon turned his head away. "Yeah. I remember."

She tapped his arm. "Here, I want you to have this, Landon."

"Why would I want your gold medal for gymnastics?" he said.

"Oh, come on. You were obsessed with this thing when I first won it." She dangled it in front of his face.

"I was like nine years old, Genevieve."

"I know, but it's special. It means something."

"To *you*." Landon tried to sound grouchy.

"And you," she said. "Remember how hard you rooted for

me to get this medal? People all around were pointing at you. You were losing your mind, you cheered so loud."

Landon felt his face overheating.

"But see, football can be your thing, Landon. You can win a prize that matters. You could get a college scholarship. Who knows? Maybe the NFL one day."

Landon shook his head.

"I'm serious, Landon. You've got a gift. People don't see it, but you have it. I know you do."

Now Landon felt like crying. He reached over and pulled his little sister into him. "I love you, Genevieve."

She laughed and squeezed even harder before stepping back. "So, you'll take it?"

Landon lowered his head and she draped the medal around his neck. "I'm the luckiest sister in the world to have a big brother like you. You have to believe in yourself, Landon. If you don't, no one else but me will believe in you."

"I'll try, Genevieve. I really will." It was all he could say.

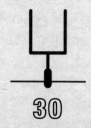

30

Landon intended to try, but helping others came so naturally to him that he couldn't help himself the next evening at practice.

He dropped a water carrier off with the skill players and then jogged over to where the hogs were stretching out in two lines facing each other across the goal line. He took up his spot out of the way in the back of the end zone. Timmy broke loose, grabbed a water bottle from Landon, gulped down a heavy stream, and then put it back without acknowledging Landon in any way. The other linemen were paired off now, two by two, so Timmy took up his spot as a third wheel along with Brett and one of the bigger linemen on the near end of the line for the "fit" drill. The drill was slow and mechanical: each hog simply stepped out of his stance, took one short power step, then a second step, and then "fit" their hands and forehead beneath the armpits and chin of the player opposite them. Coach Furster said it was the ABCs of line play.

"Right guard, left tackle, center; I don't care what position you're at," Coach would say. "Every successful play for a hog starts with a perfect 'fit.'"

Landon felt suddenly like the doors of a bus that was supposed to take him on an excellent journey were rumbling shut. He heard Genevieve's voice insisting that he had to believe in himself. He panicked and dropped the water carrier, his brain hot again because he couldn't miss this chance, not now, not with the pads on. He stepped into the fit drill across from Timmy, capping off the drill with perfectly even numbers.

Just because he was helping the coaches didn't mean he had to be left out. Why couldn't he help the team one way during some drills—as a manager—and yet in another way—as a player—during others? Even in the games, he could help with water or keeping stats when his team was on defense (if he couldn't do a simple tackling drill, he couldn't be expected to play defense) but then switch to a full-fledged hog when his team was on offense, out there rutting around in the dirt, pushing players around like a big bulldozer. It was like his father changing the plot seven hundred pages into a book. Just because other people didn't do something, or even because something had never been done before, didn't mean there was automatically a rule against it. Landon could skip the defensive drills but participate in the offensive blocking drills.

Timmy didn't seem to think so, though.

"Down!" Coach Furster barked. Timmy just stood.

"Get down." Landon tried to infuse his voice with urgency. "Your side is on offense."

Timmy shook his head while everyone else on his side of the line got into a three-point stance.

"One . . ." Everyone on Timmy's side took a power step on Coach Furster's cue.

"Come on, Timmy!" Landon patted his chest where Timmy should be getting ready to deliver a blow with both hands.

Timmy shook his head.

"Two . . ." Everyone took his second step.

"Fit!" Pads popped in unison. Landon patted his chest, desperately wanting to blend in smoothly.

"Get that fit lower, Torin. Come on, hands *inside*. Miller, that's it!" Coach Furster was working his way down the line, adjusting players who needed it, praising those who had the correct position.

Landon saw Brett in a perfect fit position, his eye cranked over to one side, watching Landon through his face mask.

"Perfect, Bell!" Coach Furster was so intent on his work that he came upon an upright Timmy in complete surprise. "Nichols! This isn't a candy—"

Nichols just shook his head and pointed at Landon, who stood shifting from foot to foot and tugging at the shoulder pad strap beneath his arm.

"I got it, Coach." Brett grabbed Nichols by the collar and slung him aside before shoving him into the exact place he himself had vacated. "I'll pair up with Landon."

"You'll . . ." Coach Furster's tongue jammed up behind his lower lip, giving him a crazy look. "Okay, Bell. Good. Nichols, you happy now? Would you like a written invitation next time?"

120

Timmy wasn't fazed by Coach Furster's gruff treatment, and he seemed perfectly content to be yelled at so long as he wasn't paired up with Landon in the drill.

"Okay, switch sides!" Coach Furster barked.

"Come on, Landon." Brett chucked him on the shoulder. "You can do this. Just stay low."

"DOWN!" Coach Furster hollered, and Landon dropped down into a three-point stance, palm flat.

"Set . . . ," the coach screamed, "one . . . two . . . fit!"

Landon took two awkward steps, stood up, grabbed the jersey beneath Brett's armpits, and banged face masks. Landon knew it wasn't right, but Coach Furster said nothing. He stepped past Landon and Brett. "Nichols! Get your arms *inside*, Nichols. Inside! I can't do it for you, son."

And on the coach went down the line.

Landon felt a tap and he looked at Brett.

"I said, look, would you?" Brett said irritably.

"Sorry," Landon said. "I didn't see you."

"Yeah, well, listen, will you? Here's how you get into a stance." Brett got down and extended his fingers like the legs of a table, before putting them into the grass. While he was down there, Landon heard him saying something, but the words weren't clear.

Landon shook his head and tapped Brett's helmet. When Brett looked up, Landon said, "I can understand better if I *see* what you say. I hear and see together."

Brett gave him a strange look, but shook his head and said, "You don't want to have your hand flat down in the grass. Use

121

your fingers. Make them stiff or you'll be too low and you can't fire out. That's why you popped up like toast."

The face mask made lipreading harder, but Landon could do it.

"Okay. Okay." Landon nodded furiously, eager to please and flooded with gratefulness. He got down in his stance, using his fingertips to support his weight, even though it felt extremely awkward. He heard Bell speaking again and popped up to see what he was saying.

"What?"

Bell shook his head, frustrated. "Just stay low. Keep your helmet below mine. Here, it's my turn. Watch what I do and do that."

Landon nodded, and Brett got down and executed the fit drill on Coach Furster's orders. The coach came down the line. "Good. Good. Head up. Good. Better. Head up, Nichols! Bell, perfect. Okay, last time, then we go live!"

Landon would have one chance only to get it right. He got down in his stance, but he couldn't see Brett in front of him, so he sank his butt, angling his torso more upright. His fingers were in the right position, but on the count he stepped forward, got too high, tripped, and belly-bumped into Brett, grabbing for his jersey. Landon ended up in a position that wouldn't be good for much of anything besides dancing.

Coach Furster blinked and then moved on without a word.

Landon watched him go and then felt a tap on his shoulder.

"It's okay, Landon." Brett reached into his face mask and

wiped some sweat from his eyes. "You'll get it. It takes time, is all."

Landon wanted to hug the kid.

Coach Furster got to the other end of the two lines and gave his whistle a sharp little blast. "Okay, ladies, like I said . . . now it is *live*! So you better be ready!"

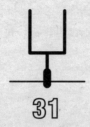

31

"Offense on my side!" Coach Furster was marching up and down behind the boys facing Landon's way like they were troops he was sending into war. "Defense on that side. Offense, you drive block their butts into tomorrow. Defensive guys, you hold your ground and shed them like a disease. Get them off you! Okay, everyone together now, and I want to see some vicious, violent hitting! Down! Set!"

Landon got in a three-point stance. Brett was hunkered down in front of him, legs quivering, face twisted with a rage Landon just didn't get.

Coach Furster gave his whistle a blast.

Landon came out of his stance in a slow rise and got a mouthful of helmet. Brett's two hands gripped the flesh in the crease of his armpits like giant crab pincers. Landon yelped. He was being lifted and driven back at the same time. His feet tangled together, and he crashed flat on his back with Brett coming down full force, pounding out whatever air remained in his lungs.

Landon choked, gagging for air. His hands and feet waddled in space, as if they could somehow suck oxygen back into his body. This was not fun. No way. No how. "Vicious and violent hitting" took on a whole new meaning when you were on the receiving end of things, and Landon was beginning to have serious doubts about his love affair with football.

The big lineman was climbing up off him, and he wasn't being gentle. Brett put a hand in the middle of Landon's soft stomach to steady himself, and he barked Landon's shin with one of his cleats as he got to his feet. Landon looked up in astonishment, expecting a sympathetic expression from the boy who'd just been so kind to him.

Instead, he saw teeth buried deep into a rubber mouthpiece and cold, cruel eyes.

Landon waited for a hand to help him up or a friendly smile, but Brett only turned and walked away.

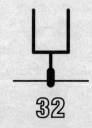

32

That was enough for Landon.

Despite what mean kids sometimes said about him, despite what he may have sounded like because of what people called "slightly garbled" speech, Landon was no dummy. He kept his helmet on, and sweat trickled down his forehead as he did his job as manager. He kept the water bottles handy for anyone who needed one, and he tried to avoid Brett Bell. No one said anything, but he sensed that everyone approved. Midway through practice, Coach West gave him a pat on the back and showed him how he could refill the bottles on a hot night from a cold tap jutting out of the bricks in the school's wall near the rear entrance.

Coach West screwed on the top of a bottle he had filled and then handed Landon an empty one and spoke slowly and loudly. "Okay, Landon. Do you want to try that?"

Landon gave him a funny look, but he nodded and refilled one of the other bottles before replacing it in the carrier.

"Good!" Coach West clapped his hands. "Good job."

"Coach, it's not that hard." Landon bent down and continued to fill the bottles.

Coach West stood watching. When Landon finished, Coach West waved both hands at Landon to get his attention, and he kept speaking in a slow and loud voice. "Landon, if you're going to be helping out like this, like kind of a manager—"

"Not the water boy," Landon interrupted.

"No, not at all. A manager for sure." Coach West seemed amused. "But if you're manager, you do not have to wear your helmet, Landon."

Landon shook his head. "Coach Furster said helmets stay on all practice."

Coach West looked even more amused. "Yes, but . . ."

Landon huffed and scooped up the water carriers. "Let's get back, Coach."

Coach West laughed. "Sure, Landon. That's great." Coach West put a hand on Landon's shoulder pad like some kind of guardian as they trudged back toward practice.

Landon wanted to shrug him off, but he also didn't want to be impolite.

When they got back into the thick of things, teammates came at Landon from all directions. As he worked like the peanut man in the Indians' stadium, his mind kept busy too. The bad thing was that he guessed he'd have to admit to Genevieve that he'd quit. The good news was that everyone seemed to like him as the manager.

It wasn't until the team was doing a drill called "Inside Run" that Landon felt a tap on his shoulder and turned to see Brett standing there. He had somehow snuck up on Landon.

"Hey," Brett said, and he seemed to be happy that Landon knew his role. He didn't look mad at all. He just accepted a bottle and squirted his mouth full of water, gulping it down without pause so that the stream sprayed his face when his mouth briefly closed. When he finished, the big lineman reached in through his face mask and wiped the water from his eyes.

"Thanks, Landon," Brett said, and then dove back into the drill, tapping out a boy who had temporarily replaced him, because that's how it worked for Brett Bell. He went where he wanted, when he wanted. He was the best lineman they had by far. It was almost like Brett and Skip could run the team on their own, without any coaches at all.

Landon ached to be like one of them. He assumed everyone did, but he wasn't even close. He watched Brett line up and destroy the guy in front of him, blasting that kid the way he'd done to Landon and turning away with the same coldhearted look in his eyes. Landon wished more than anything that he could be a star player, but he couldn't make up happy endings the way his father did. Landon was stuck with who he was, and now, *what* he was.

He tried to take comfort in the fact that he'd be the best manager ever. He'd wear his equipment, just like the rest of the team. He'd never take his helmet off, no matter how hot things got, because he was still part of the team, and Coach Furster said being a Bronxville football player wasn't for just anyone.

He'd be there for the guys when they needed him and he'd be part of a team.

He watched Timmy get flattened and felt giddy not to be in the drill. That made him sigh. If he was a powder puff because he didn't like getting pummeled, then he guessed he should be okay with that. It didn't make a lot of sense, really. Someone who enjoyed that—getting blasted around like a paper bag in a windstorm—*that* person would be the real dummy.

When practice was almost over and Coach Furster blew his whistle and told them all to line up for sprints, Landon hustled over to the bench, dumped his water bottle carriers, and stepped up with everyone else. He could do the running. It wasn't pleasant, but it didn't scare him. No one was going to knock his block off running sprints.

He felt a spark of pride as he took off on the first sprint. He'd be a part of the team in almost every way. It didn't matter to him whether he beat Timmy anymore. All Landon had to do was finish, not win. There was no fire in his gut. Timmy outran him in the last half of the sprints, and the team chanted *"Lan-don, Lan-don, Lan-don"* as he slogged through the hot air and over the finish line on the final sprint of the night.

Coach Furster was in a good mood and laughing to himself and he called them in. "All right guys, good work tonight. Good hitting. I saw some toughness from a lot of you."

Coach Furster's face suddenly clouded over. "You other guys? And you know who you are. You need to get it going. I don't want to embarrass anyone, but when you wonder what you should be doing and how you should be doing it, look at Bell and Dreyfus."

Coach pointed at his two top players. "You two guys are old-school, and I love it."

Landon looked from Coach Furster to the coach's son, Mike, and thought that having your dad praise others above you had to hurt. Mike's face went blank. Only his eyes seemed to boil, but Landon was pretty sure no one else noticed.

"All right, in on me!" Coach Furster shouted, holding his hand out for everyone to reach for and cover. "Hit, Hustle, Win. On three! One, two, three . . ."

Landon shouted with the rest of them, and the team broke apart and filtered toward the parking lot. Landon dragged his feet across the dry grass. He was exhausted from the running and in no hurry to get home and face Genevieve. He knew, despite the very good arguments he had perfected in his head over the last hour or so, that Genevieve was not going to be happy with him. That bothered him because he loved Genevieve with all his heart.

She felt the same way, and he knew it. He thought about the medal she'd given him and nearly choked. Disappointing her would be hard. Behind most of the other players, he marched uphill toward the parking lot, head pounding, hot and exhausted, feeling like his insides were swamp water. He didn't think he could feel any worse than he did at that moment, but unfortunately . . . he was wrong.

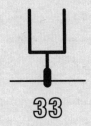

33

A woman with bleach-blond hair stood at the top of the hill. Her lips were pink and thick, reminding Landon of chewed bubble gum. Her eyes hid behind big dark sunglasses, and she was dressed like one of Genevieve's friends in a pale yellow dress dotted with little daisies, and sandals on her feet. When Xander reached her, she gave him a hug and pointed him to the car. Landon guessed she was his mom.

In one hand she held a large striped bag, like something for the beach. She was taking big blue envelopes the color of a robin's egg from the bag and handing them out to each player as he reached her. Landon slowed his pace even more to watch. Xander's mom's pink painted nails flashed along with a gleaming smile as she worked.

Landon moved close and focused hard to read her thick lips as Brett accepted one of the festive envelopes from her.

131

"We're doing laser tag for Xander's birthday, Saturday," she said. "I hope you can make it, Brett. Everyone's invited."

Landon gulped down his excitement. Laser tag was something he'd done with Scouts in Cleveland once. He was actually good at it because what you really had to do was *see* things well in the dark. The flit of a shadow here or there made all the difference, and it didn't take Landon long to learn that if you just hunkered down in a corner, you could pick people off with deadly certainty and dominate the game.

Landon picked up his pace a little because Timmy Nichols was getting his invitation and Landon didn't want Xander's mom to think Timmy was the last of the players. He took a quick glance over his shoulder and relaxed when he saw that Skip had stopped to help Mike and Coach Furster put the bags into the equipment shed. Landon was certain that Xander's mom would wait for Skip. Everyone wanted a piece of Skip.

Landon huffed and waddled and wished his padded pants weren't suddenly sagging and slowing him down. He reached back and tugged at the droopy girdle. As he crested the top of the hill, he seemed to make eye contact with Xander's mom. He couldn't be exactly sure because of her dark glasses. He was out of breath, but he wrestled his face into an enormous smile as she reached into her bag and pulled out another big, beautiful blue invitation. It was a prize worth having.

Landon was so close that Xander's mom had to be looking right at him. He grinned and he held out his hand. Then her smile suddenly dropped. She stepped aside and then actually walked down the hill to meet Skip and Mike halfway up.

132

Landon thought he could hear her chirping like a bird as she presented Skip his invitation.

Before Landon saw Skip take it, he turned toward his father's Prius. The heat squeezed him in its fist. Landon staggered a bit as he tried to hurry. When he reached the car he put his hand on the hot corner of the Prius's hood to keep himself from falling over. The metal burned his hand, but he couldn't think about that as he bent over and puked up the swamp water.

His father was suddenly there, tapping his shoulder and bending over in concern until his face filled the space outside Landon's puke-stained metal cage. "Hey, hey, big guy. You okay? I saw that running. Man, it's not easy being a football player, is it? And I used to gripe when I had to carry the *tuba*."

Landon stood up and stared at his father. From the corner of his eye he saw that Brett had stopped to look at him with his blue envelope pinched between a thumb and forefinger, frowning like he knew Landon was a super powder puff.

"Landon? Are you okay?" His father tilted his head.

Landon only nodded and pulled away. "Yes. I'm fine. Let's go."

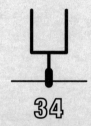

34

"Can we stop for ice cream?" Landon wasn't hungry, but his father didn't know that.

"Hey, sure. Probably hungry after losing your dinner there, huh?" His father gave Landon a cheerful look and started the car. They rolled out of the parking lot. Landon kept his eyes straight ahead and bumped up the AC as high as it would go.

His father found a place to park on the street in the center of town. Landon put his helmet and shoulder pads in the backseat and wore just his sopping wet T-shirt and football pants into the Häagen-Dazs store, where they sat at the corner table. Landon's dad accepted two menus from a waitress and watched her walk away before he spoke. "Amazing, right? I mean, look at all this. When I was a kid a banana split was a big deal, but now you got, what?" His father began to read off the menu. "Paradise with Whipped Cream? Waffle Dream? The Eiffel

Tower? Wow, Landon, you have no idea how lucky you are."

His father dipped his head into the menu, shaking his head with wonder. When the waitress returned, Landon asked for a glass of water and said he still hadn't made up his mind about his order.

"So, what's Genevieve doing tonight?" he asked when they were alone.

His father lowered the menu and raised an eyebrow. "No idea. On her computer? Texting? I was in a real writing zone and all of a sudden I saw the time. Didn't want to be late picking you up. Why?"

"No reason." Landon dipped his head. "How about this Banana Caramel Crepe?"

"Oh, didn't see that." His father got back to business.

The waitress returned with their water and Landon asked for the Seventh Heaven. His father went for the Banana Caramel Crepe. They sipped their water and watched people walk past on the sidewalk, some of them entering Häagen-Dazs to sit down, others lining up for cones at the counter. His father tapped Landon's hand, and Landon looked up.

"I gotta tell you, Landon, this book is really going good," his father said. "Nodnal is some character."

"Wait," Landon said. "I thought you weren't going to name him Nodnal."

"Well, right. It's a working name. I'll change it at the end, but for now it's really helping me. I see him as Nodnal."

Landon saw the glow of excitement on his father's face and couldn't bring himself to protest, even though he hated the idea.

"I mean, right now." His father leaned toward Landon and motioned with his hands. "He's in the dungeon. He was wrongly accused of conspiring against the king, but he's made a friend, a knight. I'm about to have them escape."

Landon tried his best to look interested, but his own life was such a mess, he just couldn't find room to care about a fictional character.

"Sounds good," he managed to say.

His father sat back, then glanced around at the other tables, but Landon could tell he was trying to decide whether or not to ask him something.

"So, football going good?" Landon's dad folded his arms on the table and leaned in again. "I mean, you like all that hitting and stuff?"

Landon shrugged. "It's not easy."

His father shook his head vigorously. "No way. It's pretty crazy if you ask me, and I don't want you to feel like you have to keep doing it if it's not for you, Landon."

Landon scowled. "Why? Did Genevieve say something to you?"

"Not at all," his father said.

"'Cause I'm not her, you know. Things come easy to her."

"Sometimes it seems that way," his father said, "but she works pretty hard, I gotta say."

The ice cream arrived. Landon dug in, truly hungry because his stomach was completely empty, and facing Genevieve now seemed far off. If she was busy on the computer or texting with her friends, he could sneak right into his bedroom and lock the door. He took a big bite, and mango exploded in his mouth.

He cut that flavor with a dash of raspberry and whipped cream.

"Mmm." He got serious about his dish and didn't look up until he paused before the final scoop.

"You beat me," he said to his dad.

His father scraped some melted goo from the bottom of his dish. "Well, it's not a contest, but wow, was that crepe good. I'm glad we stopped here."

Landon noticed a splotch of caramel on his father's shirt, and that made him think of his mom and what she'd say if she were here. "Dad?"

"Yeah?"

"If I don't get a lot of playing time—in the games—you won't care, right?"

His father's mouth turned down. "Nah. Who cares about that? It's your first time ever trying this thing. Everyone else's been doing it forever, and what's the rush? I told you, it's about being a part of something. That's what a team is. Gosh, my high school buddy Dale Higgens had no rhythm whatsoever, but there he was with that triangle—sometimes the bongos—right there, marching along with the rest of us with his chin high, all the way to Orlando one year for the Nationals. Did I ever tell you we went to the Nationals one year?"

Landon nodded. "Pretty sure you did."

"Yeah, well, we were a *band*, which is the exact same thing as a team. Like a band of brothers. A unit. A squad. Man, did we have some times. Band camp?" His father raised an eyebrow again, twirled his spoon and sighed happily before he let it drop into the bowl. "You ready?"

"Almost." Landon ate his last spoonful, and then he asked

137

the question that had been on his mind all along. "So, with the band, did anyone ever have some get-together, like a party, and not invite the whole band? I mean, that had to be normal because of how many people you have in a band."

His dad reached across the table and put his hand on Landon's. "Hey, buddy, we got plenty of room. I can fire up the grill. Burgers. Chicken kabobs. We can fit that whole doggone football team of yours right around the pool if that's what you're wondering. I like the idea. Mom won't mind."

Landon fought to control himself.

He had no idea what to say.

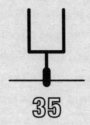

35

Landon sputtered. "No, that's okay. I was just thinking about how big a group you have with a band. I was just wondering."

"Well, yeah. I mean if you're in the band, you're in the band. Everyone just knew everyone was invited. That's what I'm talking about. That's how things work, see?" His father sat up, straight and wise. "A Cub Scout den is a different bird. I think because of all the focus on the individual skills and merit badges and stuff. I think all you did with your den was that laser tag once. Scouts isn't as much about camaraderie as a team or a band is. You sure you don't want to ask the guys over? Even after practice one night? Everybody for a dip?"

Landon shook his head and wiped his mouth. "I don't think so. Maybe some other time."

His father's hands went up in surrender. They paid the bill and headed home.

The sun was well down, and Landon's dad put the headlights on. They were nearly at the turnoff when they saw a small figure marching down the sidewalk, arms and legs flying high.

"Well, how about this for timing?" His father nodded at the furious display of limbs, and as he pulled over, Landon saw that it was his mom. She insisted on walking to and from the train each day, even with her crazy hours, because she said it not only lowered the carbon footprint of their family but also gave her a bit of exercise and the chance to wind down.

His father rolled down Landon's window. "Hey there, pretty woman. Going my way?"

Landon rolled his eyes, but looked to see how his mom would respond. She shifted her briefcase's strap on her shoulder and put her hands on her hips, smiling. "Forrest, what are you teaching our son?"

"That pretty women are hard to find and if you do find one, you pick her up! That's a lesson worth learning, I'd say."

"Oh, you would?" she teased.

"Definitely."

Landon's mom climbed into the backseat beside the football gear and then tapped Landon on the shoulder. "And my lesson is that being bold is the only way to win the prize."

Landon's dad tapped his arm. "And what a prize I am."

They went straight home, happy, without speaking. Landon digested the words his parents had spoken, sifting the lessons from the laughs. He knew Megan Nickell would be like that, joking around and happy and appreciative. He could just tell, but thinking of her made him think of Genevieve and the blowout he knew they were going to have as soon as she caught wind of him bailing out of the contact drills in exchange for carrying the water bottles.

He realized his mom was tapping his shoulder, and as they pulled into their driveway, he turned around.

"I said, how is football going?" His mom's sharp look seemed to see right into his head, like his eyes were windows without curtains.

Landon nodded. "Fine. Good."

"Isn't that great to hear?" She patted his shoulder, and they all got out. Landon heard his parents talking but didn't bother to pay attention. He got his football gear from the backseat and laid it out to dry in the garage before following them into the house. He dumped his cleats in the mud room before entering the kitchen.

"Well, we just had some pretty serious ice cream at that Häagen-Dazs store," his father said to his mom, "but I can cook something up for you if you're hungry. I made lobster ravioli. Sound good? Or, I could whip up an omelet, a little sage and white cheddar?"

Landon's mom sat on a bar stool at the granite-topped island in the middle of the kitchen. She wore a tired look. Her shoes were off and her feet were already up on the next stool. "Just some salad if you have it, Forrest."

"I always have salad," Landon's father said. He looked at Landon and winked. "I was a rabbit in another life. I ever tell you that?"

Landon gave his father the grin he was waiting for and then said, "I'm gonna shower."

141

On his way up the stairs Landon considered his mom. He couldn't remember a time when she'd been gone more or seemed so tired, and he began to wonder if she or his dad regretted coming to Bronxville. It certainly wasn't treating Landon very nicely so far. Before he crossed in front of the open hallway that led to Genevieve's room, he stopped and peeked around the corner and strained for a hint of noise. He heard nothing and tiptoed across, making it safely to his own room, where he put his ears in their drier and took a nice cool shower.

When he got out, he wrapped a towel around his waist, walked into his bedroom, and yelped with fright.

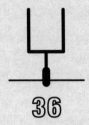

36

Genevieve jumped up off the bed, and it looked like she yelped too.

Everything was silent to Landon. He had an idea of what Genevieve was saying, though. He didn't have to read lips to know she was raving mad. Landon told himself to stay calm. He knew he just had to weather the storm. It would pass. And, a storm was always a lot less frightening when you couldn't hear the thunder.

Genevieve started pacing and flashing her phone in his face. He didn't read the text messages or the Instagram posts. He didn't have to. He knew from the pain and anger on her face that they were about him. He didn't have to read about people calling him a powder puff. He knew what they thought.

"I can't even hear you, Genevieve." Landon stood in the

same spot, folded his arms, and pointed to the ears in their drier.

"Look at me." She mouthed the words slowly. The look in her eyes was so white-hot that he couldn't look away.

She shook her head violently. "You cannot quit!"

Landon just looked down at her and shook his head. "Leave me alone, Genevieve. You don't know what you're talking about. Everything's easy for you."

"For me?" Her face twisted in disbelief. "Do you know what I've done for you?"

Landon looked away until she grabbed his arm and gave it a yank.

He could tell she'd lowered her voice as she leaned close and said, "Don't you look away. You look at me! I know you understand. I've made nice with one of the meanest girls I've ever met in my life because of you. Do you know why? So she won't *torture* you."

Landon was confused. "Not Megan."

"No, not Megan. Katy! She looks at you like a spider looks at a fly. She'd love to wrap you up and suck out every ounce of blood and leave you shriveled up like a mummy, but she won't because she wants to be my friend." Genevieve jabbed her own chest with a thumb. "Do you know how much I hate that? You think that isn't hard?

"No, you don't." Genevieve shook her head violently again, and then she grabbed him by both arms and looked up into his eyes, slowly mouthing the words, "Pain is temporary, Landon, but quitting? Quitting is *forever*."

She turned and left him alone, wrapped in his towel, still dripping.

Landon felt like she'd stabbed him in the stomach and twisted the knife. It hurt and it made him furious. He wanted to strike back, and when he saw the medal she'd given him, he snatched it off the bedpost and marched after her. She'd already disappeared into her bedroom.

He knew he should knock, but he was too mad for manners. With the medal in his hand, he cocked his arm back, ready to throw it onto her floor. He didn't need her medals and he didn't need any of his own.

He grabbed the door handle with his other hand and flung it open.

Landon couldn't hear the screams, but he knew there was screaming.

In a flash of skin and underwear and towels, he realized he'd barged in on Genevieve and her friends changing to take a night swim.

The medal slipped from Landon's hand and fell silently to the floor.

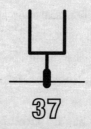

37

Landon squeezed his eyes shut and bolted back to his room.

He lay facedown on his bed with a pillow over the back of his head. His breath got hot and short, and he wondered if a person could suffocate himself. He threw the pillow off and rolled over, gasping for air, and lay there huffing for a long while. Finally, he swung his legs off the bed and sat there with the towel still wrapped tightly around his flabby waist.

He got up and dressed himself.

His hands trembled, and he dropped his ears twice before he had them on and in place. He cracked open the door and listened hard for any sounds, but the house was still. He tiptoed out and peered down Genevieve's hall. Her bedroom door stood ajar, but no light spilled from it. Quietly, he made his way down the stairs. His father's computer was on, but the chair stood crooked and empty. He rounded the corner and saw his parents sitting with Genevieve at the kitchen table. They talked in a low murmur that he hadn't a prayer of understanding. His mother held Genevieve's hand across the corner of the table. Genevieve's head hung low and her back was to him.

Landon touched her shoulder. "I didn't see anything."

Genevieve looked up in horror. "You just had to shove that medal in my face, didn't you?"

Landon's mouth fell open. He'd never seen Genevieve this mad at him. He wanted to tell her about Xander's birthday party. He wanted her to feel bad for him and comfort him, but nothing came out.

"And don't even say you didn't see anything!" Genevieve threw her hands in the air, her eyes as wild as her hair. "They totally freaked and Katy said they had to leave and she's already blabbed about it. It's *out* there."

Genevieve held up her phone as proof and then turned the phone her way, looked at it, and groaned before putting her head down onto her arm to cry.

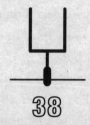

38

Landon's father looked ill. His face was pasty and he twiddled his fingers with his eyes rolled toward Landon's mom, awaiting her response.

Landon's mom stared at the tabletop, searching the rich wood grain for some kind of inspiration or truth. Finally, she sighed and looked up at Landon's dad. "Well, Landon is a normal boy, and normal boys are curious about these things."

Landon's father seemed to have swallowed his tongue. He shook his head uncertainly and gurgled.

Landon's mom looked at Landon now.

Landon shook his head. "No. I'm not curious."

"Landon? It's all right," his mom said. "It's perfectly natural for boys your age; your father will tell you that. Forrest?"

"Uh . . . of course," his father said.

"Mom! I did not see them on *purpose*!" Landon clenched his fists. "I was giving her back her stupid medal."

"Now my medal's stupid?" Genevieve raised her head. Her eyes were red, and she was livid.

Landon kept going. "That's the only reason I went to her room, and I didn't have my ears on and I didn't hear anything or anyone and I had no idea they were even *there*."

His mom removed her glasses and rubbed her eyes before looking up. "Oh . . . well . . . a misunderstanding. All of it. I'll call the girls' mothers and get it worked out."

"Good luck with that." Genevieve looked bitter, but Landon's mom was undaunted.

"I don't need luck," she said. "Just persistence."

"It's already *out* there, Mom." Genevieve groaned and lifted her phone off the table. "Katy called Landon a 'Peeping Tom,' and people are going wild with it. It's a hashtag. #PeepingPowderPuff."

"Well, every sensible person knows the internet is no place for reliable facts," their mom said.

"Like saying President Obama wasn't born in America." Landon's dad raised a finger.

Landon's mom scowled at her husband. "Well, fools are fools, and I can't help that. What I can help with, though, is this Katy Buford. We'll see how long she keeps this up after I call her mother. I'll give *her* a hashtag."

Landon stood there, lost and crushed and wanting to go back to Cleveland. Kip Meyers and his friends calling him a big, fat dummy was a piece of birthday cake compared to this.

149

Suddenly, the phone rang. They all just stared at it.

Landon's mom sighed. "Maybe she's saving me the trouble of looking up her number."

She got up slowly from her chair to answer. "Hello? Yes, this is Landon's mother."

His mom paused, and then her face turned angry. *"What?"*

Landon wondered how he could continue to sink when he'd already hit the bottom. He grabbed his cochlears and stood there, ready to pull the plug.

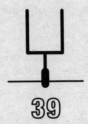

39

Landon's mom looked at him, fuming, but it wasn't him she was mad at. He could tell.

"I hate to say it," his mom said into the phone, "but I've seen things like this before. This isn't the first time Landon's been excluded from a birthday party . . . Uh-huh . . . Uh-huh . . . yes."

Landon's dad bit into his lower lip and began twiddling his fingers again.

"Wait, I'm sorry." Landon's mom's face softened. "What did you say your name was?"

She listened, nodding her head. "Courtney Wagner. Got it. Thank you, Courtney. But your son is Brett? Brett Bell? Yes, I thought about keeping my name too, but my husband is a bit old-fashioned. Ha-ha."

Confusion racked Landon.

His mom held his attention with commanding eyes. "Yes, I think Landon would be happy to talk to Brett, but it would be much easier on Skype, or we can FaceTime. Do you have an account? You do? Super. I've got it on my cell phone and I'll bring it right up. . . ."

Landon's mom tapped away on her phone. "Got it. Calling now."

His mom switched from the house phone to her cell. The Skype blurted and bleeped, and his mom came back toward the table. "Hi, Courtney. It worked! This is so nice. Let me put Landon on, and *thank you*. Thank you so much."

His mom handed Landon the phone and there was Brett, not scowling, not mean-faced, but wearing an easy smile as if he wasn't the one-man wrecking machine he had been earlier on the field.

"Hi, Brett," Landon said.

"Hey, Landon. Can you understand me okay like this? Can you see me good?" Brett asked, pointing to his own face.

"Yes." Landon felt wildly shy, aware that everyone was watching him, and having no idea what was going on. He remembered Brett's anger in the drill. Landon searched for a trick, some kind of falseness, but Brett appeared to be genuine.

"So, Saturday . . . ," Brett began.

Landon just stared.

Brett smiled crookedly, maybe from nerves. "Saturday, we're going down to New Jersey to visit my uncle. He plays for the Giants and they have the day off. He's gonna have a bunch of players over at his house—he's got a pretty big house—for a cookout at the pool. I think Rashad Jennings will be there. Eli Manning, too. Anyway, I thought maybe you'd want to come with us."

A surge of excitement and joy rocketed through Landon's entire body. "I . . . sure. But . . ."

"What's the matter?" Brett asked.

Landon couldn't help being suspicious. This sounded too good to be true. "Don't you have that birthday party, with Xander and the whole team?"

Brett gave him a funny look. "Well, if you're not going, then it can't really be a team party, right? Besides, nothing would stop me from being with my uncle and his friends."

Landon couldn't even speak. He glanced at his mom, who was beaming and nodding and mouthing for him to say yes.

"Uh," Landon said, "yes. Sure. A cookout would be awesome. Rashad Jennings is amazing. He ran for over a hundred yards last year when they played the Browns. I'm a Browns fan, but I won't say that to them."

Off-screen, his mom waved her hands frantically and mouthed for him to say thank you.

"Thanks, Brett. Thanks very much."

"Hey, no problem, Landon. And don't worry about the Browns. Everyone gets it. You're from Cleveland, right? You're supposed to be a Browns fan."

"But I can be a Giants fan too," Landon said. "You know, unless they face off in the Super Bowl."

Brett laughed and then looked at someone off of his screen

153

and then back. "My mom says we'll pick you up about eleven, if that's okay."

"That's . . . sure. Eleven would be great. Thank you again."

"Here, I'll give you my mom's cell number." Brett told him the number. "Text your address, okay?"

"Sure."

"Okay. See you at practice tomorrow, then."

"See you," Landon said. The phone bleeped and Brett disappeared. Landon looked up to see if the whole thing had really happened.

Genevieve still looked destroyed, but his father beamed and nodded like he'd won the lottery, and his mom reached out and touched his cheek. "See, Landon? See how quickly things can turn around?"

Landon handed her back her phone. "Thanks, Mom."

He didn't want to say anything more. He didn't want to talk. He didn't want to be angry about Xander's party, or sad or afraid. He practically tiptoed back to his room, removed his ears, got into his pajamas, climbed into bed, and lay there with his eyes open and the lights off. His parents came in and kissed him good night, looking at him fondly but sensing that he needed to be left alone.

He felt like he was on the top floor of a house of cards. Any misstep could bring the whole thing down, but for now, for this night, he had a friend—and not just any friend. He had Brett. And if Brett was friends with him, Megan might also be forgiving and understand when she heard his side of the story about barging in on them. She might even help him by telling people he'd done nothing wrong and that it was only a mistake and that Katy Buford was a mean, obnoxious twit.

Landon sighed.

Maybe not. But then again, maybe she would.

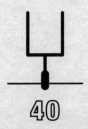

40

Friday afternoon it rained. Landon watched football technique drills and blocking highlights on YouTube while his father pecked away at the computer. Genevieve ignored him, leaving the house with nothing more than a wave. When Landon asked his father where she'd gone, his father said that she was going to the mall with Megan to shop and then see a movie.

"So that's a good sign, right?" Landon said, wishing beyond hope that the Peeping Powder Puff thing had died a quick death and everyone had gotten over it.

His father only shrugged. "Maybe. We'll see. Sometimes people surprise you, and I know your mother is on the case, so . . ."

His mom "working on it" made Landon worry more, but he chose to push it from his mind and instead dwell on the weekend invitation. He wanted to call Brett to make sure it was real, feel him out for signs that it was something his mother had put him up to, but decided that might damage what was a good thing. He needed to be patient and let it all unfold.

He closed his iPad and picked up his book.

It was nearly time for practice and still raining when Landon, sitting in his favorite chair, looked up from reading and, out of the blue, spoke across the room to his father. "Genevieve didn't seem too mad when she left?"

His father looked up from his typing and over at Landon. "The thing about your sister is that she's a lot like your mom. You never have to worry whose side she's on."

Landon waited for his father to go on, but he'd stopped talking. Landon filled the silence, saying, "My side, right?"

His father dipped his chin. "Your side times ten. She might be mad, but she'll fight for you, Landon."

Landon thought for a moment. "But who wants to have a little sister fighting for him? I mean, that looks kind of bad."

His father scratched his chin and pointed. "You seem to really like that book."

"Huh?" Landon wasn't sure if he'd heard his father correctly so he held up the book, and his father nodded. "Yeah, it's awesome."

"But look at it," his father said. "A worn-out green cover with the title and the author's name, both faded. No fireballs or dashing heroes or swords or brilliant, eye-catching colors. But inside? Wow. What could pack a bigger punch than *The Three Musketeers*? It's unforgettable."

"So, don't judge a book by its cover," Landon said.

"I never do." His father smiled and turned back to the screen and his story.

Later, at football practice, Landon watched the other kids warily. The rain hadn't stopped. Maybe that was keeping the fires of rumors under control. The temperature had dipped into the low seventies, so there wasn't as much need for water bottles. Landon found himself shifting from foot to foot, drenched from head to toe, watching the other boys battle in the muddy grass. There was a lot of hooting and hollering. Landon couldn't figure out why. Large drops swelled on his face mask, growing fat until they broke free and splattered his jersey.

No one said anything to him. The one time Landon found himself face-to-face with Skip—before practice on the sideline where Skip was retrieving a football from the ball bag—the quarterback simply walked around Landon like he was a lamppost. He took that as a good sign, but he had a sinking feeling that something might have changed with Brett. It was like their Skype the night before had never happened. He wasn't able to bring himself to tap Brett on the shoulder until after wind sprints.

Brett looked exhausted, which was no surprise. The big lineman had hustled and hit his way through practice like it was a fifty-round boxing match, if there even was such a thing. Even in the cool rain, Brett's face was beaded with sweat and his eyes sagged wearily. "Hey, Landon."

"Everything good?" It was the only question Landon could ask.

"Oh, you mean guys calling you 3P?" Brett shot a glare around at the other players slogging up toward the parking lot. "Don't worry about that junk. People are stupid."

158

"Wait, what?" Landon had no idea what he was talking about.

Brett waved a padded hand toward the heavy gray sky. "Forget it. Just jerks. You're good for tomorrow, right? My uncle's place?"

"Yeah." Landon nodded. "I'm great for tomorrow, but what's 3P?"

Brett studied him. "Landon, it's okay. Junk happens. People blow things out of proportion. The girls you walked in on? I already told Skip to keep his hands off you."

"You did?" Landon felt a surge of gratitude. "Thanks, but why would Skip . . ."

"Well, you know he and Megan are, like, this thing." Brett wrinkled his face. "Stupid, really. I think they hold hands at the movies or something. Everyone was pushing him to bust you in the mouth, but I got that covered."

"But, 3P?"

Brett tilted his head. "You really don't know? It's not nice. I don't want to even say. It's stupid."

"Wait . . ." Landon lowered his voice. "Peeping Powder Puff?"

Brett looked disgusted. "Don't worry about it. It'll die down, and no one's laying a hand on you." Brett made a fist and tapped his own chest. "They know better."

Pressure built up inside Landon because he felt like he should let Brett go. The two of them were just standing there alone now. Brett's dad was huddled up with the other coaches as they sometimes did after practice, but Landon had to ask, "Why are you doing this?"

"Doing what?"

159

"Being my friend. What's in it for you?"

Brett shrugged. "Nothing. You're my teammate. My dad says a real leader treats everyone on the team the same. The best player or the . . . the not-best player."

"You mean the worst player." Landon wondered if, despite the drills, he even qualified as a player. "The guy who plays left out."

"It doesn't matter, Landon." Brett set his jaw. "Some people just don't get it, but in my house, that's how we do things. You help people who really need it."

Landon swallowed. "And . . . because of all this stuff, I really need it?"

Brett had that hard look on his face again. "Yeah. You do."

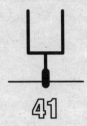

41

Landon woke early the next morning. He packed and repacked his Nike duffel bag with a fresh change of clothes, bathing suit, goggles, and towel, wanting everything to be just right, to look just right. He modeled three different bathing suits in his bathroom mirror and ended up going with the black knee-length one that had a narrow orange stripe down the side. The others, he decided, made his gut look too big.

He was ready to go by eight. His dad had pancakes going before his mom wandered down in her robe, bleary-eyed and feeling her way around the kitchen for a cup of coffee.

Genevieve appeared in a soccer uniform with her wild hair pulled back in a tight ponytail and a headband.

"You got a game?" Landon asked.

"Yup." Genevieve scanned her phone with a blank face. "That's how it works."

Their mom set her coffee cup down with a sharp sound. "What's that supposed to mean, young lady?"

Landon stabbed a pancake but dragged it back and forth across the puddle of syrup instead of shoveling it into his mouth. He wondered how much Genevieve was going to say.

"Just getting my game face on," Genevieve said with the same blank stare at their mom.

Landon stuffed the forkful of pancake into his mouth.

"Hmm." Their mom sat down and raised the coffee with both hands, closing her eyes to inhale the steam, before turning her head toward the stove. "Well, Forrest, we should go to the game."

"Right." Their dad raised a spatula without turning around. "Should be on the family calendar."

"I was hoping I wouldn't have to look at any calendar today," she said with a sigh.

Their father brought another plate of pancakes to the table and sat down beside their mom. "You don't. Just leave everything to me."

Their mom smiled and then turned her attention back to Genevieve. "How's the social media looking?"

Genevieve put her phone down on the placemat and picked up her knife. "Not too bad, actually. Looks like you did your magic."

Their mom fought back a smile. "Good."

"I just hope it's not like the French aristocracy." His sister busied herself with the syrup.

"Meaning?" their mom asked.

"We all know how that ended." Genevieve looked at their mom with a false smile. "The guillotine."

The knife dropped with a clank, and the top of her banana skittered into the puddle of syrup.

"That's an entirely different story." Their mom took a swig of coffee and set it down hard again.

Genevieve only shrugged and dove into her pancakes.

Landon tried not to think about it, but as he waited for eleven o'clock to roll around, he found himself touching his own neck as he sat in his favorite chair to read. At quarter till the hour, Landon gave up his book and positioned himself in the front window.

Finally, at 11:04, Brett and his family pulled into the driveway. Landon grabbed his bag and scrambled toward the garage. "I'm going."

His mom cut him off and straightened the collar of his bright blue polo shirt. "Mind your manners."

"I will." Landon felt his mom right behind him and he turned to see what was up.

"I'm coming out, to say hello to Courtney," she said. Before they got through the garage, she tapped his shoulder again. "Make sure you keep your ears dry—remember, wrap them good in a towel someplace out of the way, and tell everyone you won't be able to hear when you're swimming."

He was too excited to care what she said, and he just kept going.

Brett's mom got out of the big Suburban and circled around to say hello. She stood nearly a foot taller than Landon's mom, and Landon was surprised to see that she had no hair on her head, not even any eyebrows. If Landon's mom noticed, she didn't show it. The two women shook hands before Landon's mom pulled Brett's mom into a hug. "Courtney Wagner, you're my type of gal."

Brett's mom blushed down at Landon's mom, but she seemed pleased. "Well, Brett says Landon is a very nice boy, and we like nice boys."

"He is." Landon's mom gave Brett's mom's hand a squeeze.

Brett's mom pointed to her hairless scalp. "With all my treatments, we've been going through a lot, so we know what it is to look a little different, and it's always nice when people don't care."

Landon's mom beamed. "You're wonderful. Thank you again."

Landon had stopped before getting into the SUV to keep an eye on his mom because he was afraid she was going to start giving Brett's mom instructions on his ears, but she didn't. He gave her a final wave and climbed in next to Brett. In the third row of seats, two twin girls who looked to be kindergarten age wore fluffy, blue bunny ears and were focused on the iPad on the seat between them. Kiddie music jangled and the two of them looked at each other and laughed before staring down again.

"My sisters," Brett said. "Don't worry about them. One's Susie, the other's Sally, and even I have a hard time telling them apart."

"Hi, Landon." Coach Bell reached around from the front seat to shake Landon's hand as Brett's mom got in.

"Hi, Coach," Landon said. "Thank you for bringing me."

Brett's mom turned around in the passenger seat and looked directly at him. He liked what she'd said about looking different, and he was careful not to stare at her missing eyebrows or hair and to look her in the eyes when she spoke.

"It's our pleasure to have you, Landon."

Landon gave her a nod and then watched his mom wave as they pulled out of the driveway. He breathed a sigh of relief when she finally disappeared from sight.

Brett tapped Landon's chest. "Know who's gonna be there?"

"Well, you said Eli and Rashad . . ."

Brett trembled with delight. "Yup, them too, but can you guess who *else*?"

Landon shook his head. "Who?"

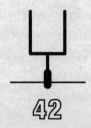

42

"Michael Bamiro." Brett spread his arms as wide as the inside of the SUV would allow him. "Biggest guy on the team and one of the top five big guys in the *whole* NFL."

"Wow," Landon said. "How big?"

Brett nodded, evidently glad to see Landon's enthusiasm. "Six foot eight. Three hundred and forty-five pounds. How about that?"

"Man . . ." Landon shook his head and then raised his eyebrows. "Did I tell you my dad is six-ten?"

"I've seen him." Brett's eyes sparkled. He directed his voice toward the front. "Dad, did you know Landon's dad is six-ten?"

Landon could see Coach Bell shaking his head, but he wasn't sure what he said in response. Landon thought it was, "That's tall." But he couldn't be sure.

"Hey," Brett said, nodding at the duffel bag on Landon's lap. "You bring your phone?"

"Yes." Landon got it out and showed him.

"You do *Clash of Clans*?"

"No."

"You want to? You should. You can be in my clan. Here, I'll set it up. It's free!" Brett took the phone from Landon and got to work.

Landon felt like he was floating as Brett leaned toward him, showing him how to get things set up and then showing him his own phone. "I've got a Town Hall 8, but I've been doing it for over a year. It takes time, but you can be in a clan and still get matched up to battle guys your own strength level."

They spent the rest of the trip with Brett schooling him on *Clash of Clans*. A couple of times, with all the talk of castles and dragons and archers, Landon felt like he had an opening to tell Brett about his father's book, but he kept quiet because he didn't want to ruin anything. And, as they pulled up the long, curving driveway and into the circle in front of Brett's uncle's gigantic house, Landon told himself to keep as quiet as he could about everything. He needed to just get through the day without botching things up. Building a friendship with Brett would be even more spectacular than creating a clan war base, but he sensed it was similar in that he'd have to do it one block at a time, with great care and patience.

They parked among a parade of glittering automobiles and walked through the house out to the backyard without even knocking. Each of Brett's parents held the hand of a twin. Brett and Landon followed behind out onto the sunlit terrace, where two large tents stood on either side of the pool to protect the colorful buffet tables laid out there. The party was already in full swing with people in shorts and bathing suits everywhere in and around the big pool. Landon not only heard but felt the thumping of music from the outdoor sound system. Several men—players, by the look of their muscles—welcomed the Bell family like old friends.

They kissed Brett's mom on the cheek, smiling at her as if she wasn't sick at all.

Then one of the players who had a beer bottle in his hand turned suddenly on Landon, laughed, and asked cheerfully, "Hey, my man? What the heck are those things?"

It seemed like the whole party suddenly stopped so everyone could stare at Landon. Just like that, his plan of keeping a low profile was destroyed.

Brett's mom gave the player an angry look and said, "Jonathan *Wagner*, what's wrong with you?"

Landon realized that the player standing in front of him was Brett's uncle. He couldn't break out in tears. He couldn't hide his face.

He had to say something.

He just had no idea what.

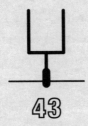

43

"I'm . . ." Landon's mind went blank.

Brett and the others looked stunned.

Landon suddenly turned and dashed back into the house without knowing what he was doing or where he was going. He passed through a great room with a TV the size of a wall and down a hallway that he thought led to the front entrance. He found himself in a huge library, reversed his course, saw a staircase, reversed again, and ducked into a marble-floored bathroom, shutting the door behind him.

He was huffing to catch his breath, and he looked at the pain on his face in the mirror. His fingers crept over his ears, caressed the battery packs, and slid along the wires to the discs magnetically stuck to the implants beneath his scalp. He should have worn his cap. He had been planning to, but the thought of walking into a New York Giants players' cookout with a

Cleveland Browns cap didn't seem right. He wanted to remove his ears—just stash the equipment in his bag and look like a normal kid—but he knew he couldn't. He'd be too cut off if he did.

He stood there for a while. Time seemed to have frozen. He jumped at the sudden sound of a knock on the bathroom door and turned the water faucet on to make it sound like he actually needed to be in there. "Just a minute."

"Landon?" It was a voice Landon didn't recognize, but he was shouting through the door and Landon thought he understood. "Hey, my man, it's Jonathan, Brett's uncle. You all right?"

Landon gathered himself and opened the door. "I just had to use the . . ."

"Hey, my man." Jonathan wore a sad face. Behind him stood Brett's dad.

Jonathan Wagner put his hands on Landon's shoulders. "I am way sorry. Listen, I did *not* mean to insult you or upset you. No way, my man. You gotta believe me."

"It's okay." Landon wanted to melt.

Coach Bell stepped forward and asked, "Landon, are you all right to stay?"

Landon nodded. "Yes."

"For sure," Jonathan said. "Come on, my man. I'm personally dressing up a couple dogs for you. What do you like? Ketchup? Mustard? Chili? How about a chili dog?"

"It's okay." Landon looked down at his sneakers. "I'm fine. Really. I just had to wash my hands."

"Landon, my sister told me your gear there is so you can *hear*," Jonathan said. "I had no idea they could do something like that, implants and all. So, think about it, you're, like, bionic. In a good way. Hey, I am too. I got this plate in my arm here."

Jonathan presented a tattooed forearm split down the middle with a shiny scar and laughed. "Sets off metal detectors in the airport. I know about hardware, my man. It's all good, right? Are you sure you're okay?"

Landon could only nod. He appreciated Jonathan feeling bad and letting Landon know that he meant no harm. He could hear his father's voice. "Forgive and forget, Landon. Forgive and forget."

But in truth, he was horrified that there had been a scene, and he didn't want to go back into the crowd.

"Hey, you gotta come on out because you know who I'm going to introduce you to?" Jonathan said.

Landon shook his head.

"You like Eli Manning?"

Landon nodded vigorously. "Yes!"

"Hey," Coach Bell said. "That's a great idea."

"Sure, everyone likes Eli. Come on." Jonathan turned, saw Landon hesitate, and took hold of his arm. "My man, you're not just gonna meet him. I'm taking a pic you can post on whatever you're into and all the kids at your school are gonna freak. Come on, now. You don't want to hurt Eli's feelings by not wanting to meet him."

Landon let himself be led because how could he resist? Jonathan was built like a battleship, with bulging biceps pushing the sleeves of his polo shirt against cannonball shoulders. Tattoos covered his arms—green, black, and orange, with all

171

kinds of designs and pictures. It reminded Landon of a graffiti-covered brick wall. As he was hauled back out into the crowd, all Landon saw were smiles.

"We worked it out, Courtney." Jonathan motioned for his sister to follow them and then turned to Landon. "My sister's a tough cookie."

Landon laughed. "So is Brett. He's the best player on our team."

Brett and his mom gave Landon thumbs-up and followed with Brett's little sisters in tow.

The crowd parted by the diving board next to the second tent, and there he was: Eli Manning. Landon felt his heart double-clutch. Manning had a can of grape soda in his hand and was talking to a player who could only be Michael Bamiro. The Giants lineman was nearly as tall as Landon's dad, only his chest was twice as wide and his legs were like tree trunks. Stylish black-framed glasses and a shaved head gave him a studious look.

Both men turned their dark brown eyes on Landon and both smiled like he was some long-lost friend.

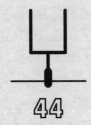

44

"Guys, this is Landon." Jonathan gave Landon a pat on the back. "I have no idea why he wanted to meet you, Eli, but I told him that if he asked for a picture with you, it would make your day."

Eli held out a hand and Landon shook it. "It's a pleasure to meet you, Mr. Manning."

"Hey, Landon." Eli spoke quietly, but Landon understood. "You know who Michael Bamiro is, right?"

"Hi, Mr. Bamiro." Landon shook the giant man's hand. "I play football too. I want to be a lineman like you and Mr. Wagner."

"Yeah," Jonathan said. "He's on my nephew's team."

"Very nice," Bamiro said. "What high school you guys play for, Landon?"

Landon blinked and stuttered. "I, uh . . . we play for a seventh-grade youth team, sir."

"Seventh?" Bamiro was surprised.

"Yes," Landon said quickly. "I'm twelve."

"You?" Bamiro laughed, flashing a set of bright white teeth. "I think you're bigger than I was at twelve. You hear that, Eli? Maybe you can last long enough for Landon here to block for you."

Eli grinned and pointed at Bamiro and Jonathan Wagner. "With you two knuckleheads in front of me, I'll be lucky to make it through next season."

The three players laughed at that together, and Landon blushed even harder when Brett stepped into their little circle. Landon had to wonder—as nice as Brett had been—if he wouldn't expose Landon for being more of a water boy than a lineman, but Brett only smiled and asked if he could get a picture with Eli too.

Rashad Jennings, the Giants' running back, suddenly appeared and threw his hands up in the air. "Manning, Bamiro, Wagner. Come on, guys. Let's get this lovefest over with. Eli won't be able to fit his head into that new Corvette he's driving."

"Well, it's a convertible," Eli said.

Rashad snapped his fingers. "Of course. Now we know why. You *already* can't fit your head in, so you gotta keep the top down."

The players all laughed again, and so did Landon and Brett.

They got a bunch of pictures with the players individually and all as one big group.

"Okay," Jonathan Wagner said. "We good? 'Cause if we are, I say let's eat. I promised my man some chili dogs."

They all piled plates with food and sat down at one of the long tables on a brick terrace under some enormous shade trees. Landon's eyes were busy, darting back and forth, trying to follow the banter between the players, who seemed to genuinely enjoy each other's company despite the constant kidding.

With winks and slaps on the back, they made him feel part of it all.

Their plates were pretty much empty when Rashad Jennings pointed at the diving board and said, "I'm fixing to light that thing up now, boys."

"Light it up?" Jonathan slapped Rashad on the back. "With a pencil dive or something?"

Everyone laughed.

Rashad kept his chin up. "How about a backflip?"

The players all hooted.

"Yeah!"

"Let's see that!"

Jonathan Wagner held up both his arms. "Who needs something fancy like that when you have the world champion cannonballer right here?"

Landon bit his lip to keep from laughing, and he couldn't help himself from shouting, "I bet I can beat you!"

"What?" Wagner tilted his head and knotted up his face. "Boy, you're gonna be big one day, but I hit that water like a twenty-ton *bomb*."

Landon shrugged. "I think I can beat you."

The players went wild, hooting and laughing, pointing at Wagner and saying Landon called him out.

Wagner stood up and pretended to be angry, throwing his napkin down on the table and pointing at Landon, but he was unable to keep from smiling. "It's on, my man. You and me. Cannonball championship of the *world*!"

Landon's spirit soared.

45

Landon changed in the same bathroom he'd tried hiding in. He looked at himself in the mirror, removed his ears, patted his belly, and grinned. He knew he could cannonball. He marched outside, and everyone was lined up around the pool. When they saw him, they cheered, waving their hands and grinning. He wished he could have heard it, but in a way, the silence helped him not to get nervous.

Jonathan Wagner stood on the end of the diving board, and it bowed beneath his tremendous weight. Landon gulped as the big man began bouncing up and down on the end of the board. After half a dozen jumps, he launched himself quite high, dipped, tucked, and plummeted into the water.

A geyser exploded. The column of water shot at a sideways angle, though, drenching a good dozen people, who scattered. Landon laughed at the sight of their happy screaming. When the crowd recovered, everyone began to clap and chant. Landon read their lips.

"Lan-don, Lan-don, Lan-don."

He was briefly reminded of wind sprints, but pushed that ugly thought from his mind and climbed up onto the board. The sandy surface scratched his feet. He strode out to the end, where he curled his toes over the lip and felt the flex of the board beneath him. He knew he couldn't get as high as Wagner and he knew he wasn't nearly as big, but technique was very important when cannonballing, and that he had.

With all eyes on him and the chant of his name on their lips, Landon got into a rhythm, up and down, flexing his legs, getting more height. When he was ready, he took one last jump for balance, launched himself, and tucked like a true human cannonball. When he hit the water, he fought to keep his form and felt the water explode beneath him. Then the suction drew his body into the void with tremendous force.

He let his momentum carry him down until his knees scraped the bottom of the pool, and there he floated, suspended in water and joy until his breath ran out and he sprang off the bottom, breaking the surface to a new round of silent cheers.

He knew by everyone's reaction that he'd won.

Even Jonathan Wagner slapped him on the back, giving him a big thumbs-up. Then Bamiro raised Landon's arm high in the air and said something while people cheered even more.

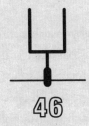

46

Landon and Brett swam the rest of the afternoon, and by the time they had to go, they were exhausted. Landon changed into dry clothes and put his ears back on, so he could hear when Jonathan Wagner stopped Brett as they were getting into the Suburban.

"Hey, Brett," the Giants' right tackle said, "you got one heck of a friend. You'll have to bring him around again."

Landon buckled his seat belt and closed his eyes, concentrating hard, because he was determined to remember the sound of those words for as long as he lived. When he opened his eyes, Jonathan Wagner was at the window and motioning for him to roll it down. Landon did and said, "Thanks for having me. It was a great time."

"Hey, my man, you are more than welcome." Jonathan reached through and shook his hand. "And thanks for bouncing back on me after my off-sides penalty with the implants there. I appreciate you not holding a grudge. It sure wasn't a smart thing to say, that's all. And I just want you to know I'm sorry. Anyway, you'll be seeing me again real soon."

"Really?"

"Yeah, well, we got a bye week coming up, and my sister, Courtney, makes this meatloaf like our mom used to make that keeps me coming back." Jonathan's face looked a bit sad for a second, but then it brightened. "I'll check you guys out at your practice. This is all *if* Coach McAdoo gives us some time off. He should, so . . ."

Jonathan held out a fist and Landon knew to give it a bump, even though his head was spinning.

"I'll get to see you and Brett in action."

And suddenly, even after the magic of the day, Landon's nerves were on edge.

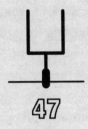

47

"I want to kiss Brett Bell."

Landon's mouth sagged open. "What did you say?" He blinked, unsure of what he'd just seen and heard, because it sounded like his sister had just said she wanted to *kiss* Brett Bell. Landon and Genevieve were out in the yard in the dying light of the day with glass jars, catching fireflies. The damp grass tickled his bare feet. In the twilight beneath the trees he easily could have mistaken what she said.

Genevieve staved him off with a hand as she crouched and then pounced with her jar, scooping it into the grass and clapping the top on in one expert motion. She held the jar up and frowned, searching in the gloom. When the bug lit up, it burned so bright Landon could make out the smile on her face and read her lips clearly when she looked at him. "I said I want to kiss him."

"That's gross."

"Oh, Landon." She rolled her eyes. "In a sister sort of way, or the way the French kiss when they meet."

"A *French* kiss?" Landon scowled at her. "Geez, Genevieve. That's even more gross, sticking your tongue in someone's mouth. What's more disgusting than *that*?"

Genevieve sighed. "Please, Landon. Nothing gross. Nothing romantic. 'Kiss' as in, he's the greatest kid in the world. That post with the split picture of you and Jonathan Wagner doing cannonballs? Michael Bamiro calling you the world champ? It's all over Instagram. That peeping thing is practically *gone*."

Landon caught a glint of light in the corner of his eye, and he spun and flailed after it, missing the fly completely. He watched it blip as it floated up into the trees, and then he turned back to Genevieve. "What about Megan?"

Genevieve nodded. "She's fine, Landon. She felt bad for you with all this."

"But she didn't come over." Landon fit the top onto his empty jar, practicing his scoop, and then hustled across the lawn when he spotted a firefly winking from a blade of grass. He pounced and held the jar up for Genevieve to see the bug blinking away.

"I got it!"

Genevieve came over and patted his shoulder. "Nice work."

Landon studied the insect as it crawled around on the inside of the jar with a wing askew and its bottom glowing, a miniature version of the sticks they carried with them on Halloween. He looked up when his sister tapped his arm.

"She's coming tomorrow to swim."

Landon's face got hot. "Tell her I'll be locked in the closet of my room when you guys are changing. Um . . . what about Katy?"

Genevieve swatted the air. "Forget Katy. She's dead to me."

"You shouldn't talk like that."

"Trust me, Landon." Even in the dim light Genevieve's eyes sparkled with anger. "What I'd like to do to her? Being dead *is* nice."

"Dad always says, 'Forgive and forget.'" Landon angled his head toward the house. In the light of the great room through the big window overlooking the backyard, they could see their father at his desk, working away.

"Forgiveness is for people who ask," Genevieve said.

"It's easier to let things go."

Genevieve shook her head violently. "You've got to fight sometimes, Landon. Fight people like Katy. Fight on the football field."

"That again?" Landon turned away.

Genevieve caught him. "You said Jonathan Wagner's going to be at practice sometime soon. What are you gonna do? Offer him water?"

"Maybe I'm just happy being on the team. Ever think of that?"

"No, Landon. Not the way you love football. No way."

Landon shook himself free from her. "We're catching fireflies, Genevieve. Let's just do that."

He turned his back on her, searching the yard, until he sensed her movement. Genevieve went into high gear. She might have been doing a dance routine, darting here and there, scooping, snatching, spinning, filling her jar. Landon watched her for a minute. Three, four, now five fireflies blinked inside their glass prison.

"Like it's so easy," he said to himself.

The solitary lightning bug flashed in his jar, but not as brightly as before.

Landon unscrewed the lid and let it go.

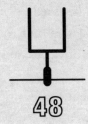

48

Sunday morning, Landon's mother was back to herself.

Gone were the bags under her eyes and the weary frown. She stood straight and moved about the stove like she had springs in her joints.

Bacon snapped beneath her spatula, filling the kitchen with a delicious smell. She was chattering at Landon's father, who presided over the toaster, waiting and watching patiently, butter knife in hand. Landon didn't know what she was saying, but when she realized he was there, she turned with the spatula in hand and beamed at him. "Good morning, sunshine."

"Hi, Mom." Landon sat down at the table at a place where someone had laid out placemats, plates, juice glasses, and silverware wrapped in checkered cloth napkins.

"Ready for a big day?" she asked.

Landon had had a big day yesterday, and this morning he'd

woken with excitement. His joy melted instantly, however, at the thought of Jonathan Wagner visiting practice only to see that his "man" was a powder puff. Landon's mind was stuck on that, and he wasn't thinking about today.

"What are we doing?" he asked.

"Well, school starts Tuesday and you and Genevieve both have games every weekend after this, so I thought we should do something special."

His mom turned to quickly shuffle the bacon and then looked back at him. "New York City. We're taking in the city. Uptown. Downtown. Soho. The Statue of Liberty. Empire State Building. A carriage ride in Central Park, maybe the zoo. Dinner at the Jekyll and Hyde Club."

"The *what?*" Landon unrolled the silverware and put the napkin in his lap.

"It's a haunted restaurant." Landon's mom made a scary face and turned her free hand into a claw. "Ghouls and mummies and such waiting on tables. Talking gargoyles."

Landon's father waved at him from the toaster. "Death by Chocolate. That's for dessert."

Genevieve appeared. "What dessert?"

"We're going to New York City to see *everything*," Landon said, teasing his mom.

"What?" Genevieve stared. "I've got Megan coming over to swim."

"Genevieve," their mom said, "it's Labor Day weekend. We're having a little family getaway, spending the night in New York. I've got us hotel rooms. There are fireworks on the Brooklyn Bridge after dinner."

Genevieve threw her arms in the air. "You don't just announce a family getaway on the morning of the getaway, Mom."

Their mom shrugged. "Well, I didn't know about it until now. I got up this morning at five and thought, yes, a family getaway to the greatest city in the world."

"Mom, this is important." Genevieve looked like she was begging.

"What's important?" their mom snorted. "Taking a swim?"

Genevieve gave Landon a knowing look. "Yes, Mom. It is."

"Not on my watch, young lady. Family first." Landon's mom pointed the spatula at his sister, and he saw that look on his mother's face, the one that said everyone better be careful. His father literally ducked down before buttering another slice of toast.

Landon's eyes went to his sister. He knew she could bite back, and he hoped she wouldn't now.

Genevieve's lips had a little wrestling match, good and bad fighting for control. Finally, she exhaled. "Fine."

The tension melted away, and Landon took a breath.

"The last couple weeks have been hard for everyone." Their mother's face softened. She turned and lifted the bacon out onto a bed of paper towels covering a platter. Beside the bacon rested another platter heaped with steaming scrambled eggs. She turned off the burner, slid a hand under each platter, and headed for the table. "This is a chance for us to reconnect as a total family. *And* do something fun. People come from all over the world to see the sights in New York City. We'd be fools not to take them in when they're right here under our noses."

Landon's dad delivered his platter of toast, and everyone

joined Landon, sitting at the table. Landon piled eggs and bacon onto his plate, got a piece of toast to help shovel, and dug in. He couldn't help focusing on his food, until he realized his mom was talking to Genevieve about the trip and he thought he heard Megan's name.

"I think it would be fun," his mom was saying.

Landon looked at Genevieve, who went for her phone on the table and began to text. "I'll ask her. I don't know if she can, but asking her makes canceling not so bad."

"Ask who what?" Landon took a swig of orange juice from his glass.

"Megan." Genevieve hit the Send button. "Mom said she can come with us."

Landon choked on his juice.

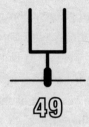

49

The trip to the city was fun. Landon had no idea something so simple and nice could cause yet another problem for him, but it did. A picture was taken after their dinner at Jekyll and Hyde by a man with a tightly trimmed beard on the Bow Bridge in Central Park. It was the five of them—Landon's family plus Megan—all crowded together, arms around one another, smiling, with the water and the incredible Central Park West skyline behind them. Genevieve had posted it on Instagram, a quaint family portrait plus a friend. #CentralPark.

By Monday evening, someone—and everyone seemed to know it was Katy Buford—had taken the image, cropped it so that Landon and Megan were standing together without anyone else in the picture, and added the caption, *Beauty and the Beast #Truelove?*

They couldn't pin it on Katy directly because the post was

on a site called ChitChat Bronxville, a horrid little cesspool on the internet where people in the small town could spew nasty rumors about one another without having to leave their fingerprints behind. It was a site where the posts were anonymous.

The picture and ensuing nasty comments had also revived Landon's 3P nickname, along with lots of other speculation about what he and Megan were up to and how she really mustn't have minded him seeing her changing after all. Landon read over Genevieve's shoulder in a state of shock until their mother took the phone to see for herself.

Landon's mother sat at the head of the kitchen table. With the look of a person about to jump out of an airplane, she started to read. Her lips moved and a frown dragged the corners of her mouth down. She began to tremble with rage. "It's vicious. It should be illegal."

Landon's father shrugged and made the mistake of observing, "It's free speech."

His mother's eyes cut Landon's father to the quick.

"But it shouldn't be," he added, hardly missing a beat.

"Well," his mom said, snapping the phone off, "we won't read it and we won't think about it. We're not going to validate this disgusting site by acknowledging that it's even there. That's what everyone should do. Would you read some nasty comment on the inside of a bathroom stall and then post it to discuss with people? That's all this is."

Landon had never seen Genevieve so defeated. She raised her head and spoke in a low voice Landon could barely make out. "Everyone else is seeing it and talking about it too. Everyone's saying to check out ChitChat Bronxville."

"Was there a site like this in Cleveland?" their mother asked. "A ChitChat Cleveland?"

"Things always start in New York or LA and bleed toward the middle of the country," Genevieve said. "So, no. I'd never heard of ChitChat until now, but Megan told me everyone here knows about it."

"And how is *she*?" Their mom puckered her lips for a moment. "Megan?"

Genevieve shrugged. "Upset, Mom. No good deed goes unpunished."

"What does that mean?" Their mom's back stiffened. "What good deed? Enjoying a getaway with us in the city? How is that a good deed?"

"Just . . ." Genevieve took a quick glance at Landon and then looked down at the kitchen table in front of her. She made a small, tight fist and banged it down. "Nothing."

Like the poison of a snakebite, the realization that Megan being nice to him was nothing more than charity seeped deeper and deeper into Landon's bloodstream, filling his body, and paralyzing it with pain. He sat for a minute, and then he staggered up from his chair and headed for the stairs. He heard his mother call to him gently, but he kept going.

As he climbed, each step brought with it the shred of a memory from the past two days: the cinnamon smell of Megan's hair next to him in the carriage ride through Central Park, the touch of her warm fingertips on the back of his hand to draw his attention to the sunset from atop the Empire State Building, the sound of her shriek when a ghoul popped up behind her chair at the Jekyll and Hyde Club, the sparkle of fireworks in those glassy blue eyes, the feel of her shoulder bones beneath his arm as he wrapped it around her for the picture that was causing all the problems.

And tomorrow?

Landon kicked his bedroom door shut and lay down.

Tomorrow was school, a disaster in and of itself. He'd asked himself before how anything could be worse than the first day of school at Bronxville. He knew now that it could be worse.

It would be so much worse.

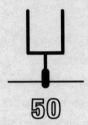

50

Landon woke with a headache and butterflies in his stomach, but knew that with his mom, if there wasn't any vomit or temperature, you were going to school. His mom was a fanatic about school attendance.

"Ninety percent of success is just showing up," she'd say.

So he did his thing in the bathroom, tugged on the khaki shorts and new strawberry-colored Izod shirt his mom had laid out for him, and clomped down the stairs. His dad sat bent over his computer in the great room. Landon waved as he passed into the kitchen, but his father was lost in his writing. Landon's mom was speaking to him, but he didn't hear a thing. He read her lips.

"Where are your ears, Landon?"

He shook his head, thought he might actually throw up from nerves, and returned to his bedroom for the ears. When he got back, Genevieve was at the table, halfway through her pancakes, and looking worried herself.

"Hey," he said.

"Hey." She put her fork down and cleared her plate. "Let's do this, okay?"

Landon forced a chuckle. "That's a little dramatic. We're not going into battle, Genevieve."

She narrowed her eyes. "Maybe *you're* not."

Landon picked at his own pancakes, cleared his plate from the table, and went to say good-bye to his dad. Landon had to tap his father three times before his fingers stopped dancing on the keyboard. He looked up, blinking. "Oh, hey, buddy. Wow. In a zone. Ready for school?"

"I guess so."

"Hey." His dad put his hands on Landon's shoulders. He nodded toward his computer before looking deep into Landon's eyes. "Nodnal is fighting the dragon right now. That's the scene I'm on. His hair and eyebrows have been roasted off his head. He's bleeding from his nose and his sword is broken. The dragon is crashing down on top of him, and do you know what's gonna happen?"

Landon watched his father's eyebrow creep up into an arch on his forehead.

"He's gonna be crushed?" Landon didn't see how it could go any other way.

His father's lips quivered into a small smile. "No, Landon. Nodnal dives to the ground with his sword like this."

Landon's dad gripped the handle of his pretend sword, one hand on top of the other like a baseball bat. "The broken sword is straight up, like a post. The dragon comes down with all his weight and impales his heart, just a nick, on the jagged tip. On reflexes alone, the dragon jumps up and away, trips, falls flat on his back . . . and dies."

Landon simply stared. After a few moments, he said, "This is real life, Dad."

"I know it is." His father mussed Landon's hair. "But happy endings abound. Where do you think happy endings came from, buddy? Real life. Go get yourself one."

Landon's dad turned back toward his screen and went to work.

Landon walked out the door. Genevieve was waiting for him in the driveway. She wore a short Abercrombie dress with a matching dark blue ribbon to hold back her thick hair from her face.

Landon took a deep breath and let it loose. "Ready?"

"Not yet." Genevieve shook her head. "Mom said for us to wait. She's going with us before she goes to the train station."

"Oh, boy."

Genevieve bit her lip. "Yup. She better not do anything crazy."

Their mom came out of the garage, heading their way with her briefcase strap over her shoulder. Her mouth was stretched as thin as a paper cut. "Okay, kids. First day of school in Bronxville. Thought I'd have a little *chat* with the principal. Ready?"

The word "chat" told them that their mom was ready for a fight. Landon and Genevieve exchanged a look.

She was already past them, headed directly for the middle school.

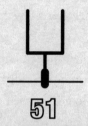

51

Landon and Genevieve sat reluctantly with their mom, staring at Mr. Sanders, who sprouted hair from his head like weeds in a garden. As if to compensate for the hair, his suit was shiny-new, his black-and-blue-striped tie crisply knotted. The principal greeted Landon's mother like an old friend. He said that after all the calls and emails, he felt he knew her.

"Mrs. Dorch, at our last teachers' meeting we discussed Landon's hearing. I emphasized that he needs to read lips to fully understand, and everyone is on board. We want Landon to feel welcome." The principal grinned widely and raised his eyebrows.

Landon's mother said, "Thank you, Mr. Sanders, but we're not here about that."

Then she proceeded to explain the situation.

Now Mr. Sanders wore a look of serious concern. "I told

you on the phone, we have a no-tolerance bullying policy, Mrs. Dorch, and I meant it."

His mom seemed to accept that just fine. "I run fifty offices across the globe. Trust me, I know that even the best leader cannot be responsible for every move her team makes. And I know there are outside forces . . . the internet. Social media."

Mr. Sanders winced at the words. "But we try and educate our students. I assure you."

"Right. But I'm here because this internet bullying is *real*. It's anonymous, but it's not imagined. It's not hypothetical. All you have to do is check out ChitChat Bronxville if you don't believe me. If you do believe me, don't check it out, because looking at those things validates them, don't you think?"

"I see what you're saying." Mr. Sanders started clicking his pen.

"We can't prove any direct accusation because it is all anonymous, but we can bet this came from a student in their grade." She looked at Landon and Genevieve. The smoldering anger in her eyes made Landon's mouth dry.

"Be alert, is all I'm asking, Mr. Sanders," Landon's mom said. "Talk to my kids' teachers. Make them aware. Landon will never say a word, but Genevieve is apt to go ballistic."

Mr. Sanders stopped clicking his pen. He glanced at Genevieve, who gave him a wan smile.

"Get what I'm saying?" Landon's mom asked.

Mr. Sanders cleared his throat and said, "We have another teacher meeting this afternoon. I promise we'll discuss this."

"Great!" Landon's mom popped up. "I'm off to work. Thanks so much for your time, Mr. Sanders."

Their mom gave them each a kiss on the cheek and then gave Mr. Sanders's hand a feisty little shake before disappearing out the door. Genevieve wasn't waiting around. She was in a different homeroom than Landon, one that was on the other side of the school. She was halfway out the door when Landon turned to the principal. "Sorry, Mr. Sanders."

Mr. Sanders circled his desk and put a hand on Landon's shoulder. "Don't be sorry. I wish every mom cared that much about her kids. You can't begin to imagine . . ."

Landon nodded, even though he wasn't quite sure he understood. "See you."

"See you, Landon. And Landon, don't worry about any of this."

Landon nodded again and turned and left the office, plunging into the sea of hostility, hoping for even a scrap of something that could help him stay afloat.

Landon walked into Room 114, and there it was.

A life jacket.

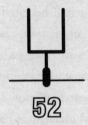

52

Brett jumped out of his chair, slapped his hand into Landon's and pulled him into a teammate hug, thumping him on the back. "Landon, come sit here." He motioned to the seat next to him. "I saved you a seat."

Landon didn't need anything else. He didn't scan the room from the corners of his eyes. He didn't worry about people dipping their heads together to whisper. He was saved.

His friend was wearing a Rashad Jennings Giants jersey and matching gym shorts.

"Dude, put your stuff down and get your schedule." Brett pointed at the desk where Landon rested his backpack. "Let's see how many classes we have together. Schedules are on Mrs. Rigling's desk."

Landon retrieved his schedule and got a smiling wink from Mrs. Rigling. Things were looking up. He returned to his desk and sat down. Brett grabbed the schedule from his hand and placed it down next to his own.

"Let's see. First, I got English. You got math. . . ."

Landon dared to look around. Half the kids were busy with their schedules. The other half he caught gawking at him like a zoo animal. He wasn't sure if it was because of Brett's warm welcome, the internet site, or his cochlear implants, but their eyes scattered when they saw him looking at them.

". . . Fourth, you got earth science. I got . . . social studies. Darn." Brett frowned and glanced at Landon. "Lunch? Nope. Hey, wait, we got gym together! That's a good thing."

Landon felt a ray of thankfulness. Gym was always a nightmare: being picked last, no one wanting to be his partner, getting beaned as the easiest target the game of dodgeball had ever known.

"No for eight. No nine either." Brett frowned and looked up. "Well, it's homeroom and gym, but you'll have some of the other guys on the team in your classes. You'll be okay."

Both of them knew that wasn't true, but Landon kept up appearances, even when Mrs. Rigling arrived at his desk to deliver printed announcements with a secret smile. He knew this came from his mother. She'd made calls and emails to Mr. Sanders because he hadn't a prayer of understanding most of what was said on a loudspeaker. Still, he hated being singled out like that. When the announcements were over, Mrs. Rigling rapped a ruler lightly on her desk, stood, and went through the disciplinary code and the policy on late arrivals to homeroom, often looking straight at Landon.

"Also," she said, "I'll have some of you for math class, and any of you—whether you're in my math class or Mr. Mazella's—are welcome to ask me questions during homeroom period. I love math, and helping you learn it is why I'm here."

When Mrs. Rigling sat down, Landon leaned close to Brett. "See you in gym."

"You got it, my man."

They bumped fists. The bell rang, and Landon took a deep breath as the day began.

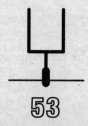

53

The seat that was most helpful for Landon to sit in—front row, middle—was empty. He kept his eyes on the teacher, Mr. Mazella, from the moment he sat down. Math was his favorite class. Numbers were always straightforward. There wouldn't be hidden meanings in a comment made offhandedly. But once Mr. Mazella got started, he often spoke with his back to the class, making it hard for Landon to keep up.

When the bell rang, Landon thought of saying something, but there was no time. Instead, he went directly to his second-period class, English, which was on the opposite end of the school. The halls were crowded, but Landon just kept his head down and plowed along. He focused on people's feet. He liked the shocking orange, blue, and strawberry-colored sneakers with fluorescent green or yellow laces. His own sneakers were electric blue with laces that were school bus yellow.

If anyone did say anything to him, it was lost in the noise. Hearing in a crowd was nearly impossible unless he was looking hard and closely at a person's lips.

When he entered the classroom for English, he froze.

Megan Nickell was in the front row, head hung down and hands folded in her lap. Her face hid behind a curtain of hair, and she seemed to be shaking. Landon walked up to her and tapped her shoulder. She looked up with wet, red eyes and sniffed. "Oh. Landon."

"Are you . . . can I sit here?" Landon pointed to the desk next to hers.

She shrugged. "Sure. Okay."

Landon sat down and took out his things. He was about to say something when he saw the teacher, Mr. Edwards, at his desk with an open book, making notes. Landon wanted to look at Megan. He wanted to do something—anything—to make her feel better. Still, all he could do was stare straight ahead feeling embarrassed.

The bell rang and Mr. Edwards climbed up onto his desk, looking down at them all with an impish smile from his corner of the room. His bright blue eyes flashed from behind gold wire-rimmed glasses. In his hand was a book.

"*The Count of Monte Cristo*. Who's read it?" Mr. Edwards raised a single eyebrow, reminding Landon of his father. "What? No one? Ladies and gentlemen, you're in for a treat. Alexandre Dumas is famous for this book, as well as *The Man in the Iron Mask*."

Landon's hand shot up, but he spoke without waiting to be called on. "And *The Three Musketeers*."

The classroom erupted with laughter. Landon looked around. Megan looked embarrassed for him, and Landon realized they were laughing at him, either because of the garbled sound of his voice or the enthusiasm of his words for something most of them couldn't give a hoot about. Landon didn't mind, though, because he felt like he had a connection with Mr. Edwards, and that was all that mattered to him. His heart was racing at the thought of learning more about books like the one he already loved.

Mr. Edwards's blue eyes sparkled. "Yes, that too; and can you tell me why Alexandre Dumas was such a successful writer?"

"He makes you care?" The words simply escaped from Landon's mouth.

"Yes!"

Mr. Edwards looked around at the class with a wild expression. Landon took a glance and soaked up the empty stares and the smirks held back by bitten lips.

Mr. Edwards either didn't see them or chose not to notice. He plunged ahead, taking Landon with him. He told them all about Dumas's life and then read quotes from the book about vengeance. Halfway through the period, he thumped a box down on his desk and began passing out paperback copies. He was waving his arms and talking about General Dumas (the writer's father) being betrayed by Napoleon when the bell rang, and everyone but Landon popped out of the seats.

"Chapters one through five for tomorrow!" Mr. Edwards shouted. "You will be quizzed."

A collective groan went up from the departing students.

Landon couldn't wait to read it, though. He checked his

schedule to see where he had to go next and then tucked the book away in his backpack. The room had nearly emptied out, and he fell in behind Megan at the door.

"Good stuff, huh?"

She turned and gave him a worried look. "Yes. Everyone talks about Mr. Edwards. Whether they love him or hate him, everyone talks about him."

"Hate him?" Landon said as they entered the fray of the hallway. "Why would anyone hate him?" He was intent on Megan's face, so he knew by her expression that something was wrong. Before he could learn what, he was suddenly shoved backward into the lockers. His head slammed against the metal with a crash.

Megan shrieked.

Landon regained his senses, and the hateful face in front of him came into focus.

"Skip?"

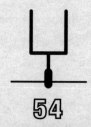

54

The freckles seemed to jump off Skip's burning, snarling face.

Landon wanted to say that they were teammates.

He wanted to say that he hadn't done anything wrong.

But he couldn't get a single word out before Skip hammered him again. Landon covered his head with both arms, and the blows struck his chest and shoulders before Mr. Edwards yelled, "Stop! Immediately!" He yelled at another teacher to get Mr. Sanders.

Megan had dropped her books, and she stood crying as Landon slid his spine down the lockers and took a seat on the floor, covering his head again with his arms and resting it between his knees. One of his battery packs hung loose, and he slipped it back behind his ear.

He glanced up to see Skip scowling as the principal raced toward them.

Megan touched his arm. "Are you okay, Landon?"

Landon almost smiled to see her. "Yes. I'm fine. I don't know why . . ."

Megan looked over at Skip, who was now being marched down the hall by Mr. Sanders. "We . . . I . . . broke up. I told him, and everyone, to leave you alone."

Landon's heart swelled.

Mr. Edwards leaned down. "Are you okay?"

"I'm fine," Landon said, hoping Genevieve wasn't among the hundred-or-so gawking students.

"Come on." Mr. Edwards helped Landon to his feet. "Let's get you to the nurse."

Landon felt a bolt of panic. He wanted this to end, and he shook himself free. "No, I'm fine, Mr. Edwards. Please. Nothing happened."

"You were taking a beating when I got out here." Mr. Edwards took hold of Landon's arm again. "Come on. Nurse. Then Mr. Sanders. This isn't the Wild West. We need to fix this thing."

As Landon marched through the open-mouthed crowd toward the nurse's office, he knew that no matter how good Mr. Edwards's intentions were, some things just couldn't be fixed.

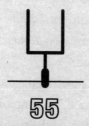

55

Landon blushed, humiliated to be slumped there on the exam table without his shirt, rolls of blubber quivering like Jell-O. He hugged himself to cover up as much as he could while the nurse probed Landon's bruised shoulders and chest. Speaking in a loud voice, she told Mr. Edwards, "Students today are trouble, and the parents can be worse. Mr. Sanders isn't going to want the Dreyfuses on his case."

"How could *they* complain? It's their son who gave Landon these bruises." Mr. Edwards's mouth fell open in disbelief.

"You said the boys were teammates, Dalton. Football?"

"They are."

Landon looked back and forth between them, thinking that it was strange to hear Mr. Edwards called by his first name, Dalton.

"Right." She gave a nod and whisked her hands together

with some Purell before turning to make some notes at her desk. "Football. Bruises. That's consistent, Dalton."

"Skip Dreyfus was using him as a punching bag," Mr. Edwards said.

"I believe you, but the Dreyfuses are apt to suggest these came from football." The nurse clucked her tongue. "Luckily these bruises aren't serious, but I know Mr. Sanders is going to have to deal with this. You can put your shirt on, Landon."

Landon wiggled into his shirt and followed Mr. Edwards to the principal's office. "I'm really okay, sir." His mom would go ballistic if she heard he'd been attacked. "The nurse is right, I might have gotten these bruises in football, or jumping in the pool. We had a cannonball contest Saturday."

Mr. Edwards looked at Landon and sighed. He seemed both disappointed and flustered. "I get it, Landon. You don't want more trouble. But sometimes trouble's what it takes."

They reached the office. "Okay, wait here."

Landon took the seat outside the principal's office and sat for quite a while before Mr. Sanders's door opened and the principal signaled him to come in.

To Landon's complete surprise, Skip was still there, shoulders hunched, head angled down, looking angry. Mr. Sanders pointed at the chair next to Skip. Landon hesitated, but Mr. Sanders gave him an impatient nod, so he sat down.

Mr. Sanders laced his fingers together and laid his locked-up hands on the desk in front of him. "Boys . . . things happen, and sometimes the best thing is to resolve them quietly and move on."

Landon nodded because he was on board with whatever. If

209

there was a way to avoid bringing his mother in on all this, he was game.

"I don't know how things worked in . . ."—Mr. Sanders searched an open file before him on the desk—". . . Cleveland, Landon, but in Bronxville we like to resolve our differences and move on. Now, I know you two got into a kind of shoving match in the hall. . . ."

Mr. Sanders looked closely at Landon. Landon was briefly confused because a shoving match wasn't anything like what had happened.

"I . . . uh, yes." Landon nodded and looked at Skip, who still appeared furious behind his clenched teeth.

"Right!" Mr. Sanders banged his hands to bring home the point. "And when shoving matches occur, we talk to the offenders and give them a stern warning and send them on their way. But . . ."

Mr. Sanders now raised a single finger and looked back and forth between them. "This *cannot* happen again."

Landon shook his head no. Skip tightened his grip on the armrests of his chair.

"Mr. Dreyfus? Are we clear on this?"

Skip didn't move his mouth when he spoke, but Landon was pretty sure he said, "Yes."

"Mr. Dorch?"

Although Landon was confused, since he'd done nothing wrong, he knew he had to agree and make all this go away. So he said, "Yes, sir." With a nod of his head, Landon prepared to rise.

"Because next time there will be detention and possibly *suspension,* for you *both.*"

Landon kept nodding and rising, and Mr. Sanders said, "Now shake hands before you go."

Landon searched Skip's face and saw a flicker of relief before he smiled a phony smile and stretched out his hand for the shake.

Mr. Sanders said, "Good. Now go."

Landon left without bothering to look back at Skip. He could only assume the redheaded quarterback was right behind him, and with the halls empty now halfway through fourth period, Landon hustled along at nearly a jog because he was seriously unsure whether or not Skip would obey the principal. Landon didn't stop until he reached Room 117 and his earth science class with Mrs. Lewis. He looked in through the window and saw everyone staring at the short, round teacher. Landon turned the knob slowly, trying to be quiet, but when he looked over his shoulder and saw Skip trudging toward him, he fumbled with the knob, sprung it open, and spilled inside, tripping and dumping himself and his backpack onto the floor.

The whole class burst into laughter.

Horrified, Landon looked up to see what Mrs. Lewis was saying to him because he could hear the drone of the teacher's voice.

"What?" Landon asked as he gathered himself and his backpack.

"*What?*" Mrs. Lewis said. "Are you making fun of me with that tone of voice?"

"No." Landon shook his head fiercely. "I didn't hear what you said. I was just asking what you said."

She studied Landon for a moment before relaxing the smallest bit. "I said, 'Fighting and clowning around is no way to begin your career as a Bronxville student,' Mr. Dorch. And you, Mr. Dreyfus, don't think you fool me with that smile. Take a seat."

Landon wedged himself into an empty seat, front row, middle, and the teacher looked past him. "Magma from deep in the earth's core . . ."

Landon tried to take his things out as quietly and smoothly as possible. By the time he had a blank notebook page and a pencil in his hand, he'd missed at least one, if not three, important points. He glanced around and saw the others writing furiously.

Landon knew he should raise his hand and ask the teacher to explain again. He knew that's what his mother would urge him—demand him, even—to do.

She'd said it a thousand times if she'd said it once. "The squeaky wheel gets the grease, Landon, and no child of mine is going to worry about making a little noise. Bang the drums! Crash the cymbals, Landon!"

Landon heard her words, and his brain steamed like a teakettle.

Several times his hand crept up the front of his shirt, fingers extended, ready to rise up, but he just couldn't do it. So, he sat and spiraled down into an ever-greater state of confusion.

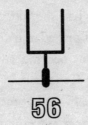

56

Earth science finally ended, and Landon headed for lunch.

It didn't surprise him that Genevieve appeared from nowhere and blocked his path.

"What *happened*?" Her face was red with fury.

"Nothing. Leave it alone." Landon looked around, grabbed his sister, and pulled her into an alcove outside the auditorium so that they could talk up close and personal. He grabbed both of her arms. "Stop it, Genevieve."

She swiped his hands away. "What *happened*?"

"Lower your voice." Landon felt desperate. "Just . . . just listen. It's all going to be fine. Megan broke up with Skip, did you know that?"

"Yes, of course I knew that." She glowered.

"So, he's upset, but Mr. Sanders said everything was going to be fine, not a big deal, but we cannot fight again." Landon made a cutting motion with one hand. "If it happens we'll be suspended, and I'm sure Skip Dreyfus doesn't want to be suspended any more than I do. So, it's over."

"Landon, seriously? How can you be okay with this? Skip is a jerk. I can't just let this go," she said.

"Right now this is off the radar. It's over. Can't we just keep it that way?" Landon was begging now, because he knew it went against everything Genevieve was about. "I don't want people on the football team mad at me because Skip gets suspended and misses a game or something . . ."

"Those jerks? Why do you care? They don't even respect you!"

"People appreciate me, Genevieve." Landon clasped his hands. "They do. Not all of them, but a lot. They say thanks to me for what I do. I'm on the team. That's all that matters. After lunch I've got study hall, then gym class with Brett and he's so cool, and I've got Megan in my English class and . . . I mean, we could even end up doing some projects together. Things are not *that* bad. I'm begging you, Genevieve."

"Landon." She sighed. "What period do you have lunch?"

"Now."

"Shoot. Let me see your schedule."

"Genevieve, you're not supposed to swear." Landon fished the schedule out of his backpack and handed it over.

"I've got lunch next period. I won't be with you."

"That's okay." Landon gave her shoulder a light punch.

"Well, we have social studies and Spanish together for the last two classes of the day, and Megan's with us too."

"Nice. She's great," Landon said.

"What do you mean?" Genevieve wore a stunned look.

Landon shrugged. "Just that she's great."

"Yeah, but you said it like . . ." Genevieve shook her head. "No, Landon. Not like that. She likes you as a friend, so do not ruin it, okay?"

"I have no idea what you're talking about."

The first bell rang.

"Yeah, Landon. I think you do know what I'm talking about." Genevieve bore her eyes into his. "Don't. That's all I can say, just don't."

"I gotta get to class. You too." Landon turned and walked away.

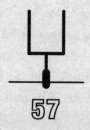

57

At lunch, Landon bought four cartons of milk before he entered the throng. He saw some faces he recognized from football: West and Furster presiding over a tableful of team-mates, Nichols at the edge. He quickly turned away, knowing better than to sit with them, and found a table in the far corner where an odd-looking girl with pink-and-blue hair sat with two undersize boys, one with a glaring birthmark on his cheek, the other with glasses as thick as bulletproof glass. They stared at him, warning him away from their territory with dirty looks, so Landon sat at the far end of that table and began unpacking his brown bag. He'd only removed two of his four meatloaf-and-ketchup sandwiches before he detected movement from the other three kids.

Without a sound or a signal, they got up and left the table.

Landon bit down hard on his sandwich and forced himself

to chew and swallow, chew and swallow, until everything was gone. In the dull roar around him, he neither looked nor tried to listen. He was just wadding up his last ball of cellophane when the bell rang and people began to scramble.

The hallways gave Landon a kind of relief because he could move in and out of people without giving them much of a chance to stare or poke fun at his ears or the way he spoke. He set his eyes on the floor, sat through a study hall, struggling with his math homework, and then practically skipped to gym class because he knew Brett would be waiting for him. After that, for the final two periods of the day, he'd have Genevieve and Megan to keep him company. And, as long as Skip wasn't there, his first day of school might not be a total disaster. He didn't even want to think about football practice.

That, he knew, would not be good.

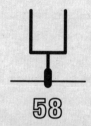

58

The school day ended on an upswing. In the last two class periods, he sat happily between Megan and his sister in the front row. When the final bell rang, Brett was waiting for Landon and the girls at Landon's locker.

"Hey," Brett said, "where we going? Diner for some pie?"

Megan shrugged. "Everyone goes to the diner. Let's do something else."

"Häagen-Dazs?" Landon nearly burst with pride when they all agreed it was a great idea.

On their way outside, it didn't seem to matter that Katy Buford sat on the steps with three heavily made-up girls trying their best to copy her by casting vicious looks their way.

"Hi, Katy." Genevieve sounded as pleasant as the first day she arrived. "We're going to Häagen-Dazs; want to join us?"

Katy was caught so far off guard, she could only snort and

sputter. They'd reached the bottom of the steps, where the trees cast their shade, before Katy got a word out. "You wish!"

Genevieve spun on a dime, still smiling. "No, not really. Enjoy your little cat club. Who's that? Lucinda Rayes? Isn't she the girl you said you'd never invite to another sleepover because she destroyed your bathroom? Probably hard for you to tell one bad smell from another, though, right, Katy?"

Megan looked like she was trying not to laugh, but Brett guffawed, slapping his leg and growing bright with joy. "Classic crush!"

Katy took out her phone and pretended to be busy, but Landon could see that her back had stiffened and her face burned beneath the skin.

They kept on going down the sidewalk and took a right toward the center of town, with Brett on one end and Landon on the other. They talked about the teachers they liked best and worst—Edwards best and Mazella worst for Landon, Edwards and others for the rest.

"I think Mr. Mazella is a good teacher," Genevieve said. "You should just ask him. I bet he'd help you, Landon. He just loves math is all. He gets excited."

Landon was looking ahead to the Häagen-Dazs when Brett stopped in his tracks.

"Uh-oh," Brett said with a weary sigh. "Here comes real trouble."

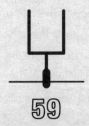

59

Skip was sandwiched between Mike and Xander. They all wore tough-guy looks.

"Going for a little ice cream, kids?" Skip said it like ice cream was for babies.

"Hey, Skip. What's up?" Brett stepped forward.

"Just get out of here, Brett," Skip said. "This has got nothing to do with you. This is me and the dummy." He nodded toward Landon.

"Mr. Sanders said no more fighting, Skip. Neither of us wants to get suspended." Landon tried not to sound afraid, even though he was.

Skip made a show of looking around. "Yeah, which is why we're standing on Pondfield Road instead of in the cafeteria. Sanders can't touch me here, and you're twice my size, so I can do whatever I have to do to protect myself."

"Who's gonna believe that?" Genevieve fired out.

Mike decided to get into the fray. "How about Xander's dad? Chief of police."

Brett shook his head. "Look, you guys don't want to do this. Do you know how stupid you're gonna look wearing your butts as hats?"

"What hats?" Skip narrowed his eyes at Brett. "What are you even talking about, Bell?"

Brett clenched his hands and took another step forward. "If you don't get the heck out of here, I'm gonna kick your butts so hard, you'll be wearing them for hats. Those hats."

"There's three of us." Mike spat his words, but he wasn't moving closer.

Brett snorted. "I only see about two. One for Skip and about a half each for you two clowns."

Furster and West looked at Skip to see how he'd respond.

"Look, Brett, we're teammates. This isn't about you."

"You're right. *We're* teammates," Brett said. "All of us."

"Not *him*." Xander pointed at Landon.

"Yes, him," Brett growled. "Last time I checked, he was on our team. And besides, he's not the one who took your girlfriend, Skip."

"I know he didn't *take* my girlfriend. He's like her big pet Wookiee." Skip laughed with his friends. "That big dork isn't gonna *take* my girlfriend."

"Yeah," Brett said quietly but with a hard edge, "'cause *I* did that."

Skip's eyes went from Brett to Megan, back and forth several times, before settling on Brett. With a blood-curdling yell, Skip launched himself.

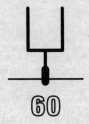

60

Xander and Mike went for Landon.

Landon never found out how serious they were about it because neither of them got their hands on him. Genevieve stepped up and kicked them, hard and directly, right in their shins, just like that, one-two. They cried out and went down like bowling pins.

Brett was amazing.

When Skip got close, Brett hooked an arm under Skip's, lifted, and flipped him to the side. Skip went down with a thud on the grass and then rolled into a tree, but he hopped up and came after Brett again. Every time he got close, Brett just side-stepped him, or tripped him, or spun him around and threw him to the ground. Before too long, Skip was out of breath and hunched over with a bloody nose.

When Genevieve went to give him a bonus kick, Brett

scooped her up and spun her around. "Oh, no you don't. None of that. He's had enough, haven't you, Skip?"

Skip only glared up at him and smeared the back of his hand with a bright swatch of blood from his nose as it dripped steadily into the grass.

"Yeah, he's had enough." Brett started to walk away. "Come on, guys. Let's get some ice cream."

Brett paused and they looked at him. "Come on."

He turned again, and this time they followed. Landon made sure the girls were with them and the bad guys weren't following before he relaxed enough to say, "Brett, what was that? Like, jujitsu?"

"Nah." Brett waved a hand through the air. "Just wrestling."

Landon shook his head. "How can you be so calm about it?"

"I'm not afraid of them, Landon. You were right. I could crush them." Brett held the door for them all. "You could too. You just don't know it."

Genevieve chimed in, "That's what I keep saying to him."

"Yeah, we gotta work on that, Landon." They all sat down at a table in the corner before Brett turned to Megan. The way he looked at her, and she at him, gave Landon a jolt. He'd assumed Brett was kidding when he said *he'd* taken Megan from Skip.

"You okay?" Brett asked her.

"Yes. Thank you," she said.

Then she put her head on Brett's shoulder, breaking Landon's heart.

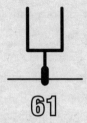

61

Later, after their friends had gone home, it was just Landon and Genevieve by the pool.

"I *told* you not to go there, Landon." Genevieve threw her hands in the air and did a can opener into the pool.

Landon sat at the table beneath the wide, green umbrella with his math homework spread out. Genevieve surfaced and he shouted at her, "I didn't *go there*. I didn't go anywhere!"

"Then why are you sulking like that? You haven't said a word since they left." Genevieve popped up out of the pool and stood dripping on terrace stones until she swiped a towel off the chair next to Landon.

"Because multiplying fractions stinks!" He realized he was shouting.

Genevieve's face turned sad, and she put a hand on his

cheek, which he shrugged away. "I get it, Landon. She's beautiful and she's so nice."

"I don't care about all that." Landon tried to focus on the problem in front of him. "Brett is my friend. My only friend. Even if I liked Megan, I'm not going to do anything stupid if my only friends likes her too."

"I tried to warn you, Landon. I saw that look on your face. I saw you thinking about her like that and I told you, don't do it." Genevieve tossed that grenade at him, and then she bounced off the end of the board and did a swan dive, slipping into the water with barely a splash.

Landon tried to ignore her and instead focus on the fractions in front of him. Genevieve climbed out of the pool, wrapped herself in the towel, and sat down across the table from him. Sunshine poked pinpricks through the wide, green umbrella above. A slight breeze carried with it the ripe promise of fall.

Landon looked up and saw her staring at him. "I'm doing my homework."

"You can't blame anyone," she said. "With people like Megan and Brett, it just happens. They're together with a common cause and they realize they like each other. And their common cause is you, so you can't feel that bad."

"I. Am. Fine." Landon banged a fist down on the glass tabletop, snapping the pencil in his hand. "Now see what you made me do?" He didn't take it back, but he said, "How the heck can you multiply something and it gets smaller, huh? What'd Mom call that? An oxymoron? I'm an oxymoron. No, I'm a just plain moron."

Genevieve stared at him for a moment. "You can't blame yourself, either. I shouldn't have said, 'I warned you.' Everyone's in love with Megan. She's gorgeous. She sweet. She's smart. She and I are probably going to be co-captains of the soccer team. She's got it all."

Landon checked his answer against the key in the back of the book. He had 3/16; the book said the answer was 1/8. He scribbled and scratched at his answer, blotting it out until nothing remained but a horrible mess and a small hole in the homework sheet.

Genevieve got up and peeked over his shoulder. She tapped him. "You added the numerators. One plus two equals three, but you were supposed to multiply them. One times two equals two. Then two over sixteen reduces to one over eight. You're close."

Landon made an arrow on his paper and wrote in the correct number above sixteen: two. "Yup, just like me and Brett and Megan. There's no room for three, just two."

"That's not true. There's room for all of us: four friends."

"You know what I mean."

"Hey." Genevieve grabbed his cheeks. "I know that I'm the luckiest sister in the world. You've got so much, Landon. You're just a late bloomer. When you come into your own, all kinds of things are going to happen."

Landon wanted to cry. "I don't know if that's even true, but in the meantime, I feel like I need to make myself as small as I possibly can, and that's not easy, Genevieve. It's not easy at all. Look at me."

"Well, stop making yourself small," she said. "Stand up for yourself. Don't worry if people notice you."

He wanted to agree with her. Instead, he hugged his little sister, wishing he was half as strong as she was. "I gotta go get my stuff ready for practice."

"I'll help Dad with dinner," she said. "I'm sure he needs it. He doesn't get off that computer, you know? I wonder if Mom will make it home."

Landon hesitated. "Do you think Brett was right? Do you think everything will be like . . . normal with Skip and everyone at practice tonight?"

"I think he gave them a lot to think about," Genevieve said. "I think if Brett wants things to be like nothing happened, they'll count themselves pretty darn lucky. Also, I think he and Megan being an item takes a lot of the pressure off of you."

A spark of hope glowed in Landon's heart. "Do you think that's all it is? Him and her helping me?"

"No, Landon." She shook her head sadly. "I think they're just both nice and they like each other. Just enjoy being friends. They like you. We don't need other friends if we've got Brett and Megan, and we can just be ourselves around them."

"And who are *we?*" Landon made a crazy face and wiggled his fingers.

They laughed and went inside together.

After dinner, Landon's dad dropped him at football practice. Landon did his thing with the water and the running, never taking his helmet off, and Brett was right. It was like nothing had happened. It made the whole first day of school

228

seem like some dream, or a TV show that Landon had seen and not been a part of.

Landon got to math class early the second day of school, and before class started he politely explained to Mr. Mazella that he needed to see what he was saying to fully understand. Mr. Mazella not only told him it wasn't a problem, he also instructed Landon to remind him if he forgot, by simply rapping on his desk. So Genevieve had been right about him.

When he saw Skip or his buddies in the hallway, even though his stomach knotted up waiting for something to happen, nothing did. That didn't mean Landon could shake the sense that they were planning something, because he couldn't. His instincts told him the feud was far from over, but he also had to admit that he might just be paranoid after a lifetime of problems with other kids.

At lunch, he ate alone again. He could handle that, though. It took him nearly the entire period to finish everything anyway, and Landon didn't need a ton of friends. He just needed people *not* to be mean.

After day two ended without a hitch, he dared to hope that life in Bronxville—with Genevieve, Brett, and Megan to rely on—might shape into something that he'd never experienced before.

But the very next day, he came out of the bathroom right before gym class to find Mike leaning against a locker, watching him. Landon looked around. There were only a dozen or so students in the hall because the first bell for the next period had already rung, so it wasn't hard to pick out Xander loitering outside a classroom also, pretending to be tying his shoe. Landon stiffened, immediately sensing trouble.

He started down the hall away from Xander, hugging the lockers on the opposite side of the hallway from Mike. The coach's son didn't move, but his eye, peering out from beneath his dark flopping hair, locked on Landon, and he wore an evil smile. Landon glanced back. Xander was on the move now, heading his way. Landon picked up his pace, glancing back and forth between the two of them and expecting Skip Dreyfus to pop out up ahead of him at any moment to cut him off. The other kids in the hall seemed to sense trouble too. Landon was aware of their nervous looks and their rush to get out of the area.

As Landon passed the spot where Mike leaned with his arms folded like a tough guy, he hurried his pace and glanced nervously ahead. Two more steps and he'd reach open hallway. He could run if he had to.

He had nearly made it past when Mike lunged.

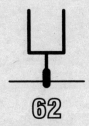

62

Landon bolted.

His arms flailed. He looked back and saw Skip, Mike, and Xander together now, snarling. He surged ahead, tripped, and spilled himself and his backpack onto the floor.

He twisted around in a panic, face burning with shame, and saw them not upon him but howling with laughter, slapping one another on the back as they backed away down the hall.

It was just a joke to them, scaring him. Landon's face burned as he clambered to his feet. Skip and Xander dipped into a classroom and Mike hurried down the hall. The second bell rang.

Late for gym, Landon got a stern warning from the teacher before he could even explain.

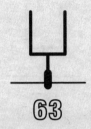

63

Friday evening's pregame practice was a dress rehearsal for their opening game on Sunday. Landon wore his game uniform with pride. The black pants glistened like wet tar and the orange-and-black jersey was bold as a Bengal tiger. Practice wasn't really much of anything. They didn't run and they didn't hit. The only thing they did was line up in positions on the various squads and team units they'd be using in the game.

There were punt teams and kickoff teams and other special teams Landon had nothing to do with. Then there were different squads for offense and defense—first string, second, and third. Landon lined up at right tackle on offense and left end on defense, both third string, which was actually a rag-tag bunch of leftovers from the second string squad and the most inept players on the team, guys like Timmy Nichols. Still,

Landon felt proud to be included. It was like he *did* have a position, like he was a real player.

But the third string was whisked on and off the field like an annoying afterthought. Landon watched the first team replace them and walk through a series of important plays. As each starter strove to show the coaches he'd mastered his job, Landon couldn't help feeling left out. That's what third string was, basically. Left out.

He paid close attention anyway. He'd seen Coach Furster chew guys out for not paying attention, and he'd always say, "You never know when someone might get hurt and we need you to step in."

Then Coach would glare all around and say, "Guys, if your number gets called, you'd better be ready."

Gunner Miller was the starting right tackle on offense, and Landon studied his every move, even the way he'd turn his mouthpiece sideways and chew on its ragged end between plays. He watched Gunner's feet and mimicked their motions on every play—a forty-five degree angle to the right on one play or a straight ahead power step on the next. After doing his little silent dance, Landon would look around to see if anyone might be watching him, but no one ever was.

Practice was short. Coach Furster blasted his whistle and gathered his flock. Landon looked around in surprise because it seemed there'd be no sprints in this pregame practice.

"Take a knee," Coach Furster said. "Helmets off."

Landon looked around to make sure he understood correctly, and when everyone else shed his helmet, Landon did

233

the same. He adjusted his skullcap and his ears, patting them gently into place.

"Guys, tomorrow I need every one of you to stay off your feet. Get plenty of rest and plenty of water. Sunday is D-Day, the beginning of a championship season, and it starts with Scarsdale. Now, I know a lot of you—and I have to admit I do this too—are looking ahead to the Tuckahoe game next week because it's a rivalry that goes back to the beginning of youth football in this town. But first we need to focus on Scarsdale." Coach Furster curled his lips like he'd eaten Skittles Sours.

"Coach West had one of his deputies film their scrimmage against Tarrytown, and we've broken them down." Coach Furster and Coach West exchanged a cunning chuckle before Coach Furster frowned. "They are good. But . . . we are better. We just have to play that way, boys." Coach Furster suddenly smiled. "So, rest up and hydrate, go over your assignments. I want you to visualize blocking and tackling, hitting, and winning. Can you do that?"

"Yes!" they all shouted.

"CAN YOU DO THAT!"

"YES!"

"Ha-ha! I like it." Coach Furster grinned. "Be here at eleven sharp Sunday morning, boys. We are gonna whip Scarsdale's butts!"

Landon looked around, chuckling and expecting others to be snickering as well because Coach had said "butts," but all he saw were serious faces, so he quickly coughed to cover his glee and put his hand in for their "Hit, Hustle, Win!" chant before he marched up the hill, heading for the parking lot.

He felt a pang of envy when he saw Brett talking to Gunner Miller about the pass protection they planned to use against Scarsdale's blitzing linebackers. He wanted to stop and talk too, but felt foolish because it seemed impossible that he'd get into the game for even a single play. As he trudged up the hill, though, he couldn't help wondering if, despite everything, tomorrow might be the day he became a true football player.

Hadn't Coach Furster told everyone to be ready?

It made him tremble from head to toe to think of going into a real game, even if it was a blowout and no one cared. And in that moment, he felt determined that if he got the chance, he would be ready.

Landon Dorch would answer the call.

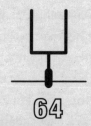

64

Saturday at the breakfast table, Landon insisted he couldn't do any yard work.

"Because?" Landon's mom asked, not looking happy.

Landon glanced at his dad, who shrugged and looked away, suddenly interested in the clock on the wall.

"Coach said to stay off our feet, Mom. I gotta rest up. I gotta go over things in my mind, visualize blocking and stuff." He studied his mom's face and knew she wasn't impressed. "Winning, Mom. You gotta visualize it to do it."

She huffed and rolled her eyes. "Forrest, do you buy this malarkey?"

Landon's dad pointed to himself and blinked. "Me? Oh, well, you know . . . I never played football, Gina. I've heard of that, though."

"Well, the lawn and the garage are your domain, Forrest. If you're willing to go without help today for your long list of things to do, then I'm not going to stop you." Landon's mom produced the list and slapped it onto the table.

"Well . . ." Landon's dad reached across the table and picked up the list. "I don't see why I can't. Some of this we can do tomorrow after the game, right?"

"As long as it's done by the end of the weekend—and I'd like to have a cookout tomorrow evening before it starts snowing around here." Landon's mom sniffed, and it was settled.

From his bedroom window, Landon looked down at his dad waving the hedge trimmer like a magic wand, shaping shrubs and bushes with no one to pick up the leavings. That inspired him to search the web for some videos of lineman drills, and he watched them all morning long, visualizing himself doing the things he saw big, beefy college players and coaches demonstrating in clinics across the country. He imagined himself as them, big and strong and, most importantly, fearless.

One thing that kept popping up was his hands. Landon knew he was supposed to deliver a blow out of his stance. He knew he was supposed to strike the defensive lineman across from him on either side of his chest, but as he watched clinic after clinic on YouTube, he knew he hadn't been keeping his thumbs up, but rather pointing in, like a traffic cop signaling to stop. After a while of worrying, he peeked out the window. His dad was raking up the last bit of trimmings and dumping them into the wagon hitched to the riding mower.

Landon hustled downstairs and out into the back yard.

"Hey!" His dad smiled warmly and wiped some sweat from his brow with the back of his hand. "Thought you were resting up?"

"Dad, can you help me?"

His father looked around like it was a trick question. "Well . . . sure. What do you need?"

"You gotta be my dummy."

"Now I'm a dummy?"

"No." Landon shook his head. "Just, like, stand there in a preset position," he said.

"I have no idea what that is." His dad laughed and shook his head.

Landon showed him how to stand, crouched over with his hands on his knees. "Now, I'm gonna fire out at you and you just stand there."

"Ah! Just like a dummy," his dad said. "Don't worry. I got it."

"See, I've got to deliver a blow with my hands, but my thumbs have to be up and I just need to do it, in case I get in the game tomorrow."

"Okay—go for it."

Landon got down in his stance. Since they had no quarterback and his dad knew nothing about football, he called the cadence aloud himself. On "hike," he fired out and struck his dad with both hands.

"Oof!" His dad staggered back. "Wow. Good hit."

"Yeah, but my hands still aren't right." Landon studied the position of his thumbs. They were still sideways instead of straight up and down the way he'd intended them to be.

"How about you just do the hand part?" his dad said. "You know, save the stance and all that jumping out at me until you've got the hands just the way you want."

"Dad, that's genius!" Landon beamed, and his father grinned back.

Over and over he shot his hands into his father's chest, and after a dozen tries, he had it down pretty good.

"Now put it all together," his dad said.

"Dad, did you play football and you're just not telling me?" Landon was suspicious because his father seemed to be speaking with authority.

"No, but this is just like band. You work on a piece one line at a time to get it right, and then you put it all together." His dad patted his chest and got down in the preset position. "Come get me."

Landon did, and it worked out pretty well. They kept going until his mom rounded the corner with a floppy hat, gardening gloves, and her pruning shears. She stopped abruptly in front of them. "What?"

Landon and his dad stood and blinked.

"What's going on? I thought you had to rest?" His mom narrowed her eyes.

"Sometimes you gotta realize what you visualize, Gina." Landon's dad put a hand on his shoulder. "That's all. Just fine tuning. And don't worry, I got the yard covered. Look . . ."

Landon's mom pinched her lips and looked around. "You missed that dead limb on the sugar maple, Forrest."

"My next stop." Landon's dad winked and motioned for him to skedaddle.

Landon laughed and started to trundle off, before turning and hugging his dad. "Thanks, Dad. You're the best."

That evening his dad made spaghetti, and they all went out to a movie as a family. Everyone was in good spirits, but Landon passed on a bucket of popcorn. Tomorrow was Sunday and his first football game, and suddenly, he wasn't so hungry anymore.

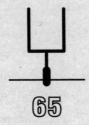

65

Landon woke early, nervous, though he couldn't really say why. Words about Scarsdale's toughness rang in his brain, but he really didn't expect to get into the game unless they were way far ahead. Even then, he couldn't be sure Coach Furster would play him. Because of his size, he knew the only position he could play on offense was right tackle. If Landon had to go against someone as big as himself (or even someone close), it was likely to end in Landon getting creamed.

He turned over the framed picture sitting on his dresser and saw himself with his family plummeting downward on the ride at Disney World. It stiffened his resolve. He knew he had to get out onto the field during a game, just to say he'd done it. It would make him feel like a real team member and not something less, which is what he couldn't help feeling like now, no matter what Brett or Landon's dad said.

At breakfast Landon could only stare at the stack of pancakes in front of him. He took two swigs of orange juice and nearly lost it.

His mom peered at him over a steaming mug of coffee. "Nervous?"

"It's game day, Mom." Landon excused himself and began getting his gear on.

Genevieve had practice, and they dropped her at the soccer field before circling the school and pulling into the parking lot above the football field. A concession trailer churned out smoke, and the smell of hot dogs was in the air, even though it wasn't yet eleven o'clock. The stands were already half full of people. The sun shone and the baking grass smelled freshly cut.

"Go get 'em, big guy." Landon's dad slapped his shoulder pad.

"Good luck," said his mother.

"Okay. See you." Landon strapped on his helmet and took off at a jog down the hillside. He fell in with the rest of his team, full of doubt and uncertainty, but also a sliver of hope.

For the first time in Landon's life, it was game day.

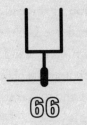

66

The Scarsdale Knights wore red helmets and jerseys, with white pants. They looked big and fast and mean. Their chants about hitting and hustling and winning that rang out over the field sounded more like a threat than a team motto. Landon looked around at his teammates as they stretched and warmed up. None of them seemed troubled by Scarsdale's battle cries, not even Nichols, but Landon fought the urge to feel thankful that he probably wouldn't get into the game.

Before he knew it, Landon found himself on the sideline watching Skip and Brett march to the center of the field with the referees and captains of the Scarsdale team. Landon turned and began to fidget with the water carriers, making sure the bottle tops were on tight and wondering if he'd been remiss in not getting to the game earlier to make sure Coach West didn't need help filling them. Either way, they won the toss, and after the kickoff Bronxville's offense swarmed out onto the field behind their quarterback.

Landon looked up into the stands, saw his parents, and gave them a small wave he trusted no one else would see. Passing the ball and running around the end on naked bootleg plays and sweeps, Skip marched the Bronxville offense right down the field for a touchdown. The stands behind Landon shook with the stomping of feet, and the cheers washed over all other sounds, so much so that Landon was startled when Coach West thumped the middle of his back.

"Huh?"

"Come on, Landon. Let's get water into these guys. A lot of them play both ways and don't have much time." Coach West had a carrier in one hand and gave the other to Landon.

Landon did his best, handing out bottles of water to the guys who needed it most, but when he presented one to Skip, the quarterback turned away and got one from Coach West instead. Landon shrugged it off and made sure Brett got a good drink.

"Hey, thanks, my man." Brett sprayed a thick stream of water into his mouth, and Landon smiled at the way Brett called him "my man," the same way Jonathan Wagner had done.

The Bronxville kickoff team did its job, pinning Scarsdale down deep, and then the defense—led by Brett with two tackles behind the line—did the same. During the next break on the sideline for Brett, Landon handed him a water bottle and said, "They're not as tough as they look, right?"

Brett cast a look across the field. "Don't say that yet. Football's a funny deal. Things can change quick."

As if Brett had a crystal ball, Skip fumbled on the first play of the next series. Scarsdale used the sudden change to throw a long pass and tie the score. Scarsdale kicked off, and Furster muffed the kickoff, giving Scarsdale the ball again. Five plays later they scored another touchdown. When Bronxville was back on offense and Skip fumbled again, Coach Furster called a time-out and marched out onto the field. Even though Skip had recovered his own fumble, everyone could see that Coach Furster was steaming mad.

Landon watched from the sideline, eager for Skip to get dressed down. He heard the yelling all around him, but didn't get that his teammates and coaches were shouting at him until Coach West grabbed his shoulder pad and spun him around.

"Come on, Landon! Get this out there!" Coach West shoved a water bottle carrier into Landon's gut.

Landon got hold of it, but then he paused in confusion.

"Go!" Coach West stabbed a finger at the Bronxville huddle out on the field, where Coach Furster was gesturing wildly to his team. "Get the water out there!"

"Oh, uh, okay, Coach." Landon felt stupid, not having realized that the time-out meant someone could take water out to the team. He turned and dashed toward the huddle. Someone tripped him, and he went down like a collapsing building. The water bottles exploded up out of the carrier, and Landon lay facedown in the grass. It sounded like some people were laughing and like others were shouting angrily. He wasn't sure which was which or how much of any of it was meant for him, but he scrambled with the water bottles, reloading the carrier and then stumbling out to the huddle.

By the time he got there, the ref was blowing his whistle to end the time-out.

Landon held a water bottle out to Brett, who only grimaced and shook his head. "Thanks, my man. No time."

"Let's go, Landon." Coach Furster grabbed the upper sleeve of Landon's jersey and yanked him out of the huddle like he was the one who had fumbled. Landon knew his coach was talking, and he zeroed in on his face. ". . . can't even hang onto the football. Heck, we can't even get the stupid water bottles right."

When he got back to the bench, Landon tried to hand out some water bottles to the guys who were mostly just watching. Some of them took water, but most shook their heads and declined. Xander gave Landon a shove and said, "Get away from me, 3P, you doofus."

It stung to hear "3P," because Landon had thought that issue was dead and gone.

He didn't take any more chances. He kept the water carrier in his hand and stood on the fringe of the players and coaches crowding the sideline, ready at a moment's notice to run out to the huddle if there was another time-out. The game went on, and at halftime the score was 20–7 with Scarsdale in the lead.

Coach Furster led the team beneath the goalpost on one end of the field, where they sat in a circle. "Landon, get that water around to everyone, will you?"

"You got it, Coach." Landon tried to sound somber since they were behind and everyone looked angry. He walked around handing out water while Coach West passed around two buckets with quartered oranges for the players to eat for energy. No one said thanks to him now. Everyone was angry about getting beat, and the coaches seemed to be keyed up and ready to explode.

After ten minutes of telling every kid who played what he'd done wrong and how he needed to be better, Coach Furster blew his whistle and told everyone to line up to get stretched out again. Landon fell into the back of the line, but Coach West tapped him and asked if he wouldn't mind helping pick up the orange peels that some players had left scattered around in the grass. Landon glanced down at the garbage, and a complaint perched on his lips because picking up after everyone else seemed to be taking the water-boy thing a bit too far. And, wasn't he supposed to be warming up? The words got stuck though. He watched the team as it began to jog out onto the field without him, and then he saw the frown on Coach West's face and said, "Sure, Coach. I can get warmed up on my own on the sideline."

Coach West gave him a funny look, and then they began scooping up peels and dumping them into the bucket. They ended up meeting the rest of the guys on the sideline, and the whistle blew beginning the second half. Reaching into the bucket of mostly peels, Landon retrieved an uneaten quarter of orange. He was undoing his chinstrap to get the juicy fruit up under his mask so he could take a bite when someone snatched it from him.

"You don't need to eat anything," Xander snarled. "You haven't done a doggone thing. Give me a break."

Landon watched Xander chomp down on the fruit and then toss the peel at Landon's feet before putting his helmet on and jogging out onto the field. Landon looked around. No one seemed to be looking, so he walked away from the garbage, refusing to add it to the bucket.

By midway through the fourth quarter, the score was 34–13, and Landon's legs ached from standing. Still, Coach Furster's words rang out in his mind. "If your number gets called, you better be ready." Landon thought maybe he should rest his legs so that he *would* be ready, if he got called upon, so he took a seat on the bench. He glanced up in the stands and saw Genevieve sitting there with his parents in her soccer uniform. Megan sat beside her, and Landon wavered between pride and embarrassment. With just two minutes to go, Scarsdale scored yet another touchdown.

It was a blowout.

Coach Furster began substituting players, and Landon started to tremble with excitement. He didn't want to get too excited, so he stuck his hands under his legs to stay calm. Just because the coach was putting people in didn't mean *he'd* get any action, but when Coach Furster slapped Timmy on the shoulder, sending him in, Landon stood up.

He knew he was next.

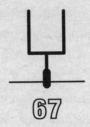

67

The clock wound down.

Scarsdale was running the ball right up the middle to keep the clock winding down. Landon kept his eyes on Coach Furster and saw Brett's dad, who for some reason had a cell phone in one hand, say something to Coach Furster. The two of them argued, but Landon got distracted by the action on the field.

He watched Timmy stand straight up on the snap of the ball and get driven nearly ten yards back before falling in a heap. Landon could do better than that. He knew he could, and he moved closer to where the coaches stood on the sideline. Brett's dad had disappeared somewhere. Landon looked around and thought that Coach Furster had said something to him.

He looked up, but the coach had his eyes glued to the field.

Landon looked at the clock, which said 00:27 and was winding down.

Landon turned and scuffed his cleats all the way to the bench. When he got there, he spun around and slumped down. Coach Furster was staring at him through the crowd of kids on the sideline, as if Landon had done something wrong. Landon could only shrug. The coach shook his head and spit in the grass.

The last play of the game was another run up the middle. Someone from Bronxville made the tackle and got up excited, even though his team had just embarrassed itself. The players and coaches lined up and shook hands, Landon among them. Then the team gathered in the end zone for a post-game speech. Coach Furster kept shaking his head and spitting as if he couldn't get the bad taste out of his mouth.

"That was just pathetic." He glared around at the players, his voice sounding like it might be hoarse from shouting. "Well, next week we've got Tuckahoe, the biggest rivalry in downstate football and our chance to regain the Pondfield Road Cup. You all know that it's practically a holiday when we play them, and the game is on Saturday, so it's a short week. I'll say this: you play like you did today, men, and we may not win a game all season, so you better come to practice Tuesday night ready to work, and be ready to *run* until you *puke*. That's all. Go. Get out of my sight."

The team broke apart, but when Landon turned, his eyes widened at a sight that horrified him much more than the thought of running till he puked.

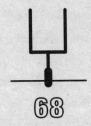

68

Landon's mom had fire in her eyes.

She grabbed him by the arm and blasted through the crowd of football players, heading straight for Coach Furster. Landon was aware that his father was sort of with her, if you could count hanging back a good twenty feet as being with her.

Coach Furster was huddled up with Coach West and Coach Bell.

Landon's mom apparently didn't care. She went straight for Coach Furster, stabbing a finger at his chest without actually poking him. "Coach, you and I need to talk. *Right now.* In private."

There was no room for anything else. The two other coaches melted away fast. Coach Bell had his face in one hand as he went, shaking his head. Landon wished he could go with them, and he actually tried to tug loose, but his mother held his arm with an iron grip. He couldn't help himself from watching.

Landon could see the anger in his mother's face. "You played every single kid on this team except *my* son, and I want to know why. Not one single play."

Coach Furster's lips quivered. He snorted and looked away as if he couldn't believe this was happening.

"Don't look away from me," Landon's mother steamed. "You look me in the eye and tell me who you think you are and what you think you're doing."

"Really, lady? You really want to have this discussion with me?" Coach Furster tugged the bill of his cap down tighter on his head.

"You bet I do."

"Really?" Coach Furster looked both angry and surprised at the same time. "Okay, here it is, lady. Your kid . . . he's fine, a little slow maybe; he's a good enough kid, but he's *soft*. You know what that means?"

"He's the biggest kid on your team, and it's *football*." Landon's mom spit her words at the coach.

"Yeah, the biggest and the *softest*, and part of my job, believe it or not, is to make sure these kids are safe." Coach Furster folded his arms and leaned down toward Landon's mom so their noses nearly touched. "And I *asked* him if he wanted to go in for the last play of the game, and you know what he did?"

Coach Furster clenched his hands and put them rigidly against his sides. "He *sat down on the bench*. That's right, turned and walked away from me when I asked him. So you just take your attitude and redirect it at your son, lady, and ask yourself what he's even *doing* out here."

Landon's mom took a step back.

"Yeah, that's right. He doesn't want to hit anyone." Coach Furster wore a mean smile, and it looked like he was suddenly enjoying himself. "He got a taste of hitting and that was enough. Since then, he drops out of every contact drill we do, but I'm a nice guy, right? So I let him hang around and wear his uniform and help out. So you huddle up with your kid and figure out what you want to do here, because I'm a volunteer and I'm not paid to take guff from some helicopter mommy with a kid who's obviously got special needs."

Coach Furster gave a final snort, turned, and walked away.

Landon's mom had nowhere else to look but at him. "Landon? Is this *true*?"

Landon looked over at his dad, who had stopped a good ten feet away in order not to catch any wrath.

"Don't look at your father; look at me!" Landon's mom glared up at him, and he didn't even think what to do. He just did it.

Landon turned and ran.

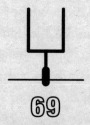

69

Landon ran all the way home.

He dashed up the stairs and threw the football helmet down on his bedroom floor. He whipped off his ears and let them clatter without a sound onto the night table before throwing off every bit of his football gear. He stood panting in the middle of his bedroom wearing nothing but a big yellow pair of boxers spotted with little blue anchors. He paced the floor until he felt the slam of a door beneath him.

Landon slipped on his ears and listened.

Feet stamped up the stairs, and a door down the wide hall-way, probably his parents' bedroom door, crashed shut. Landon froze.

He heard more stomping, but lighter feet—his mom's. She pounded on the bedroom door and even Landon could tell what she was saying, she shouted so loudly. "Forrest! Forrest, open this door!"

Landon heard a muffled response. It sounded like "no."

"You get out here! This is on *you*, Forrest! Were you not paying *attention*?"

His mother paused, but if Landon's dad answered, he didn't hear it.

"You just let some moron turn your son into a water boy?" His mother was shrieking. "Really? Do I have to do everything?"

Landon heard the door crash open and now his father was shouting.

"No! You don't have to do *everything*, Gina! But you have to do *something*! Something besides that awful job! You think this is fun for any of us? You think *I* wanted to come here? No! I did not! But I came here for you, and all you can do is work, work, work! Since when did that job become more important than *us*?"

Landon didn't want to hear any more. His hands crept for the wires connected to his head, but he didn't pull the plug. Something wouldn't let him do it.

"This is not my fault!" his mother screamed.

"And it's not my fault either!" his father screamed right back.

"Yes it is!" his mother shouted.

"Then I'll just *leave*!"

Landon heard his father's feet crashing down the stairs. He felt the front door shudder, and then everything went quiet.

He stood for a long while before slowly opening his door and creeping down the hall.

When he got to the open door of his parents' bedroom, he saw his mother curled up on top of the bed, holding herself and crying so hard that she shook.

"Don't do this, Mom." Landon had never seen his mother cry. "Please don't do this. It's not your fault. It's not Dad's fault. It's my fault, and I know how to fix it."

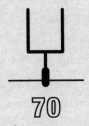

70

Landon told his mom the plan at the kitchen table, just the two of them. His mother had insisted that Landon have a glass of milk along with some Fig Newtons.

She listened to his idea, but when he was finished, she shook her head. "No, Landon, you can't quit. You can't let someone like Coach Furster break you. Once you let that happen, it never ends."

Landon's stomach, already tight, now turned. "I hate it. I don't want to do it."

"This has been your dream, Landon."

"Now it's a nightmare."

She shook her head with short little movements. "No. You don't give up like that. You muscle through it, or you'll look back for the rest of your life and kick yourself and wonder. You'll finish the season. I don't care if you never play a minute—well, I care, but you'll finish, Landon."

Landon sulked for a moment before he looked up.

He bit into a cookie, feeling trapped. He still didn't think he should return to the team. There was just no sense in it. When the phone on the wall rang, Landon's mom gave him a curious look and then got up and answered it.

"Hello, Coach Bell. I'm sorry I made a scene." His mother listened for a several minutes before she spoke again. "Thank you. Thank you. You and your son and wife have been so kind. I'll tell Landon and I'm sure he'll feel much better . . . Yes, I'm sure Landon would love to watch the Giants game with you. I can drop him off after we have some lunch. Just text me the address. Thank you again."

She hung up the phone and turned to Landon. Pointing to the phone, she said, "See? We're not the only ones who believe in you." As she spoke, his father came in through the garage door in the mudroom like nothing was wrong.

His parents gave each other a look and then smiled before his mom said, "Landon got invited to the Bells' to watch the Giants game at four. Coach Bell said I was right and wanted us all to know that he argued with Coach Furster to put Landon in with the other backup players."

Landon's mom turned her sharp eyes on him. "He says he thinks that if you just get used to the whole thing, you'll be fine. He said it might take time, but that's okay. He said Brett started out slow too. He just started much earlier, when he was eight."

Landon had to admit that made him feel better, and his

heart swelled at the notion of having anything in common with Brett at all. Still, he had a hard time believing football was for him anymore.

Landon's dad made grilled cheese sandwiches and tomato soup. Genevieve ate lunch with them, but she was quiet on the subject of football. Landon could only assume she'd been embarrassed by their mother's outburst. Maybe she even blamed him for their parents' fight. Either way, she was impossible to read. When she finished her lunch, she asked if she could go to the country club to play tennis with Megan.

"Yes, of course," their mother answered. "Landon is going to the Bells' to watch the Giants game, but let's all plan on being back for a family dinner by seven thirty."

Landon's parents dropped Genevieve off at the country club first.

"Tell Megan I said hi," Landon said.

"Sure," Genevieve said, but her face told a different story. It was clear that she was still upset. He wanted to stop her, to say he was sorry for all the drama and give her a hug, but before he could act, she was gone.

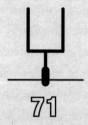

71

They rode to the Bells' house in silence, and Landon was glad to get out of the car.

Brett's mom greeted Landon at the door with a smile. "Hi, Landon. They're down in the man cave. I'll show you."

"Thanks, Mrs. Bell." He followed her through a small living room and down the stairs. At the bottom, a big, hairy dog lay sprawled out, sleeping.

"Just step over her, okay?" Brett's mom said.

Landon turned a corner and went down another small set of stairs, entering the man cave. It was a shrine to the New York Giants. Everything was red and blue. Signed pictures and jerseys covered the walls. A big, blue sectional couch surrounded the enormous flat-screen TV festooned on its edges by Giants pom-poms. Brett and his dad sat side by side on the edge of their seats, and the action hadn't even begun.

"Brett . . . Brett!"

"Huh, what, Mom?" Brett turned his head. "Oh, hi, Landon! Come sit down. Dad, Landon's here."

"Hi, Landon." Coach Bell sprang up. "Rashad's got a bum ankle and they're talking about what it means. . . . Come on over. Sit down. Right here between us. Want some chips?"

"Sure, that'd be great." Landon sat and took a handful from the bag they placed in front of him on the coffee table. Brett offered him an orange soda, and he accepted gratefully. "I guess I should have worn something blue."

"Oh, don't worry." Brett swatted the air and then pointed to the Jonathan Wagner jersey he wore. "I wear this for luck, and I keep this in my hands the whole game." Brett showed him a football that had been signed by the entire team.

"Wow. Nice," Landon said.

"Yeah. Hey, at least you didn't wear brown and orange for Cleveland. Ha-ha." Brett chucked Landon lightly on the shoulder and turned his attention to the screen.

Landon started watching and felt a little jolt of pleasure when he realized they had the closed-captioning feature turned on. Landon had thought about that on his way over, but he had decided he wouldn't mention it. Most people didn't use the closed-captioning feature, even though most new TVs had it. He looked back and forth between Brett and his dad, but their attention was on the screen.

Landon sat back and breathed easy. It choked him up a little bit to be there, just hanging out with such nice people who took his limitations in stride.

On the wall Landon saw Eli's jersey, and Rashad's, and also

older Giants like Michael Strahan and someone named Gifford. There were footballs everywhere, as well as pictures of a much-younger Coach Bell. One shelf held nearly a dozen wrestling trophies, some with gold medals slung over them, confirming that Landon was in the presence of athletic royalty.

The Giants fell behind early in the game, and Landon worried along with his hosts. After two turnovers, though, and a stunning block by Brett's uncle on a sweep, the Giants got right back into it. Once they had the lead in the fourth quarter, it was all a ground game for the Giants. They made no secret of running the ball behind big Jonathan Wagner. Several times the TV announcers ran close-up replays of the huge lineman plowing people down.

"Awesome!" Brett turned to Landon, and the two of them slapped high five.

"We should run the ball like that, Dad." Brett spoke across Landon to his father, so Landon caught every word. "Layne Guerrero is as good a runner as any in our league. We'd be better pounding the ball than all that passing garbage we did today."

Landon thought of Layne as just a quiet kid who never did anything to Landon but smile pleasantly. He hadn't known he was supposed to be a star runner. Like most of the team, Layne hadn't done much of anything in their game earlier.

Landon turned his attention to Brett's dad, who scratched his chin. "Well, I hear you, but Skip's a good quarterback, and Coach Furster likes to air it out."

Landon turned to look at Brett.

"Yeah, 'cause his mopey son is a receiver." Brett slapped the football he'd kept in his lap throughout the game.

"Okay, Brett." Brett's dad rumbled when he spoke. "Let's talk nice, okay?"

"*You* should coach the team." Brett muttered the comment under his breath, but even Landon knew what he said.

Landon wondered if that was even possible. It would be a dream come true for him, having a head coach who was actually nice to him, who *liked* him.

Landon held his breath, waiting to see what Brett's dad would say.

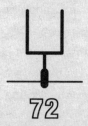

72

"Anyone want some dip for those chips?" Brett's dad pointed at them, and they both nodded before he left the TV room headed for the kitchen.

It was as if Brett had never made the suggestion.

"Why *doesn't* he coach the team?" Landon asked when Brett's father had disappeared.

"He says it's their show. They started coaching when Xander's and Mike's older brothers played. They've been doing it with Coach Furster as head coach ever since." Brett unexpectedly tossed Landon the ball.

Landon surprised himself by catching it.

"Hey, maybe you'll play tight end in high school." Brett looked serious. "Less blocking, more catching. You'd be a big target."

"I don't know if I'll end up playing anything but left out."

Landon's face tightened. "I can't believe my mom did that. Plus the coaches seem to like me handing out water more than being on the field."

"Hey," Brett said, glancing over his shoulder to make sure his dad hadn't returned. "My dad said she was right. They should've played you."

"I'm still not that good."

"Yeah, but you're there. You can line up and take a play. You need to get in the game. See what it feels like. Did you see Nichols?"

"I know I could do better than that." Landon tried to sound confident.

"Yeah." Brett nodded. "You can't do worse than that. But still . . . he got some action. You'll do it. You'll get in there. My dad will make it happen. They were just crabby because we lost. Coach Furster wants to blame everyone but himself. I'm telling you, we could run the ball like the Giants."

"I wish your dad was the head coach," Landon said. "At least the line coach. Why doesn't he coach the line, anyway? He played line."

Brett shrugged. "My dad's the best coach, period, any position. Furster *said* it was because he thinks dads shouldn't be the position coach of their own kids—which I guess makes sense—but I think it's because Furster wanted his kid to have the best coach. I don't know. You know how grown-ups are. Everything's a riddle."

They both turned to the TV set and watched the Giants offense take the field to kneel down on the ball and run out the remaining seconds.

"Giants, 1–0," Landon said.

"Yup." Brett beamed proudly. "And Coach McAdoo will be in a good mood, so the team will get off later this week and my uncle will be at practice. Wait till you see what that does to Coach Furster and Coach West. They'll pee their pants."

Landon snickered. "At the same time?"

"Oh, for sure." Brett grinned at him. "Two yellow puddles. Side by side."

Brett's dad returned with a bowl of dip. "What are you two so giddy about?"

"Giants won, Dad."

"Yeah," Brett's dad said, cracking open a can of iced tea and taking a sip. "Now let's see if *we* can get the Bronxville junior football team a win, huh?"

"*And* get Landon in the game, right?" Brett said.

Brett's dad eyed Landon. "Would you like that, Landon?"

Landon wanted to be honest. He was still just flat afraid of getting smashed around. On the other hand, it would feel so darn good to be out there, on the field, in a real game. Wouldn't that make him a football player, no matter what the rest of them said?

"Landon?" Brett's dad spoke loudly and slowly. "Would you like that? Getting in a game?"

"Yes, sir! I've got to get in the game," Landon said.

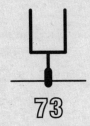

73

Monday in school, no one bothered Landon. In English class it felt like a three-way discussion about *The Count of Monte Cristo* between him, Megan, and Mr. Edwards. Landon loved it and couldn't have cared less if the other kids in the class were bored or annoyed.

Toward the end Mr. Edwards jumped off the top of the desk where he sat and wrote in big block letters on the board: DISAPPOINTMENT!

"This is what you need to know: Dumas was *disappointed*," the teacher turned to them and said. "Disappointed with friends, society, with France itself. So, what will the author do with that disappointment? What will become of Mercedes, eh? Read on. *Read on*, all of you."

The bell rang.

"And I want you each to find a partner by tomorrow!" Mr.

Edwards yelled over the hubbub. "You'll be doing a research paper on Dumas's life with a partner. Pick wisely, my friends. Pick wisely!"

As soon as they spilled out into the hallway, Megan tapped Landon's arm.

He looked into those eyes feeling dizzy.

Would she say it?

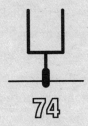

74

Megan smiled. "Partners?"

Landon felt his soul float to the ceiling. "Sure."

Lunch was lonely, but Megan's invitation carried him through the rest of the day. In gym class they played badminton. Landon was pretty bad, but it didn't matter one bit. Brett picked him for a partner. They won every game. Landon couldn't help chuckling when Mike slammed his racket on the gym floor and got detention.

After school Brett and Landon watched Genevieve's and Megan's soccer practice. When the girls were finished, the four friends walked to the diner. They were halfway up the block when Skip and his goons came out and saw them coming down the sidewalk. The three boys did an about-face and went the other way.

"Now that's what I call respect," Genevieve said.

Everyone but Landon grinned. "I don't trust him," he said. He knew Skip and his cronies weren't done with him. Then again, Landon couldn't imagine anyone wanting to tangle with Brett.

They ate french fries and milkshakes at the diner and then headed home. There was no football practice on Mondays, so Landon got all his homework done and still had time to watch some Monday Night Football.

Tuesday, Landon's stomach churned all day. Football practice was looming. The more the day wore on, the tighter his stomach twisted. He could only finish two of his four sandwiches at lunch, and he hurried home at the end of the day to sit in the bathroom for a while before trying to read in his favorite chair. When Landon's dad came up for air from his computer and asked Landon if he wanted a snack before practice, Landon took a pass.

"Ah, building up that intensity, are you?" Landon's dad looked like he hadn't taken a shower since the night before. His hair went in crazy directions atop his head, and he wore only one slipper on his feet, pajama bottoms, and a dress shirt buttoned in the wrong holes.

"Just nervous." Landon tried not to stare at the crooked shirt.

"Well, it'll all work out." His father beamed, rubbing the scruff on his chin and pointing at the computer across the room. "Your alter ego slayed the dragon today. What do you think of that?"

"Nodnal?" Landon raised an eyebrow, the wild hair and crazy clothes making sense now. "You're at the end? Dad, it's only been a couple weeks. . . ."

"Yes, Nodnal and I are close to the end, but it's not quite the end yet. I've been writing like mad. Lots left to happen still, *but* he's got people's attention. The first dragon is always the hardest." Landon's dad stopped talking, but Landon kept looking at him, waiting for him to go on.

His father scratched his belly under the cockeyed shirt. "You get that, right?"

Landon sighed. "I get it. Everything's not a story, though, Dad."

His father scowled. "No, no. That's not true, Landon. Everything *is* a story, and we are the authors of our own lives."

Landon looked out the window at the trees swaying in a stiff wind. Random leaves had gone from green to yellow.

"I don't know, Dad. I don't know if we're writing it, or someone else."

"Why would you say that?" his father asked with a sad face.

Landon stared at him and swallowed. "Sometimes . . . most of the time, I feel like I'm in a crowded room with my hands tied behind my back. I start one way and someone pushes me back. Then another person spins me around and I trip and fall. I get up and start going again and someone else gives me a shove.

"If I was writing my own story . . . it wouldn't go like this."

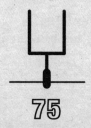

75

During Tuesday's practice Landon kept expecting something to happen, like maybe Brett or his dad would stop things and insist Landon join the contact drills. He just didn't know. Everything was the same, though. Gunner Miller growled and snarled and drove Nichols on his back three plays in a row. Brett hammered Travis in a one-on-one drill, causing the blocky center to kick the grass. Torin and Jones, who appeared to be friends off the field, mixed it up like mortal enemies.

Landon shied away from the contact drills, and the coaches let him. Landon kept watching Brett's dad as he instructed Skip or the backup, Bryce Rinehart, on a pass play or Mike and Xander on how to run a pass route. He expected Coach Bell to do or say something about Landon's situation. On the couch on Sunday, it had seemed like Landon was almost part of the Bell family, and if that was the case, wouldn't Coach Bell take him under his wing?

But the coaches were putting in a bunch of new pass plays—plays Coach Furster said he had devised to get the team a needed win—so there was a lot of teaching the coaches, especially Brett's dad, had to do. Landon reasoned that Coach Bell didn't have time to stop practice and interfere with the linemen. He didn't know what he thought Brett could do either; he just hadn't expected everything to be the same.

Wednesday's football practice was like déjà vu all over again. Landon stretched and went through agility drills and then migrated to the sideline when the hitting started. Nichols shot him a nasty look before asking the question others also seemed to have on the tip of their tongues: "Where's the water, Landon?"

He couldn't help himself. If he wasn't going to dive into the drills, and if no one was going to encourage him, he wanted to do *something*. Without answering, he went for the carrier and began supplying his teammates with bursts of cool liquid, which, pitiful as he knew it was, made him feel like he was contributing to the effort of defeating Tuckahoe. Brett, Gunner, Timmy, and the other linemen hunkered down in their stances and blasted each other with grunts and groans and flying sweat, and Landon told himself that maybe when Brett's uncle showed up on Thursday, he'd give it a try. What reason was there for him to get into the fray now?

"Landon?" Brett took a water bottle from him and spoke so gently that Landon barely heard a sound through the whistle blasts and shouting. "Come on. You should get in there."

"I . . . uh . . ." Landon thought about the hand drills he'd done with his dad. Maybe he was ready, but he glanced at his water carrier and held up an empty bottle. "Let me refill these and then maybe . . ."

Brett nodded his head. Landon thought he said, "Okay," before diving back into the drill.

Landon felt like a tug-of-war rope, stretched and straining, first going one way then the other. The discomfort of disappointing Brett pulled against the discomfort of being smashed into and knocked around like some giant kitten. Paralyzed by indecision, Landon kept the water bottles circulating around and cheerfully refilled them a second time at the spigot outside the back entrance to the school.

Practice was halfway over and they were running through plays as an entire team when Landon saw some of the other backup players nudging each other and pointing up at the parking lot. Skip Dreyfus, who wouldn't even look at Landon, shoved an empty water bottle at him, and Landon replaced it in the carrier before he looked to see whatever was distracting his teammates.

Up on the hill was a gleaming, midnight blue F-350 pickup. The enormous grille and chrome rims the size of manhole covers sparkled in the last rays of sunshine. It was the biggest, nicest truck Landon had ever seen. The door swung open and Jonathan Wagner, the Giants' starting right tackle, got out, hitched up his pants, and marched right for the junior football team's practice.

Everything stopped.

The whistle Coach Furster kept clamped between his teeth dropped from his mouth to the end of its lanyard like a prisoner on the gallows.

Jonathan Wagner wore mirrored sunglasses and a silky black T-shirt. Cowboy boots poked out from the hem of jeans that clung to his telephone-pole legs. His face was set in a concrete scowl. He *looked* like an NFL player—until he stopped and his face turned merry and he spoke in the excited voice of a kid at Christmas. "Hey, Coach Bell. How you guys all doing?"

Brett's dad hugged the Giants player and they clapped each other on the back with thundering strokes. Brett's dad turned to the other coaches. "Guys, you know my wife's brother, Jonathan Wagner?"

Coach Furster stepped right up to shake hands like they were long-lost friends. "Jonathan, heck of a way to start out the season. I've been a Giants fan since before I was born."

"Me too." Coach West got in on a handshake and puffed his skinny chest. "I'm the police chief here in town, so you just let me know if you need anything."

Landon glanced at Brett, who snickered and mouthed, "I told you so."

Coach Furster had his hand on the enormous player's back like they were buddies as he turned to address his team. "Guys, this is Jonathan Wagner. We all know him. He's Brett's uncle and the two-time Pro Bowl tackle for the New York Giants."

Jonathan looked around, nodding and smiling. "Brett, come here, you."

Brett went to him and Jonathan gave him a one-armed hug before his eyes roved over the rest of the team. Landon slowly set the water carrier down in the grass. He didn't want Brett's uncle to see what he really was.

"Where is he?" Jonathan looked around until his eyes locked on Landon. "Hey, *my man*! How you doing, Landon?"

Landon saw the entire team look his way with utter disbelief swirling in their eyes.

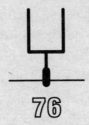

76

Jonathan Wagner pumped Landon's hand once and turned to Coach Furster. "Okay, Coach, don't let me disrupt practice. You guys get back to it and I'll just hang here. Coach McAdoo would have a fit if he saw a football practice stop in its tracks. Seriously, you guys get to it. I'm just here to watch."

Coach Furster's face fell in confusion and maybe disappointment, but he recovered his wits and his whistle and gave it a blast. "Let's go! First team offense, second team defense!"

The players scrambled back to their respective huddles. Coach West held up a card with a diagram that told the defensive players where to line up, mimicking the Tuckahoe team they'd face on Sunday. Coach Furster didn't even check his practice script. He signaled a pass play that had the quarterback throwing a long bomb to his son, Mike, who easily outpaced the second-string cornerback and sailed untouched into the end zone.

"Money!" Coach Furster shouted and pumped a fist before taking a glance at Jonathan Wagner to see if he too appreciated Mike's skill and the brilliance of the coaching.

All Jonathan did was nod slowly without comment.

Practice continued for a time before the second-string offense was put in to get a few reps running the new plays Coach Furster had designed for Tuckahoe. Landon shifted his weight from one foot to the other. The NFL superstar stood next to Brett's dad. Both big men had their arms crossed and both stared intently at the action.

Landon felt equal parts relief and disappointment. The tug-of-war in his brain continued, and he had started to wonder if this was what it was like to go crazy when he saw Jonathan Wagner turn to Coach Furster after a broken running play up the middle. With his thumb, the Giants player pointed at Landon. "Coach? Why don't you get Landon in there? I bet he could've made that inside trap really go. What position does he play?"

Coach Furster's face did a dance, and then he sputtered, "Well . . . he's . . . big, yeah, but . . . he's . . ."

Coach Furster ran out of ideas, and then he gave a short laugh and said, "The kids call him 3P, something about a powder puff. He pretty much plays left out. Heh heh."

Jonathan Wagner simply looked at Furster. No one knew what his eyes were saying behind the sunglasses, but Landon sensed his anger. "He's bigger than Brett, Coach. Kid as big as that? I mean, the kid's a truck. Even for short yardage plays.

What do you think? Maybe I can whip him into some kind of usable shape."

"Whip?" Coach Furster's face colored a bit and he laughed a nervous little laugh. "What do you mean? *Work* with him?"

"Yeah," Jonathan Wagner said, unamused. "Has anyone gone through the fundamentals with him? Flat back, power step, head up, stay low?"

Coach Furster's face turned a deeper shade. He lowered his voice, but Landon read his lips. "Well, he's deaf, right? And he has trouble with things and . . . well, he's got two left feet and he doesn't really *want* to hit, but if you can get something out of him—wow, great. By all means."

"Nice." The Giants' tackle turned toward Landon. "I'll take him to the sled."

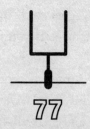

77

Landon was nearly dizzy from the mixture of pride and worry as he tramped along behind Jonathan Wagner. The big NFL lineman swung his hips as he walked atop great bowed legs. His hands hung low like tremendous meat hooks from their long arms. When they got to the blocking sled, Jonathan removed his sunglasses, slapped the top of the dummy on the end, and turned to face Landon with a big smile. "Okay, let me see what you got."

Landon shook his head. "I got nothing."

"Well, you've seen the other guys, right?"

Landon nodded. "And about a million YouTube videos."

"Well, just give me the best stance you can and fire out on my count and block this bad boy, and I'll see where you're at and we can go from there." The NFL player studied Landon's face. "If you could do it perfect already, you wouldn't need me."

"Did you help Brett get so good?" Landon asked.

"Me and his dad." Jonathan nodded. "Brett's a natural. Maybe you are too. Let me see."

"I'm not a natural." Landon got down in his frog-like stance, looking up at Jonathan. "Okay, ready."

"Whoa. No. Not ready." Jonathan grabbed Landon's shoulder pads and raised him up like a sack of beans, and then he pushed him back a bit so they stood facing each other. "Okay, get your feet shoulder-width apart, like this. Keep your feet straight, like you're on skis."

Landon did as he was told.

"Good. Now bend your knees just a bit and slide your right foot back so it's even with the heel of your left foot so you're staggered, like this."

Landon watched Jonathan slide his foot straight back and did the same.

"Not that far," Jonathan said. "That's it, so your toe is even with the heel of your other foot. Good. Now, rest your forearms on your thighs like this. This is your preset stance, and you have to have a good preset stance to have a good stance because we're gonna drop right down into our stance."

Landon watched the enormous player drop down into a three-point stance. A thrill shot through him. Jonathan was the real deal. An NFL player was right in front of him, showing him how it was done. Landon dropped his hand down and got into the stance, proudly remembering to use his fingers as a bridge the way Brett had showed him.

Jonathan stood up and assessed him. "Hmm. Better, but get that hump out of your back. Look, watch me. See how my back is flat. You should be able to have a picnic on the back of a good lineman in his stance."

Landon tried, but it was hard.

"Move your hand out a little. You don't want to be too far forward, but get a little bit longer. That'll help with your back." Jonathan moved Landon's hand and ran a finger down his spine. "That's much better. See? Everything starts with the stance, Landon. You keep flat and you turn that big body into a battering ram that can destroy people. Now you're ready to fire out and hit that dummy."

Landon fired out and struck the dummy.

"Hey, good work with your hands, thumbs up and everything. I like that placement. See? You got this, Landon," Jonathan's voice rumbled. "Okay, again."

On and on it went. For half an hour Jonathan Wagner tutored Landon on blocking before he stood tall and said, "Okay, you're ready."

"I'm ready?" Landon blinked at him.

Jonathan laughed. "Oh, yeah. You come out of that stance like I have you doing? Keep your head tilted up but low? Deliver a blow with your hands and chop your feet the way you've been doing on this dummy? You'll be a beast. You gotta do it with heart, though. Get a little mad about it. Punish people."

Landon thought. "Brett always seems like he's mad when he's blocking. He knocked me over and was like . . . snarling."

"Brett *is* mad when he's blocking. That's a good thing if you've got it."

"I don't think I have it like him," Landon said.

"But you really don't know, do you?" Jonathan said. "You

can't know until you've got the right technique. You've been flopping around like a fish in the bottom of a boat. Now you're gonna swim, and we'll see what happens. I know one thing. . . ."

"What?" Landon asked.

"You're determined."

"I am?" Landon thought about all those YouTube videos he studied. Maybe that counted?

"I watched you in that cannonball contest. You held your form even when you tilted too far and smacked your bare back on the water. That had to hurt, but you held it anyway. Because why?" Jonathan looked at Landon, waiting for the answer.

"Because I wanted to win?" Landon wasn't sure it was the right answer, but it was the truth.

"Yup. That's determination. Bring it to your game on the line. With your size, it'll be enough to dominate these guys. Well, everyone but my nephew." Jonathan put his big hands on his hips. "And if you've got any nasty in you at all, you'll be in the starting lineup."

"Nasty?" Confusion washed over Landon.

"There's this part of you where, like, you see red or you hear the whoosh of a train in your brain and you just lose it." Jonathan twirled his finger beside his head. "You go batty and . . . people better watch out."

Landon snorted at the joke.

"I'm serious, Landon," the NFL player said. "Not a lot of people walking around as big as you who can tuck and hold a cannonball. You learn how to use what you got? You bring a little nasty to the dance?" Jonathan shook his head and broke into a small smile. "My man, I'll be your agent."

The big lineman turned and marched toward the rest of the team and Landon followed. When they reached Coach Furster, he signaled a play to Skip and then turned to face the Giants player.

"Well, Coach," Jonathan said, putting a hand on Landon's shoulder pad, "he's ready."

Coach Furster laughed, but his grin faded when he saw that Jonathan meant it. "You want me to put him in there?"

"Why not?" Jonathan shrugged and looked at Brett's dad, who also shrugged.

"Uh, well. He has no idea what the plays are," Coach Furster said. "He really won't know what to do."

"What's the next play on your script?" Jonathan pointed to Coach Furster's clipboard.

Coach Furster glanced down. "Uh, pro right forty-four veer."

"Great!" Jonathan clapped his hands once. "A run play. Landon, you know what to do on the forty-four veer, or do you need me to tell you?"

"I know." Landon nodded his head. He'd seen that play so many times he could run it in his sleep. He knew the blocking assignments. He knew what the running backs did, and the quarterback too. It was no big deal to Landon, but judging by the look on the coaches' faces, it was a surprise that he had any idea at all what was going on.

"Yeah," Jonathan said. "No more left out. Get him in there at right tackle and let's see how good of a job I did."

"Well, we're running the first team right now." Coach Furster looked like someone had told him the stock market crashed.

"Yeah, that's okay. He can do it." Jonathan Wagner gave Coach Furster a stone-cold stare he probably saved for the Philadelphia Eagles.

Coach Furster bit into his lower lip, but then he wagged his head and shouted, "Miller, go to left end on defense!"

"Coach?" Gunner Miller gave Coach Furster a puzzled look.

"Just do what I say!" Coach Furster barked at the dejected-looking player before he turned to Landon and forced a smile.

"Go ahead, Landon. Get in there."

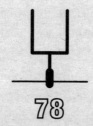

78

Landon marched to the line of scrimmage.

As he lined up in his spot at right tackle, Landon looked at the defender across from him. Gunner Miller was no Brett Bell, but he was the team's starting left defensive end *and* the starting right tackle on offense and a hitter for sure. Gunner did not look happy about Landon taking his spot. Landon turned to look behind him. Jonathan Wagner stood next to Coach Bell with his arms folded across his chest and his biceps bulging like water balloons. He wore the face of a lion on a high rock, separated from other life forms, but he offered Landon a thumbs-up.

Landon turned back to the line and realized Skip had already begun his cadence. Landon got down into his stance a second behind the other linemen. The defense was ready too, with Gunner hunkered down and trembling with rage right in front of Landon. He could barely hear Skip's voice, and in that instant he was struck by the thought that Skip was being quieter on purpose, because Landon couldn't hear as well as the others by a long shot. Landon pushed the thought away. He checked himself quickly to make sure his stance was correct, looking down through his face mask at his feet.

Just as he glanced up, action exploded all around him and Gunner fired out, cracking Landon's pads. Landon winced, but he took his power step. His hands blasted up into Gunner's chest and Landon stayed low like he'd been told. They were neutral for a moment, and then Landon began to chug his feet, up and down, up and down, plowing forward, and almost in slow motion Gunner began to go backward. Landon kept chugging. Layne Guerrero flashed past in a blur with the football tucked under his arm.

Landon kept blocking, driving Gunner down the field. Gunner tried to separate, but Landon had his hands clamped up under the breastplate edges of his shoulder pads. Gunner turned and squirmed and desperately began swatting Landon's helmet. Landon heard the distant sound of what might have been the whistle, but he wasn't sure, so he kept doing what Jonathan had told him to do, and he did feel a little mad at Gunner for swatting him in the earhole.

Finally, Landon saw that he was alone with Gunner in the middle of the field. No one was around, and he figured it was time to stop because the whistle was really shrieking now.

Landon turned to see Coach Furster's boiling face, teeth

clamped tight on the whistle, marching straight for him.

The coach whipped Landon around by the shoulder pad and gave him a shove. "Are you . . . just . . . stupid?"

Landon saw that everyone had stopped to stare. He shook his head. "No."

"Well, you just got us a fifteen-yard penalty for unnecessary roughness, did you know that?"

"No." Landon felt his insides quiver, but he also felt . . . mad.

There was a flash of movement as Jonathan Wagner dashed up and put a friendly hand on Coach Furster's shoulder. "My bad, Coach. This is on me totally." Jonathan laughed. "I *told* him to keep driving his man until he heard the whistle. Landon asked me what to do if he didn't hear it, and I told him I'd rather see him get a penalty than not finish his block. It's a lineman's code of conduct type of thing. My bad. I'm sorry."

Coach Furster's face softened, but not entirely.

"Did you see that block my man made, though?" Jonathan's eyebrows jumped. "Wow, my grandmother could've run through that hole."

"Yes, it was a . . ." Coach Furster seemed to be choking on a fish bone. "It was a good one. A good block. True, but we can't have a fifteen-yard penalty on every play. You can't have *that*."

Landon knew what was happening. It had happened to him all his life. Just when someone gave him a chance, just when things looked like they were going his way, someone like Coach Furster stepped on him like a bug.

The only difference here was that Landon's savior was a six-foot-six, three-hundred-and thirty-pound All-Pro lineman for the New York Giants.

If the cruel cycle of Landon's life was ever going to be broken, it was now.

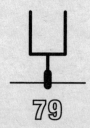

79

"So, Landon." Jonathan turned to face him. "Forget what I said before. You block for five seconds and then stop. That's the length of an average play. Can you count that in your mind? Just one, two, three, four, five; then you get off the block. That'll fix it. Can you?"

"Sure," Landon said.

Coach Furster opened his mouth to protest, but nothing came out except, "He . . . uh . . . uh . . ."

"Coach, you line my man and Brett up next to each other?" Jonathan shook his head with the slow wag of a dog. It looked—and kind of sounded to Landon—like he whistled. "Man oh man. You got yourself a juggernaut. Yes sir, one of them unstoppable, rolling battering ram things that just crushes everything in its way. You tuck your runner up behind 'em? My man!"

"It's an idea." Coach Furster seemed to slowly be regaining

his control of the situation. "Let's see how he does, though. Let's see about this five-second thing."

Jonathan clapped his meaty hands. "I like it, Coach. That's just what Coach McAdoo would've said."

Coach Furster lost his fight not to smile at the comparison, and the toot of his whistle was a little less strong than usual before he barked, "Okay, let's get it back in the huddle. Forty-eight sweep! Let me see it!"

Jonathan winked at Landon and shooed him toward the huddle.

It all happened so fast. Skip called the play in a mutter. Brett pointed at him and smiled from the other side of the huddle. They stepped to the line. Gunner Miller hunkered down in his stance with trembling legs, ready to explode, ready to take revenge. Part of Landon was scared. Part of him wanted to explain to Gunner that he only wanted a true place on the team, not to actually take his job. But part of Landon got mad, and he asked himself, why should he go through life being picked on and being left out? Why shouldn't *he* win the day? Win the battle? Win the war? Landon saw the other linemen drop, so he did too, more ready this time for action.

And in that instant, he felt it.

He went batty with anger.

Nasty.

Even though he couldn't really hear the cadence, Landon exploded at the first sign of movement, low and hard. This time there was no neutral, momentary stand-off. This time Landon plowed through Gunner so fast and hard he fell down. Landon went over him like a lawnmower, let go, and pitilessly grabbed the next body he came upon, Timmy Nichols. Landon manhandled him, driving him three yards back before tossing him to the dirt.

He was huffing and puffing and he stopped and stood up straight, fearful that he might have gone over a five-second count. In truth, he hadn't counted at all. All he knew was that Layne Guerrero was wiggling his butt in the end zone. Landon turned.

Coach Furster looked amazed, but when Landon detected the small smile in the left corner of Jonathan Wagner's mouth, it filled him with joy and pride. Brett was slapping him on the back. Landon turned.

"Dude! You crushed them. Two pancakes in the same play? Ha-ha! I never had *two* pancakes!" Landon's cheeks burned. He shrugged and headed back toward where he knew the huddle would be, unable to keep a huge grin from blooming around his mouthpiece.

Practice went on just like that.

Get the play. Line up. Five seconds of nastiness. Do it again.

Landon kept expecting something bad to happen, some problem to pop up and ruin everything, but by the end of the evening Jonathan Wagner had taught them all four new running plays from an unbalanced line that put Landon and Brett right next to each other to open massive holes in the defense to run through. Landon could see that Coach Furster didn't really like the whole thing, until Jonathan showed them a counter-play that had the quarterback handing the ball off to the wide receiver on an end around to the weak side.

That was a play where Mike would shine.

"See?" Jonathan explained excitedly. "The defense is going to *have* to shift to this unbalanced line, and when they start getting chewed up by your two monster hogs, they'll *over*-shift. Then you come back at them with this wide receiver end around, and they may just lay down on you and quit."

They ran the play, and the grin on Coach Furster's face when his son scampered into the end zone could have lit a Christmas tree.

"We really are a passing team, though." Coach Furster scratched his head.

Jonathan shook his head and frowned. "There's no such thing, Coach. You can ask Coach McAdoo or Eli Manning. You can ask Peyton Manning or Aaron Rodgers or Tom Brady. Even the so-called 'passing' teams know you gotta run the ball to set up the pass. No one ever won a championship any other way."

Landon looked back to Coach Furster to see his reaction.

What he saw, he never expected.

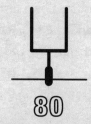

80

Surrender.

That was the best word Landon could think of, and he never thought he'd see it on Coach Furster's face. He never imagined Coach Furster was even capable of it, but in the presence of a man as big and powerful and immovable as Jonathan Wagner, Coach Furster was reduced to a regular dad, chewing on his knuckle.

As the team gathered around, no one could hear them talking, but Landon read the NFL player's and his coach's lips.

Coach Furster said, "I was thinking to myself that we needed to get back to basics. I mean, losing to Scarsdale?"

"It's a funny-shaped ball," Jonathan said. "It doesn't always bounce your way, but you're right about basics. I think you've got something here, Coach. Something that could really give people headaches."

Coach Furster held out a hand. "This has been an honor."

"And a pleasure for me." Jonathan shook the coach's hand.

"Hey, would you mind saying a few words to the team?" Coach Furster asked.

"Sure." Jonathan Wagner turned to the team. He didn't speak until everyone was standing totally still. Only then did he look around like that ferocious lion again. "Guys, you've heard it before. There's no 'I' in 'team.' And that means if you want to be a champion, you have to realize it's about everyone around you. Look around."

He waited until they really did look before he continued. "From the best player to the worst, you're a team, so act like one. Treat each other well and you won't just win, you'll *be winners*."

Coach Furster waited to make sure Jonathan Wagner was finished before he turned to the players, who now stood waiting in anticipation for wind sprints, and shouted, "All right, men. It's not every day you get an NFL player showing up at your practice, so I'm gonna let Jonathan Wagner decide just how many sprints you guys will run. Let's go! On the line!"

Coach Furster blasted his whistle and everyone lined up shoulder-to-shoulder on the sideline.

Jonathan stepped forward and raised his voice. "I like what you guys are doing. I like the way you worked, and when the New York Giants work really hard and have a really good practice, sometimes, *sometimes*, Coach McAdoo says, 'You did your running during practice men, *see you tomorrow*!'"

Everyone around Landon cheered. He looked to make sure that's what it was before joining in.

"You heard him!" Coach Furster shouted, waving them off the field. *"See you tomorrow!"*

More cheering, and the team moved in a wave up the hill toward the parking lot. Landon saw Mike Furster and Skip Dreyfus without their helmets, each with a hand on the shoulder pads of a crestfallen Gunner Miller. Xander West walked backward, talking to them all. Landon was breathless at the sight, and he hesitated. He wanted to thank Jonathan Wagner, but he didn't want to be a pest and Coach Furster was now having his picture taken with the Giants player, so Landon turned and slogged up the hill.

When he got into the car, his father looked at him from his hunched-over position and asked, "What's everyone so excited about, buddy?"

Landon carefully removed his helmet and the skullcap and adjusted the hearing apparatus clinging to his head. He dumped the helmet into the backseat and sat looking down at his hands. Tears rushed into his eyes. He couldn't speak, but only shake his head.

"Hey, hey." Landon's dad gave him a gentle shake until he looked up. "What's wrong, buddy? Hey, what happened? You can tell me."

Landon sniffed and spoke in a choking voice. "*I* happened, Dad. I did it. I did it."

Landon looked through the kaleidoscope of tears. "I'm a football player."

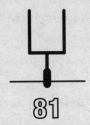

81

That night at home and the next morning before school, Landon didn't boast about it. He didn't even tell Genevieve, not because she didn't deserve to know but because Landon wanted to caress the idea of who he now was in the privacy of his own thoughts.

As Landon dug into his oatmeal, Genevieve pounded her hand on the table between them to get his attention. "Are you okay?"

"Yeah, great." Landon did his best to look normal.

"Something's going on." She stared at him.

Suddenly he could hold it no longer. Landon burst into a smile. "I did it, Genevieve, I showed them all I can play. Really play."

The feel of her arms wrapped around him in a tight hug stayed with Landon all the way to school. Nothing around him seemed to have changed, but he felt somehow taller, and it didn't bother him that he stood out.

Landon got to English class early. Mr. Edwards was making some final notes for his lesson when Megan arrived, and she got right in Landon's face. "I hear you're the new big thing on the football team."

Megan looked to be as delighted as Landon felt. He offered a shy nod.

"Landon, I'm so happy for you. Brett couldn't stop raving." Her laugh was a pleasant jingle of bells. "We were texting all night and then he had to meet me before homeroom to tell me again in person."

Landon felt a mixture of pride and envy. He couldn't help wishing it was him Megan was texting far into the night and him she'd met up with in the hallway before homeroom.

"Seems good so far," he replied.

"I'll say." With a nod she sat down and took out her copy of *The Count of Monte Cristo*.

Landon had a hard time focusing in English—and in all his classes. As he pushed through the hallways from one class to another, he stole glances at the kids around him in a way he never had before. It had always been safer and easier to ignore the looks people gave him because they'd rarely been anything but unkind. Now though, he could only imagine it was a matter of time before news of his new prowess spread, and instead of disgust, he'd be seeing admiration in the faces of his fellow students.

At lunch he half expected someone or other to sit down at his empty table. When no one did, he assured himself it was just a matter of time. He recalled the way heads and eyes magnetically turned toward Jonathan Wagner when he pulled up in his big truck. In time, and of course to a lesser degree, that would happen for Landon. He just knew it.

He hustled right out of study hall so he could make his usual pit stop on the way to gym and realized as he went that he really was standing taller and straighter and that his height allowed him to look down on everyone from his own private rooftop.

He slipped into his usual stall, the last one in a row of five. The chipped gray paint on the inside walls and door of the stall were marked with messages and insults, old and new. As they had every day since he'd found this private spot, two round Ping-Pong-ball eyes drawn in Sharpie stared at him with pupils no bigger than dots. Their heavy lids seemed bored with his business, and he wondered if the crooked line below was an accident or a twisted smile.

Suddenly he stiffened at the sight of a shadow flickering through the thin crack between the door and its frame. He cleared his throat to let the intruder know the end stall was taken, but instead of a departing shadow, Landon saw the tips of two running sneakers.

He strained for even the hint of a sound and then proclaimed, "This one's taken."

The sneakers shifted. He sensed more movement outside the stall before an iPhone appeared beneath the door, attached to a selfie stick and directed at him.

He could see himself on the screen as he stared in horror, and then it blinked.

His mouth fell open in disbelief, and by the time he realized what had really happened—that someone had taken a picture of him sitting on the toilet with his pants down around his ankles—the phone was gone. There was a flurry of shadows in the crack of the stall door and more on the floor as the feet scrambled for the exit.

Landon yanked up his pants and fumbled with his zipper and the stall door at the same time. He heard what sounded like a crazed cackle of laughter and the slam of the bathroom door. Bursting from the stall, he grazed his head against the door, dislodging his cochlear, and saw only the flash of a backpack disappearing into the hall.

"Help!" Landon shouted at the top of his lungs. "Stop!"

He knew it was useless.

He stopped in front of the mirror and looked at the reflection of a huge boy with his pants unbuttoned and his shirt crumpled above the white of his belly. The battery pack from one ear dangled from the wire connecting it to the disc on his skull. His insides trembled with anger and dread.

A moan escaped him because he knew that this would now ruin everything.

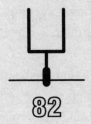

82

The sounds of a commotion out in the hall hurried Landon's fingers. He fastened his pants, tugged his shirt into place, and slipped the battery pack back behind his ear. After hoisting his backpack, Landon took a deep breath and swung open the scarred wooden door.

He blinked and gasped at what he saw.

Mike Furster lay sprawled out on the floor. His backpack and its contents had been flung about. Genevieve had a knee planted in his back, a handful of his spiked hair in one hand and his iPhone in the other. Xander hadn't gotten far, and he now turned back to rescue his friend, closing in fast on Genevieve.

Landon stepped forward to help Genevieve, but he was spun around by Skip.

"Stay out of it, you big slob." Skip yanked Landon's arm,

causing him to stumble into the lockers with a bang.

Landon's eyes darted toward his shrieking sister.

Xander had her in a headlock and he was grabbing for the phone. Skip was moving in.

Landon felt it. Without warning, at the sight of his little sister being manhandled, that nasty blew right through his brain.

Landon got hold of Skip from behind, lifted, and flung him with one motion, through the air and into the lockers with a cymbal crash Landon could *feel*.

Landon grabbed Xander by the neck and tore him free from Genevieve, raising him and tossing him to the floor. Landon roared. Looking at Mike, his head shook with fury. Mike had flipped himself over. With terror in every muscle, he scrabbled backward on the floor like a crab. Landon roared again and Mike took off, without his phone.

Xander started to follow, but Landon grabbed him by the neck again.

That's when Mr. Edwards appeared with his own look of shock and terror. His eyes went up toward Xander, squeezed in Landon's grip.

Mr. Edwards held up both hands the way you'd fend off a monster. "No, Landon. Put him down! You're hurting him!"

Landon dropped Xander to the floor, where he fell in a heap. Genevieve had ahold of Landon's arm, and he looked down.

"What'd they do?" Genevieve's face was aflame. "Take a picture of you in the bathroom?"

Landon nodded.

Genevieve gritted her teeth. "Well, too bad for them."

Even as the principal rounded the corner flanked by two teachers, Genevieve dropped the phone to the floor and stomped the life out of it.

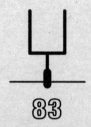

83

Megan was the one who had told Genevieve what was going on. She'd overheard Skip bragging about their plan to Katy after lunch. It embarrassed Landon that Megan knew what had happened, but he couldn't help also feeling grateful that she had helped save him from what would have been a disastrous new assault. Those were Landon's thoughts as he and Genevieve sat in the principal's office waiting for their father.

It took over forty minutes for him to finally arrive, ducking through the door and clicking his tongue. His first words were worried. "Oh, kids. Are you okay?"

Mr. Sanders popped through the door, all business. "Mr. Dorch? Somehow I was expecting your wife."

Landon's dad bit a lip and his cheeks reddened. "Oh, she's on her way. I told her it was an emergency. She'll walk through that door at any minute."

Landon's dad turned a hopeful face toward the door.

Mr. Sanders considered Landon and Genevieve. "I'm not sure it's an *emergency*, but a suspension does go on their disciplinary record."

"Suspension?" Landon's dad looked shocked.

"Your son was *warned*," the principal said, and then he nearly gagged on his next words. "Landon was *choking* another student, Mr. Dorch."

Landon wanted to look down, but then he'd never know what they were saying. When people were angry or serious, their tones always dropped, rendering his cochlear implants nearly useless on their own. So, he watched his father react with shock, sadness, and worry, until he realized that Genevieve was spouting off.

". . . picture of Landon using the bathroom, which is totally *illegal*!" Genevieve's face was on fire.

"You're not a lawyer here, miss." The principal shifted his scowl from Landon to his sister. "You're a young lady in a lot of hot water. Assaulting a fellow student? Destruction of property?"

"I didn't assault him." Genevieve glared right back at the principal. "I *tackled* him because he took a picture of my brother using the *toilet* and he was going to *post* it. Is that okay with you?"

Landon kept his eyes moving to see who would speak first. It was a standoff.

Then the door flung open and their mother burst into the room.

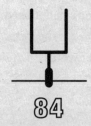

84

Landon had never seen his mother's hair so out of place.

"Why are those other boys not in here?" Landon's mom demanded.

"Those boys were the *victims* of this assault, Mrs. Dorch." The principal stood up to show just how outraged he really was. "And the discipline of children besides your own isn't any of your business, madam."

"Justice is my business." Their mom slapped her iPad down on the principal's desk. The page read: CODE OF CONDUCT AND DISCIPLINE. Beneath that was a seal and then: BRONXVILLE SCHOOL DISTRICT. "Take a look at your own handbook, Mr. Sanders. Those 'victims' were not victims. They're bullies who've tormented my son since before school began, and you will *not* continue to turn a blind eye to that. Being inept is no excuse for a middle school principal paid by my tax dollars."

"You're not going to tell *me* how to do my job, madam. This meeting is over. You can head right out that door, or I'll call security and have you removed." Mr. Sanders trembled and then snatched up the handset of the phone on his desk.

"Good." Their mom held up her cell phone. "I'm calling the newspaper."

"Wait! What?"

"That's right." Landon's mother continued to tap the screen of her phone. "And then I'm calling the superintendent, but first, the newspaper. Bullying is a big issue these days."

"Mrs. Dorch, put the phone down." Mr. Sanders's eyes sputtered like wet candles. "Please."

Landon's mom didn't put it down, but she stopped tapping. "Do you know what that handbook says?"

"Which part?" Mr. Sanders asked.

"The part on page forty-two about aggravated harassment, followed by internet harassment on page forty-three, and especially possession of indecent material on page sixty-seven. I'm not sure about disseminating indecent material because I'm not sure if the perpetrator sent the picture to anyone before he was stopped by this brave young lady who happens to be my daughter." Their mom nodded toward Genevieve.

Everyone in the room stared at Landon's mom with open mouths, none more astounded than Mr. Sanders. "You . . . you . . . but, the camera—the phone, I mean—was broken."

"That's what the cloud is for." Landon's mom folded her

arms across her chest. "If my husband and I want to push this, I think we need to involve the district attorney, don't you? I'm sure you remember the presentation that the DA's office made to the kids last year warning them about crimes like these? It's on your website, Mr. Sanders. It's part of why I chose to move into Bronxville. According to the website, the DA said that disseminating a picture that reveals a private part of a person's anatomy is a Class D felony. You should know that." Their mom wore a look of disgust.

"Of course I know that." Mr. Sanders stood upright in a futile attempt to regain his authority. The principal looked at Landon's dad and then at his mom. "Mrs. Dorch? I think we can settle all this quietly and to everyone's satisfaction, don't you?"

"First you'll admit you've got the wrong kids sitting in your office." Their mom didn't blink.

Mr. Sanders looked like he'd been hung by his thumbs.

Landon's dad glanced at their mom. "I know my wife, Mr. Sanders. I know how she thinks and how she feels, and I have an idea that just might satisfy her, but it won't be easy to pull off. Maybe, just maybe, if you're willing to work with us, my wife and I might find a way to let you resolve this *without* involving the DA."

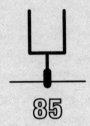

85

Landon's mom didn't say yes, but she didn't say no either. What she said was that she wanted to think about it with the family—at home.

Landon sat with his family around the kitchen table, trying to decide what to do. His dad tried to persuade his mom that an apology from the boys would do.

"See, the thing is, Gina," Landon's dad said, "Saturday's the big game against Tuckahoe. It's a huge tradition. The whole town goes out to watch."

Landon's mom narrowed her eyes. "What does that *mean*, Forrest?"

Landon's dad sputtered. "Well . . ."

"Not to them. What does it mean to *me*? What do you think?" his mother asked.

"Well . . . if we get the DA involved, they may cancel the

game. The whole thing would blow up, and our kids would be in the middle of it." Landon could tell his dad felt like he was on dangerous ground, because he was scratching his neck and blinking a lot.

His mother thumped a small fist onto the table. "What those boys did is a crime. Crimes are meant to be punished."

"But sometimes people forgive and forget?" his father suggested quietly after a pause.

"Has anyone involved asked for forgiveness?" His mother tightened her lips and shook her head.

"Not yet," their dad said.

Their mom's eyes blazed. "Sometimes people cross a line they shouldn't, and if you want them to know you mean business—so it won't happen again, Forrest—then you take action."

Landon's dad hung his head, and Landon knew how he felt, that desire to just have it all go away. Landon knew things did go away too. He'd experienced it. If you just kept your head down and kept going? People would generally leave you alone. But for the first time he could remember, Landon had experienced something better than just being left alone. He had friends. He had people who believed in him. Maybe he even had a gift that people would *admire,* and admiration? It was quite a prize.

His dad came up with another idea. "Listen, I know you say their fathers encourage this kind of bullying, the way they act as coaches. What if they agreed to quietly resign?"

"Coach Bell would bring the right spirit to the team," Landon's mother agreed.

"Look, they don't want this going to the courts any more than Mr. Sanders does. I bet they'll agree."

"And Coach Bell can be the head coach." Landon tried not to sound too excited, because he knew his parents' mood was somber.

"Will they even do that?" Genevieve asked. "I mean, Mr. West is the chief of police."

Landon's dad grinned. "Well, we're just gonna have to find out."

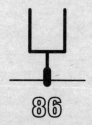

86

The next day, school spirit was soaring. Signs praising Bronxville football plastered the hallways in black and orange. From a distance, Landon saw Mike Furster walking and talking intently to Skip Dreyfus. Landon slowed down so as not to catch up to them. As soon as they disappeared around the corner, he hurried to homeroom, excited.

Brett grinned and jumped up, slapping a piece of paper down in front of Landon. "Here, check this out. My dad drew these up for short yardage. Just what my uncle was talking about. You and me like a *steamroller*."

Landon looked up from the diagrams of Xs, Os, and arrows. "Really? But we didn't practice them."

"Ahh, in the NFL they put plays in on the sideline." Brett swished a hand. "Everyone knows what to do. How awesome is it that my dad is running things?"

Genevieve had filled Megan and Brett in on what had happened.

Now, Landon looked into Brett's eyes for some sign, a flicker of doubt maybe. Brett stared right back at him, stone-cold serious.

"How many players will we even have Saturday?" Landon asked.

Brett shrugged. "You and me. Guerrero, Miller, Rinehart will be there. There will be others. Lots. Skip, Mike, and Xander will apologize. You'll see. And if they don't? They only have themselves to blame, not you."

Landon looked around the homeroom. No one was watching him, but he leaned close to Brett anyway. "Are they really not going to show up? Coach Furster and Coach West, I mean?"

"I heard your mom scared the heck out of them. I heard they apologized and agreed to resign if your parents didn't press charges against their kids." Brett frowned, but then he smiled brightly. "My uncle said *he'd* help, so who needs them?"

That spark of news lit a small fire in Landon's heart. "If your uncle's there, I think everyone will want to play. I mean, who gets to play for an NFL player? Even if it's just for one game?"

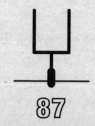

87

In English class, Megan threw Landon several worried glances.

He just couldn't get into the discussion. All he could think about was the game and what would happen. It was the Megan and Mr. Edwards Show, but neither of them could be discouraged. They went back and forth about revenge, its different forms, and the similarities between Dumas and Edmond Dantès, now the Count of Monte Cristo. After the bell, Mr. Edwards took Landon by the arm and steered him toward his desk. "I heard about everything that's going on. You stay strong, Landon."

"I am," Landon said. "Thanks."

Megan was waiting for him outside the class. "You okay?"

He nodded. "Really. I'm fine. I'd be better if everyone wasn't so worried for me."

Megan gave him a crooked smile, and her blue eyes blazed

with kindness. She reached around his middle and pressed the side of her face into the bottom of his rib cage, hugging him tight. "I know what you mean, Landon."

He could feel her fingers sinking into the flesh of his back and was so flustered he couldn't speak. A scent like flowers and honey drifted up from her glossy hair. He wrapped his arms around her too, and her compact frame reminded him of Genevieve and his mom. His nose dipped toward the wonderful smell so that it brushed the top of her head.

"Come on, we'll be late for third period." Megan released him, smiled up, and turned to go. Landon followed.

As they navigated the crowded hallways, Landon felt himself standing a little taller again, and he noticed that the glances people gave him weren't full of loathing but of respect, maybe even fear. He wondered if that had anything to do with him overpowering the kids who'd tormented him, or if it was because his mother had those same kids' parents pinned to the mat and wasn't letting up. Either way, Landon thought he liked it and that it might lead to other things, other friends, someday.

Megan paused outside Mr. Mazella's math class. "See you later, Landon."

Landon's cheek still burned from the hug, and he said a quick thanks before ducking into class.

Buoyed by the image of Megan looking up at him, the smell of her shampoo, and the touch of her hair, which Landon's mind replayed over and over in every spare moment, the day flew by. Once he nearly bumped into Xander in the hallway.

"Hey." Xander's face was frozen. "I'm supposed to apologize to you, so that's what I'm doing. Sorry."

"Uh . . . okay."

And that was it. Xander coasted right on past, leaving Landon's heart at a gallop.

By the end of the school day, Mike Furster had also apologized, but the only thing Landon got from Skip was a hateful stare from the other side of health class. When the last bell rang, it felt to Landon like a prison break. He burst out the front doors of the school and breathed deeply.

Outside, the rain had stopped and the sky had rolled back its clouds. The sun sparkled on the wet grass and dying leaves of the trees. Brett and Landon sat with Landon's dad in the bleachers to watch the girls' soccer game. They too played Tuckahoe, as did every other fall sport, and the crowd was bigger than normal for a middle school girls' soccer game. Genevieve scored twice to defeat the big rival 2–1, and Megan was a force on defense. After the final whistle, the Bronxville girls bounced up and down in a giant group hug, screaming so loud that even Landon heard them.

Landon's dad walked Landon and his sister and Brett and Megan home, distracted and muttering to himself as he sometimes did at his desk when he was writing. The four of them had pizza at the kitchen table. Landon could tell everyone was trying to keep him distracted from what would happen tomorrow, but worry hung like a heavy chain around his neck and his smiles were forced.

When their friends had gone home and Landon's mom arrived from work, the Dorch family assembled at the kitchen table.

"Well?" Landon's dad asked. "Where are we at, Gina?"

Landon's mom had a slice of pizza on a paper plate along with a diet soda for her late dinner. She chewed well, swallowed, and washed her bite down with soda before looking hard at Landon. "Did those boys apologize?"

Landon nodded. "Yup."

"Really apologize?" she asked.

"Mom, they said they were sorry." He didn't tell her about Skip.

"Three apologies?" his mom asked.

Landon looked down. "No, but I didn't see Skip, so maybe he's waiting until tomorrow."

"Well, that's a good start. Now let's see what tomorrow brings," she said before taking another bite.

"I just hope they'll play if their dads aren't coaching," Genevieve said. "Everyone really wants us to win. The whole school's gone crazy about the game."

Landon's mom finished her bite and washed it down before answering. "I spoke to Courtney Wagner on the phone this afternoon, and you know what she said?"

Genevieve just shook her head.

Landon's mom looked at him, and her emerald green eyes sparkled. "She said we don't even need those bullies. She said her brother thinks we can beat the pants off Tuckahoe with our run game."

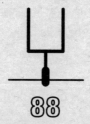

88

Sometime during the night, in a snarl of bedsheets, exhaustion finally overtook Landon, and he woke the next morning with a buzz in his brain that had nothing to do with his cochlear implants. He went through the motions of getting ready with jittery hands and stomach, passed on breakfast, and strapped himself into his football gear as if he were getting ready for a moonwalk. He even buckled up his helmet because he wanted his ears to be perfectly positioned inside the padding, and then stood staring at his father, who flipped French toast on the griddle until he realized Landon was there.

"Oh, hey." His father held the spatula upright and with pride, like a scepter, and then touched each shoulder pad. "I dub thee Landon the Great."

Landon shook his head. "This is serious, Dad."

His father's face lost its smile. "I know, son. And you're going to do great. Want me to drive you over?"

"Think I'm gonna walk, Dad."

"This early?" His father checked his watch.

"Yeah. I want to be there early. I want to hit the sled a little. Make sure I'm ready."

"What about wearing down your cleats?"

"One time won't hurt. I'll try and walk on the grass."

"Well, we will be there and cheering you on," his dad said.

"If I don't get blown up."

"You're not going to get blown up, Landon. You're going to shine." His dad shrugged. "It's just the way this story has to end."

"End?"

His father laughed and scratched at his chin. "Well, for one story to start, another story always has to end. Today is going to be a new beginning for you. It's like the sequel to *Dragon Hunt*."

"Sequel? Wait, you finished?" Landon forgot about football for a minute.

His father's cheeks colored. "You haven't seen me do much else, have you? It's two hundred and thirty pages, and it kind of wrote itself."

Landon's mind snapped back to reality. "This isn't a novel, dad. Today is real life."

His father shrugged again. "I know, but I keep telling you, you're the author of your life."

Landon sighed. "Okay, gotta go."

Before he got out the door, he felt a tap on his shoulder and turned to see that his father had followed him and stood like a fairy-tale giant blocking out the light. "I'm proud of you, Landon. However the story ends."

Landon peered at his father. In the gloom of the mudroom it looked like his eyes were glinting with moisture. His father pulled him into a hug, and then he turned him around and sent him on his way like a wind-up toy soldier.

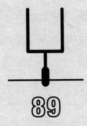

89

The clouds above crowded in on one another, piling up high and leaving almost no room for the blue to peek through. The air was brisk and a small breeze found its way through the cracks in Landon's pads. Still, he felt little, steamy swamps building up in the pits of his arms and the palms of his shaking hands. As he approached the field, cut grass sweetened the swirl of warm blacktop. There wasn't a soul to be seen. Not even a dog.

Landon tramped down the hillside and put a hand on the blue-padded blocking dummy fixed to the single sled they rarely used. The piston behind let loose a rusty squeal as he jiggled it back and forth. Landon looked around and saw only swaying trees and the lifeless windows of the houses bordering the school grounds. A yellow jacket searched the metal tube of the sled for a home and buzzed right for Landon. He jumped and swatted, filled with panic and anticipating a sting, but the bee ticked off the side of his helmet and sailed away into the breeze.

Landon laughed at himself and looked around. He imagined the stands filled with fans and the sidelines crowded with players. Still caught in the daydream, he hunkered down into his stance and heard Jonathan Wagner in his mind.

"Shoulder-width apart."

"Flat back."

"Power step. Head up. Hands inside. Feet chopping."

Landon fired out of his stance, and the dummy squealed the high-pitched cry of a little girl on a swing. He chugged his feet, driving and driving with the clock going in his head.

One, two, three, four, five. He stopped, looked around, lined up, and did it again.

Again and again he drove the sled, zigzagging this way and that, all across the grassy field beyond the end zone until he heard the faint sound of a shout. Landon turned to see Timmy.

"What are you doing here?"

Landon shrugged. "We got a game."

Timmy looked around. "Fat chance. Not much of a game without your quarterback. Thanks to you. I doubt the rest of the team's even gonna show."

Landon stuttered and then said, "It's Tuckahoe. People aren't gonna miss that. You're here."

Timmy scowled. "My mom dumps me off so she can do the *Times* crossword puzzle at the coffee shop. I'm not dumb enough to think I can make myself better the day of a game just by hitting that stupid thing."

Landon shrugged again, saying, "It never hurts to practice."

He turned away and attacked the dummy again. When he finished driving, Timmy was right behind him. He pointed at the sled. "That's pretty good, actually."

Landon studied Timmy's pudgy, angry face through the cage of his face mask for signs of contempt, but saw none. "Thanks."

"Not that it matters. Tuckahoe's gonna crush us even *if* we have enough guys to play." Timmy looked around, expecting an empty field. "Hey, Guerrero's here." His jaw dropped. "And there's Mike and Xander."

Landon followed the direction of Timmy's finger and saw that their first-team running back was jogging down the hill, and his parents weren't far behind, dressed in Bronxville colors with two pom-poms and traveling mugs of coffee. Mike and Xander were at their heels. Another vehicle pulled into the lot. It was the Bells' Suburban, and out hopped not only Brett but Travis and a fullback named Stewy Stewart, as well as Brett's dad.

"Looks like you're the only one who thinks we're gonna get crushed." Landon couldn't help jabbing Timmy. He wanted to knock that smug look off his face.

"We'll see." Timmy wasn't backing down, but for some reason he stayed close to Landon as he pushed the sled around.

Coach Bell dumped a bag of balls on the sideline and began tossing one back and forth with Layne and Stewy Stewart. Xander and Mike took a ball and started their own game of catch. The other linemen huddled up in the end zone and Brett waved Landon over. Timmy followed.

"Hey, guys," Brett said. "Let's line up and run through

those new plays. We got five linemen already. That's all we need to get started. Timmy, you play left tackle, 'cause I'm right guard next to Landon today. Travis at center and Gunner at left guard."

"I'm right tackle." Gunner stood tall.

Tension sucked the wind out of Landon and he forgot to breathe.

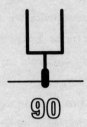

90

Brett shook his head. "Landon has to play there. He's Double X. It's in the rules. Play guard, Gunner. What's the big deal?"

Gunner gave Landon an impatient look and grumbled that it was a stupid rule, but he lined up at left guard all the same. Brett's dad marched over to the end zone with Guerrero and Stewart and flipped the ball to the center. "I'll take the snaps and hand off to Layne. Good idea to get some extra reps, guys."

With seven players and one coach, they began to run some plays. As more players arrived, they filled in at the tight end and receiver positions. Soon they had a full squad and a scout defense to run against. When Torin Bennett, the normal starting left guard, arrived, Gunner and Torin looked at Coach Bell.

"Yeah . . . okay, Torin, you're starting on defense today, but not offense. Gunner's got left guard. We're running a new offense because I don't think we're gonna have Skip to pass it today."

A couple of guys gave Landon dirty looks, but both Mike and Xander stared straight ahead, and the frowns from other guys didn't last. They got to work with Bryce Rinehart under center. Their backup quarterback was excited to be the starter, and handing the ball off to Guerrero instead of throwing passes was fine with him.

When the Tuckahoe bus pulled into the parking lot above, Landon began to worry that Timmy had been right. Skip, one of their best players and the starting quarterback, was obviously boycotting the game instead of offering his apology to Landon. An army of Tuckahoe players filed off the bus and marched in two perfect columns down the hill and through the far goalposts.

The Tuckahoe team snaked around the field on a silent jog, swishing past Landon and his teammates without a single glance before coming out through the far goalposts again and filing into seven columns of seven for warm-ups. Landon couldn't keep from watching. When they were all assembled, the Tuckahoe captain, a boy nearly as large as Landon, barked once, and the entire team roared something Landon didn't understand. Just as suddenly, they broke into jumping jacks, counting them out with sharp sounds that ended in a cascade of clapping.

Landon turned to Brett, who waved a dismissive hand in the air. "Their bark is worse than their bite. If this was a cheerleading competition, we wouldn't stand a chance, but when we start smacking them in the mouth, it won't be about cheering anymore."

Landon wished he could feel some of Brett's swagger, but as they ran through more plays, he couldn't help being slightly disheartened by the loud and disciplined nature of the Tuckahoe team.

The lot was swelling with cars and trucks, and the stands began to fill up too. Landon's family arrived, and he watched his mom with her head held high as she stamped up the center aisle of the stands and took a seat right in the middle of everything like she owned the place. The Tuckahoe stands began to overflow, and their green-and-black-clad fans started to line the fence on their side of the field.

Bronxville's high school marching band suddenly spilled from the school with blasting brass instruments and clanging drums to take up position not far from where Landon and his teammates stretched out. The air vibrated with the sounds of a military march, which ended abruptly. The Bronxville stands were packed. Landon guessed there were close to a thousand people. Coach Bell kept the pregame going as if he'd been their head coach all along. Brett ran the lineman drills efficiently, as if he were Coach Furster's ghost.

During warm-ups, Brett's mom set up a table behind the bench and unpacked a couple dozen bottles of Gatorade for the team to drink. Coach West usually brought the water bottles and carriers, but Landon didn't think anyone would mind Gatorade instead. He knew he didn't, and no one would have to worry about refilling them.

On the next practice play they ran, Landon fired out at the defensive end in front of him when he heard a shriek behind him. He spun and saw everything had stopped. Bryce was lying in a heap behind the line. Guerrero stood over him with the ball, saying he was sorry.

Coach Bell jumped forward.

Bryce rolled and clutched his ankle, howling. As Landon watched the scene unfold, he realized that Guerrero had stepped on Bryce's foot and wrenched his ankle. Bryce's dad was there now, helping his son off the field along with another parent.

Now, they had no quarterback at all.

Landon turned to Brett. "So . . . what are we gonna do?"

Brett turned and looked toward his dad. Landon turned too, and saw Coach Bell out at midfield talking with the referees and the Tuckahoe head coach. The whole group of men checked their watches together. The head ref said something, and Coach Bell nodded and walked back toward the Bronxville bench with his face in a knot.

The Bronxville players huddled around Coach Bell. "Well, guys, we've got no quarterback. They said they'll give us ten extra minutes to figure something out, but we've got to be ready. So . . ."

Everyone held his breath, waiting to see what possible solution Coach Bell might have.

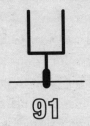

91

Brett's dad exhaled loudly and looked at his son. "Brett, let's have you take a few snaps and see what you can do."

"What?" Brett went rigid. "You want *me* to play quarterback?"

Brett's father squeezed his lips together. "You know the plays and you know the game as well as anyone. You got a better idea?"

"I . . ." Brett looked around at them. "Okay."

Gunner eyed Nichols and raised his hand. "But, Coach, if we don't have Brett on the line, won't these guys bury us?"

"You've got Landon," Coach Bell said. "Torin, you're back at left guard, and Gunner, you go to right guard. Come on. Have some confidence."

"I know, Coach, but it's Tuckahoe." Gunner sounded like they'd lost already.

As if on cue, the band struck up a marching tune from the end zone.

"It's a funny-shaped ball, guys." Coach Bell looked around at his team. "Lots of things can happen. Brett, take some snaps and let's get some handoffs going to Layne."

Brett teamed up in an open patch of grass with Travis to snap, and Layne got behind him to go through the basic mechanics of their running plays. Even Landon had to admit that it looked kind of silly to see a player as big as Brett line up at quarterback, but everyone seemed to be willing to give the whole thing a try.

Landon looked up into the stands. Megan had joined his family along with Brett's mom in a carnival of black and orange. Landon thought about his father's words, about writing your own story, but this just wasn't fair. The whole notion of the team running the ball down Tuckahoe's throat behind him and Brett just wouldn't happen if Brett was being wasted at quarterback.

A rumble like thunder from the parking lot made Landon turn his head. Jonathan Wagner's enormous, gleaming pickup pulled into the parking lot and out onto the grass, the lineman making up his own spot before he hopped out of the truck and hurried down the hill swinging his big bowed legs like backhoe buckets. He arrived out of breath while people in the stands pointed, whispered, and stared. "Sorry, guys, but I made it!"

Jonathan looked around. "Brett at QB? Okay, that'll work. I'll handle the line, Coach Bell."

330

The presence of the Giants' star lineman raised everyone's spirits, but it also seemed to somehow add to the mayhem.

The good thing about all the confusion was that Landon didn't have the chance to worry. When Bronxville lost the toss, they kicked off, and Jonathan Wagner switched Gunner to defensive tackle before shoving Landon out onto the field with the starting defense to play end. "Go get 'em, Landon. Use your size."

Landon didn't have a chance to even think as he found himself lining up at left end on defense; he had to just play.

"Just stay low, Landon!" Jonathan Wagner bellowed from the sideline. "Use your hands and get rid of the guy and go get the ball!"

Landon lined up, determined to stay low. On the snap, the Tuckahoe lineman fired out low and hard. Still unsure of himself, Landon caught the block rather than attacking his opponent. He got driven back two yards before he could cast the lineman aside, but by then the runner had crossed the line and was into the defensive secondary before he was tackled.

"Lower!" Jonathan hollered, waving his hands, and Landon knew who he was talking to.

On the next play Landon did stay low, and his foe didn't move him an inch. The ball went the other way, though, and Landon didn't get close before Brett tackled the runner for a small gain. The play after that, Landon did even better, driving his opponent back, which tripped the runner and allowed Gunner Miller to catch him from behind and strip the ball. The fumble landed right at Landon's feet, and he simply flopped down on top of it in a moment of burning excitement, buried beneath a pile of bodies.

When the ref peeled everyone away and Landon stood holding the ball up in one hand, the crowd cheered. They *cheered* for *him*!

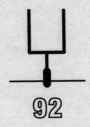

92

Breathless with joy, Landon ran off the field before he realized Coach Bell and Jonathan were waving him to go back. Landon stopped in his tracks, realized he needed to play offense now, and turned back toward the huddle. He heard a noise from the crowd and wondered if it was laughter. For once, he didn't care if people were laughing at him, because only moments before they were *cheering*, and that felt like it had been tattooed onto his heart, where it would remain the rest of his life.

In the offensive huddle, teammates kept congratulating him, and he was miffed when Brett stepped into the huddle and told them to shut up. "It was a good play," Brett said, staring around, "but we've got a long way to go, guys. A long way."

Brett couldn't have spoken a bigger truth.

The Tuckahoe defense was on fire, and by the end of the first half, Bronxville was losing 14–0.

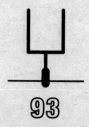

93

Down in the corner of their end zone, the Bronxville team sat flopped down in a small cluster around their coach and his brother-in-law, wheezing to catch their breaths between mouthfuls of orange slices.

"You guys can *do* this!" Jonathan Wagner pounded a fist into his hand and paced like a caged panther.

"Catch your breaths, guys," Coach Bell said. "Get some Gatorade and let's talk about what's going on. Linemen, you've gotta cut those guys on the back side. You don't have to block them, but you've gotta cut their legs out to keep 'em from busting clean into our backfield. Can you do that?"

The offensive line nodded fiercely. Coach Bell and Jonathan Wagner huddled up, just the two of them while the players gasped for breath. The coaches exchanged heated ideas before they nodded together and turned to the team.

The high school band finished their halftime show and filed past, grinning and snickering like fools at the sight of the exhausted kids.

"Okay, listen up!" Coach Bell barked. "We gotta have someone else play quarterback. We gotta try. Anyone, Gunner, Torin, I don't care, but we gotta get Brett back on the line or we don't stand a chance. Someone *has* to be able to take a snap and hand it off to Layne. Someone . . ."

Coach Bell and Jonathan Wagner looked around, expecting a reply.

Behind them, someone jostled the line of band members and finally pushed through to say, "I've got a quarterback for you, Coach."

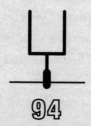

94

Everyone stared at the man in the brown tweed sports coat and expensive-looking dress shoes. Gold cuff links and a watch that looked a lot like Coach Furster's glinted from his wrists. This man was thin and taller than Coach Furster, though, with freckles on his somber face that crept up and over his shiny bald head. He reached around behind himself and produced a Bronxville football player, dressed and ready to go, but with eyes cast toward the ground.

It was Skip Dreyfus.

Mr. Dreyfus took his son by the neck and steered him toward the team. "Is Landon Dorch here?"

All eyes were on Landon, and he felt his face burst into flame.

"Landon, my son has something to say to you." Mr. Dreyfus looked from Landon to the coaches. "Sorry for being late to the party, guys. I just flew in from Hong Kong and got an update from his mother on the drive home from the airport. Skip and I talked, and he's eager to apologize to Landon and move forward with no bad feelings. Aren't you, Skip?"

"Yes, sir." Skip kept his eyes down. "I am."

"You are, what?" Skip's father asked.

"I am sorry, sir."

"Good, now say it to Landon."

Skip stepped forward, and Landon felt sick.

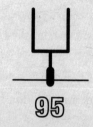

95

When Skip held out his hand, Landon shook it.

"I'm sorry, Landon." Skip didn't raise his eyes.

"Okay," Landon said.

"And nothing like it will happen again," Mr. Dreyfus said. "Isn't that right, Skip?"

"Yes, sir."

"There you go." Skip's dad gave Coach Bell a salute and disappeared as suddenly as he had arrived.

Jonathan Wagner's grin lit up the world and he slapped Skip heartily on the back. "Nice."

Skip only nodded, looking wildly embarrassed.

"Okay, bring it in." Coach Bell held a fist in the middle of them all, and everyone put his hand in. "Now we can really do this, guys! Here we go! HIT, HUSTLE, WIN, on three . . ."

"HIT! HUSTLE! WIN!"

It was a roar even Landon could clearly hear.

They jogged to the sideline, where Coach Bell pulled Landon and Brett aside. "Guys, it's bulldozer time. We are gonna line up and cram this ball right down their throats behind the two of you. Once we establish that they can't stop us, it'll open up the counter and the naked bootleg with Skip. Wow, wait till Tuckahoe gets a mouthful of this."

Brett's dad brandished his fist, and his uncle grinned and hovered beside Brett, nodding like a fool.

Bronxville had the ball. Landon studied Skip's face in the huddle. Skip wouldn't meet his eye, but he didn't offer Landon a sneer either. He was just neutral, and it made Landon wonder at the power of the quarterback's father.

"Okay," Skip said. "Heavy right, twenty-six dive on one."

"And say the count *loud*." Landon glared at Skip, who looked up at him in total surprise.

They stared at each other for a moment before Skip smiled and blushed and said, "Okay, Landon. I'll make sure it's loud."

Everyone looked at Landon with disbelief.

"Thank you," Landon said, and they broke the huddle.

Brett bounced up to the line, jittery and muttering to himself. Suddenly, he turned and grabbed Landon's face mask, pulling him close. "We're gonna *do* this, Landon. We are gonna *do* this, my man!"

Landon caught the thrill. "Let's go."

At the line, a Tuckahoe defender sneered at them, laughed, and mocked Landon in a garbled voice, crooking his arms and waving his hands like there was something wrong with him. "*Let's go. Let's go.* What are you gonna do, you big, fat dummy?"

Brett nearly jumped out of his cleats. "You're gonna see what he's gonna do, 'cause you just lost your free ride into our backfield. Time to pay up, wimp."

"Pay this." The defender slapped his own butt.

Brett just growled.

They lined up. The cadence rang out loud and clear. On "one," Landon and Brett fired out together like the double blade of a monster snowplow, lifting and ripping and grinding, driving the two players in front of them back until they crumbled and went down, and then they plowed right over them looking for more defenders.

It was a scrum, but Guerrero picked up eight yards. They lined up and did it again for six, then again for four, before Guerrero hit a crease on the next play and picked up seventeen. They ran the same play over and over, twenty-six dive. It was almost unthinkable, but Bronxville marched down the field. Tuckahoe's head coach was pulling at his hair, throwing his hat, and screaming at his defense from the sideline like a madman. They stacked up linebackers and blitzed the gaps, but with Landon and Brett foot to foot, there was just no stopping them from pushing defenders back or down to the dirt.

When they punched it in from the three-yard line, Landon turned and hugged Brett and Guerrero at the same time, howling to the sky.

Brett yelled, "We are gonna win this thing, Landon. We're gonna win it!"

When things settled down, there was Skip, blocking Landon's path back to the bench.

"Hey." Skip showed no emotion, but he wasn't letting Landon by.

"Hey, what?" Landon asked.

Skip stared hard at him with his lips pursed tight and his eyes swirling with emotion. "I want to tell you something."

"O-kay." Landon let the word drag out of his mouth and still he waited for Skip to speak.

Skip took a deep breath. His eyes skittered around the field before settling on Landon's face and locking in. "Landon, I really am sorry. I'm not just saying it."

Landon studied Skip's face, and a lifetime of reading expressions told him it was true. Skip *was* sorry.

Landon smiled widely and put a heavy paw on the quarterback's shoulder. "That's okay, Skip. Forgive and forget. That's what my dad says . . . and it's true."

"That's . . . nice. Thank you."

"I like right tackle," Landon said.

"Right tackle likes you too." Skip laughed.

"No more left out." Landon felt like he *was* writing his own ending, and he knew it when Skip shook his head, put a hand on his arm, and answered him loud and clear.

"No way. Right tackle only. . . . No more left out."

AUTHOR'S NOTE

It was during a book tour that I first met two deaf boys who were fans of my stories and, like me, avid readers and football players. Anyone who's heard me speak to students at a school knows the thrust of my message is that reading not only makes us better students, but most important, better, kinder people. Kindness begins by understanding and believing that each person is just like you on the inside and disregarding the differences on the outside. When someone is sick or disabled, those differences can be profound. I wanted to write a story about a character we could all identify with, one who dreams of success and acceptance but who was also profoundly different.

While the two deaf boys I met, Brett Bell and Layne Guerrero, appear as characters in this book, it is the main character, Landon Dorch, who more closely resembles them and, more important, their experiences. I want to thank Brett and Layne for sharing their stories, their dreams, and their hardships with me. I hope the result is that you, the reader, will develop the same bond with Landon as I have. And, most important, that when you see someone who is deaf or has cochlear implants, that you reach out to let them know that YOU know it doesn't matter.

Finally, I want to thank Kristi Bell, Brett's mom, who gave me so much time and shared so many personal anecdotes, which I know breathed life into this story.

**TURN THE PAGE FOR A SNEAK PEEK
AT TIM GREEN'S NEXT FOOTBALL STORY**

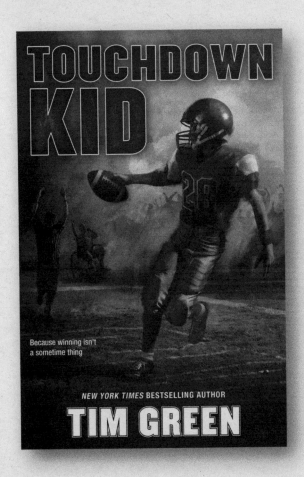

Summer sunshine baked the blacktop in the street.

Like his best friend, Liam O'Donnell, Cory wore only his football pants, socks, and cleats. Sweat drizzled down their bare twelve-year-old chests. Vents on the roof of the corner market whined, coughing hot air so the coolers inside worked, the ice pops didn't melt, and the soda stayed frosty cold.

It was a long walk uphill to Glenwood Park. Helmets and shoulder pads had been tucked inside practice jerseys that were twisted at the belly and slung across their backs, acting like small sacks. Cory secretly eyed his friend's bare chest. Liam was like a small tank, with the compact muscles of a weight lifter bulging from skin tanned by a shirtless summer. Despite his training, Cory was short of a six-pack. The sheen of sweat on his body reminded him of the walrus at the zoo.

"Wish Coach Mellon didn't decide who starts Saturday

based on looks," Cory said, only half kidding.

Liam flexed his arm, showing a bulge Cory could only dream of. "Pretty, right?"

Cory snorted.

"How do you know I'll start?"

"You will." Cory kicked a stone. "Mellon-head loves you."

"He might love *you* if you didn't argue with him all the time." Liam gave Cory's shoulder a soft punch.

"I can't help it." Cory knew his friend was right. Just two days ago he'd gotten into it with their coach. "An outside sweep is a thirty-eight or a forty-eight. A thirty-six is off-tackle whether there's a tight end or not."

"He's our coach, Cory."

"And it's not smart to make players go through an entire practice without water. That 'old school' stuff doesn't cut it with me. Everyone knows you maximize performance by staying hydrated. Even a Mellon-head should know that."

Liam patted his back. "You gotta relax. Save all that smart stuff for the courtroom, when you're a real lawyer."

"I'll try."

Liam's family had moved into the poor Irish neighborhood on the city's west side at the very end of fifth grade. Most people didn't know Liam as well as Cory did, and they sometimes mistook him for a high schooler.

Cory knew different. Liam was just a silly kid like most of the rest heading into sixth grade. The world, their neighborhood, and even his older brother's belt slipped past Liam like butter off a hot knife. Liam just let it all go, looking out on it all with that big grin and always finding something funny about things, even the welts that made Cory wince.

"I go into the army one day. I'll go straight to sergeant with these stripes," he said once, grinning and pointing to the raised strips of skin on his left arm. "No Private O'Donnell for me."

So when they rounded the street corner and saw Liam's older brother, Finn, with some friends cluttered around the metal back door of the Shamrock Club, Liam grinned and waved while Cory looked down at the laces on his cleats. And when Liam's older brother motioned for them to come close and be quiet, Cory tried to grab his friend by the arm, but it was too late.

Liam veered right off the sidewalk and over the crumbs of broken pavement and glass, trying to look easy.

The whole thing said trouble in a million different ways.

More than the stench of the dumpster told Cory to just run without looking back, but that would have meant leaving Liam behind. Coach Mellon would make the whole team run till they barfed if Cory showed up to a Saturday morning practice without Liam. They had a big game Sunday, and Liam was their star player. Coach Mellon said teammates had to look out for one another. They were a football family.

More than that, though, tomorrow was going to be the turning point in Liam's life. Everyone knew the HBS varsity head coach was coming to the game, and everyone knew what it could mean for Liam. Cory and Liam shared the same dream: high school superstars and Division I all-Americans, all leading to the NFL. Getting a scholarship to attend HBS, Howard Bissinger School, the elite private school known for its football program, was a big first step.

4

Liam had already been to visit HBS and even met the people he'd be living with. All scholarship kids had a host family. He just needed this last good game to seal the deal.

Liam was the only one who didn't seem all that excited. Why else would he even *think* about stopping for some trouble on his way to practice? Cory cared, though. He cared for Liam, and then there was the tiniest little gem of an idea sparkling in the corner of his mind that tomorrow's game could mean something for him as well.

So Cory followed, studying the situation without letting Liam's brother or his friends catch his eye.

Finn was an older, elongated version of Liam. His face had the same features—but he was always scowling. His muscles were taut, like his little brother's, only stretched-out over a six-foot-three frame. Nearly a foot taller than Liam, he didn't have to work to be menacing.

Finn's friend Hoagie was as wide as he was tall, but he wasn't named after a sandwich. His last name was Hogan. His pants were hanging halfway down his wide butt and he looked not only mean but stupid, with droopy brown eyes.

And then there was Dirty. Any one of the three boys could give Cory bad dreams with just a look, but Dirty had a special stink of evil. The oldest and shortest in the bunch, Dirty had small, beetle-black eyes with a nasty, scrunched-up face. His long, dirty-blond hair hung like a curtain, covering one eye. He'd twitch his neck like a horse shooing a fly whenever he wanted to see the world with two eyes.

Dirty flicked his cigarette onto the ground and then slipped a piece of rebar—a long, rusty piece of steel that looked like a giant pretzel rod—into a padlock on the back door of the Shamrock Club. He yanked it down, snapping the lock, before he handed the rebar to Liam. "Wow. You broke it open, Liam." He looked at Cory. "You an' your friend Flapjack better keep an eye out while we get some stuff inside that needs gettin'."

Cory got called "Flapjack" because he'd eaten too much at the church pancake breakfast two years ago and got sick on Father Haywood's shoes.

"You keep watch." Finn shot Liam a meaningful look.

Liam swallowed and nodded fast. "Okay."

The older boys all laughed and disappeared inside quick as smoke.

"We shouldn't do this," Cory whispered as he watched the semi-closed door while Liam watched the sidewalk and the street.

"They won't be long." Liam giggled. "You see their faces? Hoagie looked like he's about to pee his pants. Besides, I don't need any stripes on my backside before the big game tomorrow. Guess that's how the old man did it before he skipped town. Finn doesn't want me growing up the wrong way."

Liam laughed, but it was a laugh muddy with pain.

They waited, watching. After five long minutes, Cory said, "You go to practice. I'll watch."

"Where I come from you don't just leave a friend behind." Liam sounded insulted.

"Just go." Cory sighed. "Coach doesn't care if I'm there or not."

"Don't say that. He doesn't like you, but he knows how good you are," Liam said. "Heck, you're as good as me."

6

"You think that?" Cory's jaw dropped. He believed he had talent—talent his grumpy coach didn't appreciate—and he'd been working hard. But even he didn't believe he'd reached Liam's level.

"Well, almost as good." Liam kissed his biceps and laughed. "Let's shoot for it. We'll let fate decide."

Liam started pumping his fist up and down. "Rock, paper, scissors . . ."

"Shoot." Cory held out a flat hand to Liam's scissors. "Scissors cuts paper. Get going."

"Okay, but you better watch good." Liam handed him the rebar, a tone of warning in his voice. "I'm serious about the butt-whipping if someone isn't on lookout when he comes back."

Cory snatched the rebar. "I never messed you up before, did I?"

"That's why you're my best friend." Liam grinned and took off on a jog toward Glenwood Park, where they practiced three nights a week and on Saturday mornings.

Too much time went by before Cory crept back to the door. He strained to hear the sound of ransacking inside the Shamrock Club's kitchen. All he heard was the walk-in refrigerator straining against the heat.

"Finn?" He said it softly first, then louder before pushing the door open and stepping over the rotted threshold.

Through the club, past the bar he could see the front door. It hung open with hot sunlight forcing its way in. Cory felt both relieved that his job was over and annoyed that they'd left him waiting like that.

7

He thought of Coach Mellon and bolted out the back door just as an enormous figure filled it.

Cory bounced back off the policeman's iron gut, tripped, and sat down hard on the linoleum floor.

The rebar clattered into the silence as Cory looked at the policeman. He was white haired, with pale green eyes and a nametag
that read THORPE. The cop eyed Cory with what might have
been amusement. "You can't be fourteen."

"I'm twelve," Cory said, knowing how it all looked.

Thorpe nodded at the rebar before shaking his head. "Used
to be burglary was a grown man's profession."

"I-I-I'm not," Cory said. "I didn't."

"Get up." Thorpe sounded tired and annoyed.

Cory left the rebar and stood. The policeman raised his
hand and Cory flinched.

"You heard too many stories." Thorpe brushed a dust bunny
off of Cory's bare shoulder. "I don't hit kids, even if they are
burglars."

Cory shook his head violently.

"Oh yeah? Well, someone busted this door in, and you got the rebar. I'm no Sherlock Holmes, but you don't have to be on this side of the city. If you didn't do it, you better tell me who did."

Cory closed his lips tight.

"Oh, that's a big boy. You take the fall. You and I both know you'll go in front of the family court judge and he'll slap your wrist and send you home. You might end up in counseling at school. No need to go through that. I'll let all that trouble slide, but you gotta tell me who the bad guys are." Thorpe bent down and put his hands on Cory's shoulders. "You see, my partner's a rookie. He's gonna want to go by the book. He gets excited."

"FREEZE!"

Cory and Thorpe spun around to find a second policeman with his gun drawn and pointed their way from the sunny opening on the front side of the club.

4

"Kenny! Put the gun down!" Thorpe glowered at his partner.

Officer Kenny marched through the doorway with both hands on his gun, now pointing it at the floor. "They broke in through the front. I thought they might be in here, still."

"They broke *out* the front, Kenny." Thorpe nudged the rebar with the toe of his dusty black shoe.

Kenny sniffed the air. "Smells like someone peed."

"It's a Westside bar, Kenny," Thorpe said. "Let's take this kid home."

"But down to family court first, right?" Kenny turned his eyes on Cory like a cat sizing up a fat, juicy robin. "So we can book him? I heard they got room in Hillbrook."

Cory felt his throat tighten. Hillbrook was the name of the infamous juvenile detention center. It was only for the very worst kids, kids who committed violent crimes but were too young for jail. But even though it was a place for kids, it was reputed to be a horror show. When kids came back from Hillbrook, they were never quite right. Just the name sent chills down Cory's back.

"Maybe he gives up who did this and we bring him to his momma. You got a momma, kid?" Thorpe asked.

Cory nodded, thankful they didn't ask about a dad. That was too long of a story.

"Good. Now all you got to do is tell us who the real criminals are," Thorpe said.

Cory still shook his head. He was afraid of the police and of Hillbrook, and he was afraid of his mom, too—but not as afraid as he was of Dirty and Finn. He'd never tell.

Still, the policemen made a show of having Cory cover his belly by putting on his practice jersey. Then they put him in the back of their black-and-white squad car and turned on the siren. Cory hung his head and turned away as people on the sidewalks stopped to stare. The cops drove him downtown into the parking lot of the Public Safety Building. It was a stone fortress. Everyone on the Westside knew they kept the real criminals there.

The cops sat in the car, grilling him.

"You don't want us to take you in this place," Kenny said. "Just give us the names and we'll drive you home."

"Look, kid, just tell us what they looked like." Thorpe spun around in his seat. "You can do that much."

Cory remained silent.

Kenny shook his head in disgust. "You need to wise up, kid. Once you go through those doors, there's no going back."

"He's right," Thorpe said. "It'll be a lot better for you to tell us . . ."

Cory's silence continued to flood the inside of the police car.

"Let's book him, Thorpe." Kenny pounded a fist into his other hand.

"Wait."

Silence.

"C'mon," Kenny whined. "Let's book him."

Cory's lips remained closed, though. He knew his options, but even Hillbrook couldn't be as bad as waiting for Dirty to jump out of the shadows at some unknown moment.

Finally, Thorpe sighed and fired up the car engine.

"What're you doing?" Kenny's jaw dropped. "C'mon, Thorpe. Kid's a burglar."

Thorpe had both hands on the wheel, and he looked back at Cory before addressing his rookie partner. "Really, Kenny? You and your Hillbrook. You're gonna tell me what to do?"

"Well, no," Kenny mumbled. He sulked the whole way to Cory's house, a run-down place he and his mom rented on Hope Avenue. The policemen escorted him to the door while the neighborhood kids oohed and aahed and squealed with delight at the sight of Cory in a cop sandwich.

"Flap-jack got arrest-ed . . . Flap-jack got arrest-ed." Their singsong voices danced in the heat.

After several rings, his mom answered the door. Seeing the police, she gasped and snatched Cory to her side like a lost puppy. He wished she had clobbered him like most of the other moms on Hope Ave. would have done. Cory saw how the police looked at her bright yellow bathing suit beneath the open white dress shirt she'd taken from her last boyfriend. His mom must have been in the backyard.

"What's this?" Cory's mom was small and fragile as a bird, but life had made her tough. She glared accusingly at the police.

Thorpe huffed and rested Cory's football gear on the cracked stoop. "He was involved in a burglary, ma'am."

"A *what*?" Cory's mom stiffened, and her grip on his arm tightened.

Cory winced. "I didn't, Mom. Some big kids made me be the lookout. I didn't have a choice."

"Why don't you go catch *them*?" She turned her glare back at the police.

"We may have some more questions for him, ma'am." Officer Kenny tore his eyes loose from the yellow bathing suit and had a sudden interest in his belt buckle.

Thorpe had no problem meeting Cory's mom's stare and matching it with his unblinking pale green eyes. "We could have charged him with criminal trespassing and burglary third, but my sense is that he wasn't the mastermind in all this. He was there, but I'm not sure he had any intent to commit a crime."

Cory's mom frowned. "Of course he didn't."

"Well . . ." Thorpe tipped his hat and turned to go.

Cory watched them leave amid hooting and giggling from the younger neighborhood kids who had spilled back into the street. He saw the sad, knowing head wags of the adult neighbors tucked away on their front porches, hiding from the sun.

Cory's mom disappeared into the house without a word.

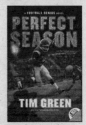